Acclaim for H A J I N *'s*

Waiting

"A remarkably austere love story, suffused with irony and subtlety. . . . It is a vivid bit of storytelling, fluid and earthy . . . a graceful human allegory."
—*Chicago Sun-Times*

"*Waiting* turns, page by careful page, into a deliciously comic novel. [Jin] casts a wise, rather than a cold, eye on his characters' struggles."
—*Time*

"Spare but compelling. . . . Jin's craftsmanship and grasp of the universal language of the human heart make the book a worthwhile read."
—*USA Today*

"A wry, lovely novel. . . . The true subjects of *Waiting* are the cruelty of time, the obduracy of desire and the imperfection of human circumstances, whether these are dominated by custom, revolutionary enthusiasm, or the falterings of the individual heart."
—*Newsday*

"*Waiting* has the stripped-down simplicity of a fable. . . . It casts a spell that doesn't break once. . . . Jin has the kind of effortless command that most writers can only dream about."
—*The New York Times Magazine*

"A delicate rendering of the universal complications of love. . . . Ha Jin's natural storytelling quietly captures the texture of daily life in a dual Chinese culture. . . . No detail is extraneous in this sad, funny, and often wise novel."
—*The Village Voice Literary Supplement*

"Remarkable . . . compellingly ingenious . . . gorgeously cinematic."   —*The Philadelphia Inquirer*

"A wonderfully ironic novel . . . complex and sad as life. . . . It captures the difficulties of love in totalitarian China with sharp prose and a convincing portrayal of human vagaries."   —*Minneapolis Star Tribune*

"Subtle and complex . . . his best work to date. A moving meditation on the effects of time upon love."
                                                —*The Washington Post*

"[Jin] reveals some startlingly original insights on human life and love . . . in a narrative that dazzles the reader with its simplicity and grace."   —*Providence Sunday Journal*

"A high achievement indeed."
                                          —*The New York Review of Books*

HA JIN

Waiting

Ha Jin left his native China in 1985 to attend
Brandeis University. He is the author of two
books of poetry; three collections of stories,
Ocean of Words, which won the PEN/Hem-
ingway Award in 1997, *Under the Red Flag,*
which won the Flannery O'Connor Award
for Short Fiction in 1996, and *The Bride-*
groom; and *In the Pond,* a novel. *Waiting,* his
second novel, won the 1999 National Book
Award and the 2000 PEN/Faulkner Award
for Fiction. He lives near Atlanta, where he is
a professor of English at Emory University.

INTERNATIONAL

Waiting

HA JIN

VINTAGE INTERNATIONAL
Vintage Books
A Division of Random House, Inc.
New York

FIRST VINTAGE OPEN MARKET EDITION, AUGUST 2000

Copyright © 1999 by Ha Jin

The Library of Congress has cataloged the Pantheon edition as follows:
Jin, Ha, 1956–
Waiting / Ha Jin.
p. cm.
ISBN 0-375-40653-0
1. China—History—1949–1976—Fiction.   I. Title.
PS3560.16W34   1999
813'.54—dc21   99-21334
CIP

Vintage Open Market ISBN: 0-375-72586-5

www.vintagebooks.com

Printed in Canada
10 9 8 7 6 5 4 3 2 1

FOR LISHA

ALONE AND TOGETHER

Waiting

PROLOGUE

Every summer Lin Kong returned to Goose Village to divorce his wife, Shuyu. Together they had appeared at the courthouse in Wujia Town many times, but she had always changed her mind at the last moment when the judge asked if she would accept a divorce. Year after year, they went to Wujia Town and came back with the same marriage license issued to them by the county's registry office twenty years before.

This summer Lin Kong returned with a new letter of recommendation for divorce, which had been provided for him by the army hospital in Muji City, where he served as a doctor. Once more he planned to take his wife to the courthouse and end their marriage. Before he left for home, he had promised Manna Wu, his girlfriend at the hospital, that this time he would try his best to make Shuyu stick to her word after she agreed to a divorce.

As an officer, he had a twelve-day leave each year. Since the trip home took a whole day—he had to change trains and buses at two towns—he could stay in the countryside only ten days, saving the last day for the return trip. Before taking this year's leave, he had thought that once home, he would have enough time to carry out his plan, but by now a whole week had passed and he had not yet mentioned a word to his wife about the divorce. Whenever the subject came to his tongue, he postponed it for another day.

Their adobe house was the same as two decades before, four large rooms under a thatched roof and three square windows facing south with their frames painted sky blue. Lin stood in the yard facing the front wall while flipping over a dozen mildewed books he had left to be sunned on a stack of firewood. Sure thing, he thought, Shuyu doesn't know how to take care of books. Maybe I should give them to my nephews. These books are of no use to me anymore.

Beside him, chickens were strutting and geese waddling. A few little chicks were passing back and forth through the narrow gaps in the paling that fenced a small vegetable garden. In the garden pole beans and long cucumbers hung on trellises, eggplants curved like ox horns, and lettuce heads were so robust that they covered up the furrows. In addition to the poultry, his wife kept two pigs and a goat for milk. Their sow was oinking from the pigpen, which was adjacent to the western end of the vegetable garden. Against the wall of the pigpen a pile of manure waited to be carted to their family plot, where it would go through high-temperature composting in a pit for two months before being put into the field. The air reeked of distillers' grains mixed in the pig feed. Lin disliked the sour smell, which was the only uncomfortable thing to him here. From the kitchen, where Shuyu was cooking, came the coughing of the bellows. In the south, elm and birch crowns shaded their neighbors' straw and tiled roofs. Now and then a dog barked from one of these homes.

Having turned over all the books, Lin went out of the front wall, which was three feet high and topped with thorny jujube branches. In one hand he held a dog-eared Russian dictionary he had used in high school. Having nothing to do, he sat on their grinding stone, thumbing through the old dictionary. He still remembered some Russian vocabulary and even tried to form a few short sentences in his mind with some words. But he couldn't recall the grammatical rules for the case changes exactly, so he gave up and let the book lie on his lap. Its pages fluttered a little as a breeze blew across. He raised his eyes to watch the villagers hoeing potatoes in a distant field, which was so vast that a red flag was planted in the middle of it as a marker, so that they could take a break when they reached the flag. Lin was fascinated by the sight, but he knew little about farm work. He had left the village for high school in Wujia Town at the age of sixteen.

An oxcart emerged down the road, loaded high with millet sheaves and swaying as it rolled along. The lead animal was a mere heifer, slightly lame in her hind leg. Lin saw his daughter Hua and another girl on top of the load, both partly buried in the fluffy sheaves. The girls were singing and laughing. The driver, an old man in a blue serge cap, was holding a pipe between his teeth and flicking his short whip over the shaft bullock's hindquarters. The two iron-rimmed wheels were screeching rhythmically on the bumpy road.

As the cart came to a stop at the front gate, Hua dropped a bulging burlap sack to the ground and jumped down. "Thanks, Uncle Yang," she called out to the driver. Waving at the plump girl atop the load, she cried, "See you this evening." Then she brushed bits of straw from her shirt and pants.

Both the old man and the plump girl looked at Lin, smiling at him without a word. Lin vaguely remembered the driver, but couldn't tell what family the girl belonged to. He was aware that they didn't greet him the way the villagers would do one another. The man didn't shout, "How's your day, buddy?" And the girl didn't say, "How are you, Uncle?" Perhaps this was because he was wearing the army uniform, he thought.

"What's in the sack?" he asked his daughter, getting up from the grinding stone.

"Mulberry leaves," she said.

"For the silkworms?"

"Yes." Hua seemed reluctant to talk with him. She raised some silkworms in the shack behind their house, in three large wicker baskets.

"Is it heavy?" he asked.

"No."

"Can I help?" Lin hoped she would say a few words to him before she went in.

"No, I can carry it myself."

With both hands she swung the large sack over her shoulder. Her round eyes gazed at his face for a moment, then with a casual gait she walked away. He noticed that her forearms were sunburned, spotted with whitish peeled skin. How tall and strong she was, obviously a good farmhand.

Again her gaze disturbed him. He was unsure whether her petulance had been caused by his attempt to divorce her mother. He felt that was unlikely, because he had not yet broached the subject this year. He was unhappy that his daughter seemed somewhat estranged from him now. When she was a baby girl, she had been very attached to him and they had often played together whenever he came home. As she grew older, she became more reticent and remote from him. Now she seldom said an unnecessary word to him, and at most she would give him a thin smile. Does she really hate me? he wondered. She's grown up already, and in a few years she'll have her own family, no need for an old man like me.

In fact Lin looked quite young for his age. He was in his late forties, but he did not seem like a middle-aged man. Despite the uniform, he resembled an official more than an officer. His pale face was smooth and handsome with a pair of black-rimmed glasses on his straight nose. By contrast, his wife Shuyu was a small, withered woman and looked much older than her age. Her thin arms and legs couldn't fill up her clothes, which were always baggy on her. In addition, she had bound feet and sometimes wore black puttees. Her dark hair was coiled into a severe bun on the back of her head, giving her a rather gaunt face. Her mouth was sunken, though her dark eyes were not bad-looking, like a pair of tadpoles. In every way the couple did not match.

"Shuyu, can we talk about the divorce?" Lin asked his wife

after dinner. Hua had just left to study with her friends, preparing herself for the entrance exams for a trade school in Harbin.

"All right," his wife said calmly.

"Can we go to town tomorrow?"

"All right."

"You always say 'all right,' but you'll change your mind afterward. Can you keep your word this time?"

She turned silent. They had never quarreled, and she would agree to anything he said. "Shuyu," he went on, "you know, I need a home in the army. It's hard to live by myself there. I'm no longer a young man."

She nodded without a word.

"Will you say yes to the judge this time?" he asked.

"All right."

A hush fell in the room again. He resumed reading the county's newspaper, *Country Constructs,* while his fingertips silently drummed the tabletop.

Shuyu was making a jacket for their daughter, cutting a piece of black corduroy with a pair of scissors and a stub of French chalk. Two yellow moths were circling around the 25-watt bulb hanging from the papered ceiling. On the white-washed wall, the shadow of the lamp cord severed the picture of a baby boy, fat and naked in a red bib, riding a large carp in billowing waves. On the mat-covered brick bed were two folded quilts and three dark pillows like huge loaves of bread. The sound of frogs croaking came from the pond at the southern end of the village while cicadas' chirping seeped in through the screen window. A bell tolled from the production brigade's office, summoning the commune members to a meeting.

Twenty-one years before, in 1962, Lin had been a student in a military medical school in Shenyang City. One day in the summer he received a letter from his father, which said his mother was very ill and their house had been neglected because the old man had to work in the fields of the commune most of the time. His father wanted Lin to get married soon so that his bride could look after his mother. Out of filial duty, Lin agreed to let his parents find a wife for him.

After a month's talking with an old matchmaker, they settled on the eldest daughter of the Lius, a family that had recently moved to Goose Village from Lokou County. Since Lin was a college student and would soon become a doctor and officer, Shuyu's parents did not ask for any gift or money and were pleased to marry her to him. Lin's parents mailed him a black-and-white snapshot of Shuyu, and he agreed to be engaged, feeling she was a fine, normal girl. She was twenty-six, just a year younger than himself.

But when he returned home in the winter and saw his fiancée in person, he was dismayed—she looked so old, as if in her forties, her face wrinkled and her hands leathery. What is more, her feet were only four inches long. This was the New China; who would look up to a young woman with bound feet? He tried reasoning with his parents to get out of the engagement, but they were adamant and said he was silly. How could they break the engagement without proving that Shuyu couldn't be a suitable wife? Had they done that, the whole village would have turned against them.

"Can good looks feed a family?" his father asked sullenly.

"My son," his mother said from her sickbed, "a pretty face fades in a couple of years. It's personality that lasts. Shuyu will be a good helper for you."

"How can you tell?" Lin asked.

"I know that in my heart."

His father said, "Where can you find such a kindhearted girl?"

"Please," the mother begged. "I'll die happy if I know you agree to marry her."

So Lin yielded to his parents. But despite accepting Shuyu as his bride, he believed she was absolutely unpresentable outside his home village. That was why, after they were married the next summer, for two decades he had never let her visit him at the army hospital. Furthermore, for seventeen years, since the birth of their only child, he had remained separate from his wife. Whenever he was home, he would sleep alone in his own room. He didn't love her; nor did he dislike her. In a way he treated her like a cousin of sorts.

Now his parents had died long ago, and their daughter Hua had graduated from middle school. He felt that the family didn't depend on him anymore and that it was time to move along with his own life. For better or worse, he should disentangle himself from this loveless marriage.

Early the next morning the couple caught a tractor that was going to Wujia Town to fetch an electric motor for the village's new millhouse. Together with them in the trailer sat Shuyu's younger brother Bensheng, the accountant of the production brigade, who had heard about their going to the divorce court. For more than ten years, every summer Bensheng had gone to the courthouse with them, though he had remained silent in the court. From the very beginning, Lin had believed that it was Bensheng who had made Shuyu change her mind at the last moment. Yet the two men, sitting against the panels of the trailer, didn't show any animosity toward each other. Quietly they were smoking Lin's Glory cigarettes.

Wujia Town was eighteen miles west of Goose Village. On both sides of the road many fields had been reaped, bundles of wheat and millet were piled like thousands of tiny graves. Several horse carts were being loaded in a field by the commune members, the tines of their pitchforks glinting in the sun. The tractor passed a meadow, where a dozen milk cows were browsing, a few calves skittering. In the north stretched the Songhua River, broad like a lake; on its surface a brownish steamer was crawling east, leaving behind strips of black smoke. A pair of pelicans were flying beyond the water, bobbing on the horizon.

The tractor jolted along slowly on the rutted road. Halfway through the eighteen miles, Lin began to feel a backache, which he hadn't had in past years. I'm getting old, he said to himself. This case shouldn't drag on forever. I must brace myself for the judge and get it settled this time.

At the entrance to the county town, the road was blocked by a column of horse carts transporting bricks, and the tractor had to follow them at a walking pace. Bensheng and the driver, nicknamed Dragonfly, grew impatient and couldn't help cursing time and again. Not until half an hour later did they reach the town center. It was market day, so the sidewalks of Central Street were occupied by vendors. They were selling poultry, vegetables, fruits, eggs, live fish, piglets, clothes. Everywhere were wicker baskets, chick cages, oil jars, fish basins and pails. A bald man was blowing a brass whistle, a sample of his wares, and the noise split the air and hurt people's ears. Some young girls at watermelon stands were smoking self-rolled cigarettes while crying for customers and waving goose-feather fans to keep flies away.

The tractor driver dropped his passengers at the black brick courthouse, which was at the west end of Central Street, opposite New China Bookstore. Then he drove away to pick up the motor at the repair shop.

Divorces were rare in the county. The court would handle about a dozen cases a year, and only two or three would end in a divorce. Most of the time the court tried to help the couples resolve their marital problems and get them back together.

The judge was a rotund fiftyish man in a police uniform. At

the sight of Lin and Shuyu, he made a face and said, "Again?" He shook his head, then waved at a young policewoman at the back of the courtroom to come to the front and take notes.

After everybody was seated, Lin went across to the judge and handed him the letter of recommendation.

Following the formality, the judge asked him to present his case to the court. Remaining in his seat, Lin said, "There has been no love between us, so we are applying for a divorce. Please don't take me for a heartless man, Comrade Judge. My wife and I have been separated for seventeen years. I've always been good to her and—"

"Let's get this straight first," the judge cut him short. "You said 'we are applying for a divorce,' but the letter of recommendation only mentions your name. Is your wife applying for a divorce too?"

"No, I'm sorry. I apply for it myself."

The judge was familiar with this case, knowing Lin had been involved with another woman in Muji City, so he didn't bother to question him further. He turned to Shuyu and asked if the husband's statement was true.

She nodded, her "yes" almost inaudible.

"You two have not slept together for seventeen years?" asked the judge.

She shook her head.

"Yes or no?"

"No."

"Would you accept a divorce?"

She didn't answer, her eyes fixed on the wide floorboards, which warped in places. Lin stared at her, thinking, Come on, say yes.

For a minute or so she made no sound. Meanwhile the judge was waiting patiently, waving a large fan, on which a tiger stretched its neck howling with a mouth like a bloody basin. He said to her, "Think hard. Don't rush to a decision."

Her brother raised his hand. The judge allowed him to speak.

Bensheng stood up and said, "Judge Sun, my sister is an illiterate housewife and doesn't know how to express herself clearly, but I know how she feels."

"Tell us then."

"It's unfair for Lin Kong to do this to her. She has lived with the Kongs for more than twenty years, serving them like a dumb beast of burden. She looked after his sick mother until the old woman died. Then his father fell ill, and for three years she took care of the old man so well that he never had a single bedsore. After his father was gone, she raised their daughter alone and worked inside and outside the house like a widow, although her husband was still alive. She has lived a hard life, all the villagers have seen it and say so. But during all these years Lin Kong kept another woman, a mistress, in Muji City. This is unfair. He can't treat a human being, his wife, like an overcoat—once he has worn it out, he dumps it." Bensheng sat down, his face red and puffing out a little. He looked a bit tearful.

His words filled Lin with shame. Lin didn't argue, seeing his wife wipe her tears. He remained silent.

With a wave of his hand, the judge folded up the tiger fan and clapped it against the palm of his other hand. Then he brought his fist down on the desk; dust jumped up, a few yellowish skeins dangling in a ray of sunlight. He pointed at Lin's face and said, "Comrade Lin Kong, you are a revolutionary officer and should be a model for us civilians. What kind of a model have you become? A man who doesn't care for his family and loves the new and loathes the old—fickle in heart and unfaithful in words and deeds. Your wife served your family like a donkey at the millstone. After all these years, the grinding is done, and you want to get rid of her. This is immoral and dishonorable, absolutely intolerable. Tell me, do you have a conscience or not? Do you deserve your green uniform and the red star on your cap?"

"I—I've tried to take care of my family. I give her forty yuan a month. You can't say that I—"

"This court declines your request. The case is dismissed."

Before Lin could protest more, the short judge got up and strode away to the side hall, where the bathroom was. His fat hips swayed while the floor creaked under his feet. His cap still perched on the desk. The policewoman eyed the back of the judge, a faint smile playing around her lips.

It was noon. The sun was blazing outside. Because many people had left the fair, the street was less crowded now. Harness bells were jangling languidly in the distance. A group of schoolgirls skipped and danced over a chain of rubber bands on the sidewalk, singing a nursery rhyme. The cobbled street, whitish in the hot sunlight, had puddles of rainwater here and there. Seeing a young woman selling plait ribbons, Lin stopped to buy a pair for Hua. But he wasn't sure of what color his daughter liked. Shuyu told him "pink." He paid half a yuan for two silk ribbons.

Together they went into Sunrise House at a street corner, a small restaurant that offered mainly wheaten food. They sat down at a table by a window. The oak tabletop looked greasy, its center marked with a few grayish circles. A ladybug was crawling along the rim of a glass jar containing a bunch of chopsticks, its wings now rubbing each other deliberately and now revolving like a pair of miniature rotor blades. A waitress came and greeted them pleasantly as though she had known them, saying, "What would you like for lunch today? We have noodles, beef pies, leek pancakes, sugar buns, and fried dough sticks."

Lin ordered a plate of cold cuts—pork liver and heart

cooked in aniseed broth—and four bowls of noodles, two of which were for his brother-in-law. Shuyu and he would each have one bowl.

In no time the dish came and then the steaming noodles, which were topped with starchy gravy made of minced pork, snap beans, scallions, coriander, and egg drops. While stirring the noodles with a pair of chopsticks, Shuyu spilled a blob of gravy on her left wrist. She raised her hand and licked it clean.

They ate quietly. Lin didn't want to talk, his heart numb. He had tried to hate his brother-in-law when they left the courthouse, but he hadn't been able to summon any intense emotion.

After finishing his first bowl of noodles, Bensheng broke the silence, saying to Lin, "Elder brother, don't take to heart what I said in the court. Shuyu's my sister and I had to do that." His thin eyes were glittering as he chewed a piece of pork heart.

"I understand," said Lin.

"So, no hard feelings?"

"No."

"We're still one family?"

"Yes."

Shuyu smiled and sucked her noodles vigorously. Lin shook his head and heaved a sigh.

The tractor driver, Dragonfly, had promised to wait for them at the crossroads by the post office, but when they arrived there after lunch, there was no shadow of the tractor. Apparently it had left for home, so they had to walk a mile to the bus stop in front of Green Inn. Bensheng couldn't stop cursing Dragonfly all the way.

Manna Wu had been in love with Lin Kong for many years, still waiting for him to divorce his wife so that they could get married. Summer after summer he had gone home and tried to carry through the divorce, but never succeeded. This year Manna did not expect a breakthrough either. According to the army hospital's rule, established by Commissar Wang in the winter of 1958, it was only after eighteen years' separation that an officer could end his marriage without his wife's consent. The commissar had died of hepatitis the next summer, but for twenty-five years the rule had been strictly observed in the hospital.

By 1983, Lin and his wife had already been separated for seventeen years, so with or without Shuyu's agreement, he would be able to divorce her the next year. That was why Manna was certain that he wouldn't make a great effort this time. She knew the workings of his mind: he would always choose an easy way out.

The day after Lin was back from the countryside, he went to Manna's dormitory and told her about the court's rejection. She responded unemotionally, "Before you left, I knew it wouldn't work out."

He clasped his hands around his knee and said, "Don't be so upset. I really did my best."

"I'm not upset."

"Come on, next year I'll divorce her, whether she agrees or not. Let's just wait another year, all right?"

"Another year?" Her voice turned rather shrill. "How many years do you have in your life?"

He remained silent for a moment, his chin propped on his palm. Then he said, "After all, we've waited so many years. Only one year more."

She lifted her face, staring at him. "Look at me, Lin. Am I not becoming an old woman?"

"No, you're not old, dear. Don't be so grouchy."

True, she wasn't old, just in her early forties. Her face had a few wrinkles, but her eyes, though a little wide set, were still bright and lively. Despite some gray hair, she had a fine figure, tall and slender. Seen from behind, you could easily take her for a woman of thirty.

The door opened and Manna's roommate Nurse Hsu came in, humming "On the Sun Island," a popular song. Seeing Lin sitting on the edge of her bed, which was opposite Manna's, Nurse Hsu stuck out her tongue and made an apologetic face at the couple. "Sorry for disturbing you," she said.

Lin said, "I'm sorry for taking your space in here."

"That's all right." Nurse Hsu went over to her bedside cupboard and took out a large tomato. Hurriedly she walked out, crooning the song again.

Lin got to his feet and closed the door. Silence followed, as though neither of them wanted to talk anymore.

He began washing his hands in Manna's yellow enamel basin supported by an iron washstand in a corner. He threw a few handfuls of water on his face, then said to her, "I have to go to work. I'll see you this evening, all right?" He wiped his face with her white towel.

She nodded without speaking.

They both worked in the Medical Department of the hospital, Lin as a physician and Manna as a head nurse. Though they were an acknowledged couple, they couldn't live together and could only eat at the same table in the mess hall and take walks on the hospital grounds. The hospital's regulations prohibited a man and a woman on the staff from walking together outside the compound, unless they were married or engaged. This rule had been in force for nineteen years since 1964, when a nurse got pregnant by her boyfriend, who was an assistant doctor. After the pregnancy was discovered, the couple confessed they had met several times in the birch woods east of the hospital. Both were expelled from the army—the man became a village doctor in his hometown in Jilin Province while the woman was sent to Yingkou City, where she packed seafood in a cannery. Then the Party Committee of the hospital made this rule: two comrades of different sex, unless married or engaged, must not be together outside the compound.

The rule was devastating to many nurses at the time, because, fearful of being punished, unmarried male officers in the hospital soon turned their eyes on young women in the city and nearby villages. Most of the nurses resented it, but for nineteen years the rule had been strictly observed. Whenever offenders were discovered, the leaders would criticize them. Because Lin was a married man and Manna couldn't become his fiancée, they were not allowed to walk together outside the hospital grounds. By now, after so many years of restriction, they had grown accustomed to it.

PART

1

1

Lin Kong graduated from the military medical school toward the end of 1963 and came to Muji to work as a doctor. At that time the hospital ran a small nursing school, which offered a sixteen-month program and produced nurses for the army in Manchuria and Inner Mongolia. When Manna Wu enrolled as a student in the fall of 1964, Lin was teaching a course in anatomy. She was an energetic young woman at the time, playing volleyball on the hospital team. Unlike most of her classmates who were recent middle- or high-school graduates, she had already served three years as a telephone operator in a coastal division and was older than most of them. Since over 95 percent of the students in the nursing school were female, many young officers from the units stationed in Muji City would frequent the hospital on weekends.

Most of the officers wanted to find a girlfriend or a fiancée among the students, although these young women were still soldiers and were not allowed to have a boyfriend. There was a secret reason for the men's interest in the female students, a reason few of them would articulate but one which they all knew in their hearts, namely that these were "good girls." That phrase meant these women were virgins; otherwise they could not have joined the army, since every young woman recruited had to go through a physical exam that eliminated those with a broken hymen.

One Sunday afternoon in the summer, Manna was washing clothes alone in the dormitory washroom. In came a bareheaded lieutenant of slender build and medium height, his face marked with a few freckles. His collar was unbuckled and the top buttons on his jacket were undone, displaying his prominent Adam's apple. He stood beside her, lifted his foot up, and placed it into the long terrazzo sink. The tap water splashed on his black plastic sandal and spread like a silvery fan. Done with the left foot, he put in his right. To Manna's amusement, he bathed his feet again and again. His breath stank of alcohol.

He turned and gave her a toothy grin, and she smiled back. Gradually they entered into conversation. He said he was the head of a radio station at the headquarters of the Muji Sub-Command and a friend of Instructor Peng. His hands shook a little as he talked. He asked where she came from; she told him her hometown was in Shandong Province, withholding the fact that she had grown up as an orphan without a home-town—her parents had died in a traffic accident in Tibet when she was three.

"What's your name?" he asked.

"Manna Wu."

"I'm Mai Dong, from Shanghai."

A lull set in. She felt her face flushing a little, so she returned to washing her clothes. But he seemed eager to go on talking.

"Glad to meet you, Comrade Manna Wu," he said abruptly and stretched out his hand.

She waved to show the soapsuds on her palms. "Sorry," she said with a pixieish smile.

"By the way, how do you like Muji?" he asked, rubbing his wet hands on his flanks.

"It's all right."

"Really? Even the weather here?"

"Yes."

"Not too cold in winter?" Before she could answer, he went on, "Of course, summer's fine. How about—"

"Why did you bathe your feet eight or nine times?" She giggled.

"Oh, did I?" He seemed bewildered, looking down at his feet.

"Nice sandals," she said.

"My cousin sent them from Shanghai. By the way, how old are you?" He grinned.

Surprised by the question, she looked at him for a moment and then turned away, reddening.

He smiled rather naturally. "I mean, do you have a boyfriend?"

Again she was taken aback. Before she could decide how to answer, a woman student walked in with a bucket to fetch water, so their conversation had to end.

A week later she received a letter from Mai Dong. He apologized profusely for disturbing her in the washroom and for his untidy appearance, which wasn't suitable for an officer. He had asked her so many embarrassing questions, she must have taken him for an idiot. But he had not been himself that day. He begged her to forgive him. She wrote back, saying she had not been offended, instead very much amused. She appreciated his candor and natural manners.

Both of them were in their mid-twenties and had never taken a lover. Soon they began to write each other a few times a week. Within two months they started their rendezvous on weekends at movie theaters, parks, and the riverbank. Mai Dong hated Muji, which was a city with a population of about a quarter of a million. He dreaded its severe winters and the north winds that came from Siberia with clouds of snow dust. The smog, which always curtained the sky when the weather was cold, aggravated his chronic sore throat. His work, transcribing and transmitting telegrams, impaired his eyesight. He was unhappy and complained a great deal.

Manna tried to comfort him with kind words. By nature he was weak and gentle. Sometimes she felt he was like a small boy who needed the care of an elder sister or a mother.

One Saturday afternoon in the fall, they met in Victory
Park. Under a weeping willow on the bank of a lake, they sat
together watching a group of children on the other shore flying a large kite, which was a paper centipede crawling up and
down in the air. To their right, about a hundred feet away, a
donkey was tethered to a tree, now and then whisking its tail.
Its master was lying on the grass and taking a nap, a green cap
over his face so that flies might not bother him. Maple seeds
floated down, revolving in the breeze. Furtively Mai Dong
stretched out his hand, held Manna's shoulder, and pulled her
closer so as to kiss her lips.

"What are you doing?" she cried, leaping to her feet. Her
abrupt movement scared away the mallards and geese in the
water. She didn't understand his intention and thought he had
attempted something indecent, like a hoodlum. She didn't remember ever being kissed by anyone.

He looked puzzled, then muttered, "I didn't mean to make
you angry like this."

"Don't ever do that again."

"All right, I won't." He turned away from her and looked
piqued, spitting on the grass.

From then on, though she didn't reproach him again, she
resisted his advances resolutely, her sense of virtue and honor
preventing her from succumbing to his desire. Her resistance
kindled his passion. Soon he told her that he couldn't help
thinking of her all the time, as though she had become his
shadow. Sometimes at night, he would walk alone in the compound of the Sub-Command headquarters for hours, with his
1951 pistol stuck in his belt. Heaven knew how he missed her
and how many nights he remained awake tossing and turning
while thinking about her. Out of desperation, he proposed to
her two months before her graduation. He wanted to marry
her without delay.

She thought he must have lost his mind, though by now she

also couldn't help thinking of him for an hour or two every night. Her head ached in the morning, her grades were suffering, and she was often angry with herself. She would lose her temper with others for no apparent reason. When nobody was around, tears often came to her eyes. For all their love, an immediate marriage would be impracticable, out of the question. She was uncertain where she would be sent when she graduated, probably to a remote army unit, which could be anywhere in Manchuria or Inner Mongolia. Besides, a marriage at this moment would suggest that she was having a love affair; this would invite punishment, the lightest of which the school would administer was to keep the couple as separate as possible. In recent years the leaders had assigned some lovers to different places deliberately.

She revealed Mai Dong's proposal to nobody except her teacher Lin Kong, who was known as a good-hearted married man and was regarded by many students as a kind of elder brother. In such a situation she needed an objective opinion. Lin agreed that a marriage at this moment was unwise, and that they had better wait a while until her graduation and then decide what to do. He promised he would let nobody know of the relationship. In addition, he said he would try to help her in the job assignment if he was involved in making the decision.

She reasoned Mai Dong out of the idea of an immediate marriage and assured him that she would become his wife sooner or later. As graduation approached, they both grew restless, hoping she would remain in Muji City. He was depressed, and his despondency made her love him more.

At the graduation she was assigned to stay in the hospital and work in its Medical Department as a nurse—a junior officer of the twenty-fourth rank. The good news, however, didn't please Mai Dong and Manna for long, because a week later he was informed that his radio station was going to be transferred to a newly formed regiment in Fuyuan County, almost eighty miles northeast of Muji and very close to the Russian border.

"Don't panic," she told him. "Work and study hard on the front. I'll wait for you." Though also heartbroken, she felt he was a rather pathetic man. She wished he were stronger, a man she could rely on in times of adversity, because life always had unexpected misfortunes.

"When will we get married?" he asked.

"Soon, I promise."

Despite saying that, she was unsure whether he would be able to come back to Muji. She preferred to wait a while.

The nearer the time for departure drew, the more embittered Mai Dong became. A few times he mentioned he would rather be demobilized and return to Shanghai, but she dissuaded him from considering that. A discharge might send him to a place far away, such as an oil field or a construction corps building railroads in the interior of China. It was better for them to stay as close as possible.

When she saw him off at the front entrance of the Sub-Command headquarters, she had to keep blowing on her fingers, having forgotten to bring along her mittens. She wouldn't take the fur gloves he offered her; she said he would need them more. He stood at the back door of the radio van, whose green body had turned gray with encrusted ice and snow. The radio antenna atop the van was tilting in the wind, which, with a shrill whistle, again and again tried to snatch it up and bear it off. More snow was falling, and the air was piercingly cold. Mai Dong's breath hung around his face as he shouted orders to his soldiers in the van, who gathered at the window, eager to see what Manna looked like. Outside the van, a man loaded into a side trunk some large wooden blocks needed for climbing the slippery mountain roads. The driver kicked the rear wheels to see whether the tire chains were securely fastened. His fur hat was completely white, a nest of snowflakes.

As the van drew away, Mai Dong waved good-bye to Manna, his hand stretching through the back window, as though struggling to pull her along. He wanted to cry, "Wait for me, Manna!" but he dared not get that out in the presence of his men. Seeing his face contort with pain, Manna's eyes blurred with tears. She bit her lips so as not to cry.

Winter in Muji was long. Snow wouldn't disappear until early May. In mid-April when the Songhua River began to break up, people would gather at the bank watching the large blocks of ice cracking and drifting in the blackish-green water. Teenage boys, baskets in hand, would tread and hop on the floating ice, picking up pike, whitefish, carp, baby sturgeon, and catfish killed by the ice blocks that had been washed down by spring torrents. Steamboats, still in the docks, blew their horns time and again. When the main channel was finally clear of ice, they crept out, sailing slowly up and down the river and saluting the spectators with long blasts. Children would hail and wave at them.

Then spring descended all of a sudden. Aspen catkins flew in the air, so thick that when walking on the streets you could breathe them in and you would flick your hand to keep them away from your face. The scent of lilac blooms was pungent and intoxicating. Yet old people still wrapped themselves in fur or cotton-padded clothes. The dark earth, vast and loamy, marked by tufts of yellow grass here and there, began emitting a warm vapor that flickered like purple smoke in the sunshine. All at once apricot and peach trees broke into blossoms, which grew puffy as bees kept touching them. Within two weeks the summer started. Spring was so short here that people would say Muji had only three seasons.

In her letters to Mai Dong, Manna described these seasonal changes as though he had never lived in the city. As always, he complained in his letters about life at the front. Many soldiers there suffered from night blindness because they hadn't eaten enough vegetables. They all had lice in their underclothes since they couldn't take baths in their barracks. For the whole winter and spring he had seen only two movies. He had lost fourteen pounds, he was like a skeleton now. To comfort him, each month Manna mailed him a small bag of peanut brittle.

One evening in June, Manna and two other nurses were about to set out for the volleyball court behind the medical building. Benping, the soldier in charge of mail and newspapers, came and handed her a letter. Seeing it was from Mai Dong, her teammates teased her, saying, "Aha, a love letter."

She opened the envelope and was shocked while reading through the two pages. Mai Dong told her that he couldn't stand the life on the border any longer and had applied for a discharge, which had been granted. He was going back to Shanghai, where the weather was milder and the food better. More heartrending, he had decided to marry his cousin, who was a salesgirl at a department store in Shanghai. Without such a marriage, he wouldn't be able to obtain a residence card, which was absolutely necessary for him to live and find employment in the metropolis. In reality he and the girl had been engaged even before he had applied for his discharge; otherwise he wouldn't have been allowed to go to Shanghai, since he was not from the city proper but from one of its suburban counties. He was sorry for Manna and asked her to hate and forget him.

Her initial response was long silence.

"Are you okay?" Nurse Shen asked.

Manna nodded and said nothing. Then the three of them set out for the game.

On the volleyball court Manna, usually an indifferent player, struck the ball with such ferocity that for the first time her comrades shouted "Bravo" for her. Her face was smeared with sweat and tears. As she dove to save a ball, she fell flat on the graveled court and scraped her right elbow. The spectators applauded the diving save while she slowly picked herself up and found blood oozing from her skin.

During the break her teammates told her to go to the clinic and have the injury dressed, so she left, planning to return for the second game. But on her way, she changed her mind and ran back to the dormitory. She merely washed her elbow with cold water and didn't bandage it.

Once alone in the bedroom, she read the letter again and tears gushed from her eyes. She flung the pages down on the desk and fell on her bed, sobbing, twisting, and biting the pillowcase. A mosquito buzzed above her head, then settled on her neck, but she didn't bother to slap it. She felt as if her heart had been pierced.

When her three roommates came back at nine, she was still in tears. They picked up the letter and glanced through it; together they tried to console her by condemning the heartless man. But their words made her sob harder and even convulsively. That night she didn't wash her face or brush her teeth. She slept with her clothes on, waking now and then and weeping quietly while her roommates wheezed or smacked their lips or murmured something in their sleep. She simply couldn't stop her tears.

She was ill for a few weeks. She felt aged, in deep lassitude and numb despair, and regretted not marrying Mai Dong before he left for the front. Her limbs were weary, as though separated from herself. Despite her comrades' protests, she dropped out of the volleyball team, saying she was too sick to play. She spent more time alone, as though all at once she belonged to an older generation; she cared less about her looks and clothes.

By now she was almost twenty-six, on the verge of becoming an old maid, whose standard age was twenty-seven to most people's minds. The hospital had three old maids; Manna seemed destined to join them.

She wasn't very attractive, but she was slim and tall and looked natural; besides, she had a pleasant voice. In normal circumstances she wouldn't have had difficulty in finding a boyfriend, but the hospital always kept over a hundred women nurses, most of whom were around twenty, healthy and normal, so young officers could easily find girlfriends among them. As a result, few men were interested in Manna. Only an enlisted soldier paid her some attentions. He was a cook, a squat man from Szechwan Province, and he would dole out to her a larger portion of a dish when she bought her meal. But she did not want an enlisted soldier as a boyfriend, which would have violated the rule that only officers could have a girlfriend or a boyfriend. Besides, that man looked awful—owlish and cunning. So she avoided standing in any line leading to his window.

2

In the mid-1960s the hospital had only four medical school graduates on its staff. Lin Kong was one of them. The rest of the seventy doctors had been trained by the army itself through short-term courses and experience on battlefields. In addition to his diploma, Lin carried on each shoulder one bar and three stars, having the rank of captain and a monthly salary of ninety-four yuan. Understandably some nurses found him attractive, especially those new arrivals who didn't know he kept a family in the countryside. To their disappointment, they would find out later that he was already married. Word had gone about that his wife was eight years older than he and had been taken into his family as a child bride when he was just seven. It was said that she had been his nanny for many years. For all the rumors, nobody could tell exactly what his wife was like.

From their days in the nursing school, friendship had developed between Lin and Manna. He had been a teacher but without any airs, unlike most of the other instructors. For that she had respected him more. Now as they worked in the same department, she gradually grew attached to this tall, quiet man, who always spoke amiably to everybody. When others talked with him, he would listen patiently and give weight to their ideas. Different from most young officers, he seemed very mature for his age, which was thirty. His glasses made him look urbane and knowledgeable. People liked him, calling him Scholar or Bookworm, and every year he had been elected a model officer.

When Manna told Lin that Mai Dong had broken their engagement, he said, "Forget him and take good care of yourself. You'll find a better man."

She was grateful for his kind words. She was certain that unlike others, he would not gossip about her misfortune behind her back.

One day in the summer, she stopped by his dormitory to deliver the journal *Studies in Military Medical Science* and some pills for his arthritis. Lin was alone in the bedroom he shared with two other doctors. Manna noticed a tall wooden bookcase beyond the head of his bed, against the wall. On the shelves were about two hundred books. Most of the titles were unfamiliar to her—*Song of Youth, Cement, The History of International Communism, War and Peace, The Guerrilla Detachment on the Railroad, White Nights, Lenin: World's First Nuclear-Powered Ice-Breaker,* and so forth. On the bottom shelf there were several medical textbooks in Russian. That impressed her greatly, since she had never met a person who could read a book written in a foreign language.

By contrast, Lin's two roommates, as though illiterate, owned no books. On one of their bedside desks, a brass artillery shell, a foot in length and four inches in diameter, stood beside a lamp, which was made of conch shells glued together. Yet they both had flowered quilts and pillows, whereas Lin's bedding was in plain white and green—a standard army set. His mosquito net was yellowish, its bottom edge frayed. It reminded Manna of a whisper among the nurses that Lin was so tightfisted he would never buy an expensive dish. She didn't know whether that was true, but she had noticed that unlike other men who would bolt down their meals, Lin often ate in a fussy manner like a woman doing needlework.

To her surprise, Lin bent down and pulled a washbasin out from under his roommate Ming Chen's bed, saying, "We have some fruit here." In the basin were about twenty brown apple-pears, which the three doctors had bought together the day before.

"Oh, don't treat me like a guest," she said.

"No. You're lucky today. If you come tomorrow, they'll all be gone." He picked up a large pear and with his foot pushed the basin back under the bed. The metallic rasp on the cement floor grated on her a little. "I'll be back in a second," he said and went out to wash the pear.

She picked up a book from his bed, which was written by Stalin, entitled *The Problems of Leninism*. Opening it, she found a woodcut bookplate on its inside front cover. At the bottom of the plate was a foreign word, *EX-LIBRIS*, above which was an engraving of a thatched cottage, partly surrounded by a railing and shaded by two trees with luxuriant crowns, five birds soaring in the distance by the peak of a hill, and the setting sun casting down its last rays. For a moment Manna was fascinated by the tranquil scene in the bookplate.

When Lin came back she asked him, "What does this mean?" She pointed at the foreign word.

"It's Latin, meaning 'from my collection.' " He handed her the pear. She noticed he had long-boned hands, the fingers lean and apparently dexterous. He should be a surgeon instead of a physician, she thought.

"May I look at some of your books?" she asked.

"Of course, you're welcome."

She took a bite of the pear, which was juicy and fragrant and reminded her of a banana she had eaten many years ago. She began flicking through several books. They all carried the same woodcut plates behind the front covers, and some thick volumes had Lin's personal seal on their fore edges. She was impressed by his caring for the books and would have loved to see more, but she couldn't stay longer because she had a package to deliver to another doctor.

After that visit, she started to borrow books from Lin. The hospital had a small library, but its holdings were limited to the subjects of politics and medical science. The two dozen novels and plays it had once owned had been surrendered to the bonfires built by the Red Guards before the city hall two months ago. Strange to say, Lin's books remained intact. No one seemed to have reported him, and none of the hospital's revolutionaries had suggested confiscating Lin's books. Manna soon discovered that several officers were using Lin's library in secret; sometimes she had to wait for a novel to come back from another borrower.

She wasn't a serious reader and seldom read a book from cover to cover, but she was eager to see what Lin and his friends were reading, as though they had formed a clandestine club she was curious about.

On National Day, October 1, she ran into Lin before the hospital's photo shop, which was run by an old crippled man. Lin asked her if she could help him make dust jackets for his books. He explained, "It's not safe to show their titles on the shelf. Everybody can see them. I've wrapped up half of them already."

"I'll come and help. You should've told me earlier," she said.

When she arrived at his dormitory that evening, Lin's roommates, Ming Chen and Jin Tian, were there, bent over a chessboard, playing a war game and drinking draft beer, which they poured from a plastic lysol can sitting on a desk. Ming Chen was an acupuncturist and Jin Tian an assistant surgeon, both trained by the hospital. Lin took out a thick roll of kraft paper, a pair of scissors, and a packet of adhesive tape. Together he and Manna began working on the books while his two roommates were battling noisily on the chessboard.

"Foul," Ming Chen shouted. "My colonel killed your captain." He had rancid breath, which Manna could smell three yards away.

"Come on," Jin Tian begged, "let me take back a move this once, all right? I let you do that just now when my land mine blew up your field marshal."

"Give me that piece, Bean Sprout." Ming Chen reached across the desk for Jin Tian's fist, which had grabbed the captain.

Dodging his opponent's hand, the spindly Jin Tian said, "Watch your mouth!"

"I watch your mother's ass."

"Knock it off, man! We have a lady comrade here."

"From now on no false move!"

"Okay."

Lin and Manna were working quietly. The books were lying on his bed. One by one they placed them on the table, wrapped them up, then returned them to the bookcase. Three or four times her hand touched his as they reached out simultaneously for the scissors. She tried to smile at him but felt herself blushing, so she kept her head low. In the presence of his boisterous roommates, she had lost her natural manners. If the other two men hadn't been around, she would have talked some with Lin, which was what she was eager to do.

Within two hours every volume was cloaked in a kraft jacket. Standing together on the shelves, the books now looked indistinguishable to Manna.

"My, how can you tell one from another?" she asked Lin, drinking a bottle of mineral water he had opened for her.

"No problem, I always can tell which is which." He smiled rather shyly, two pink patches on his cheeks. She felt he avoided her eyes.

In addition to wrapping the books up, he thumbtacked a piece of white sheeting to the bookshelf as a curtain. Now he seemed to have closed his library forever. She couldn't help wondering how he could get along with his two roommates, who were so different from him. He must be very good-natured.

Two days later, the hospital's Political Department ordered all the staff to hand in their books that contained bourgeois ideology and sentiments, particularly those by foreign authors. Lin told Manna that he had turned in a dozen books, most of which had been extra copies. She was surprised that the leaders didn't demand that he surrender all his novels. It seemed that he must have known about the imminent orders, or else he wouldn't have asked her to help him jacket the books in a hurry and closed his library right before the confiscation. Why should he run the risk of keeping them? He could be publicly denounced for doing that. Everybody knew Lin owned many foreign novels; why didn't the leaders have them confiscated? She dared not ask Lin, but she stopped borrowing books from him.

3

In the winter of 1966 the hospital undertook camp-and-field training. For some reason a top general in Northeastern Military Command had issued orders in October that all the army had to be able to operate without modern vehicles, which not only were unreliable but also could soften the troops. The orders said, "We must carry on the spirit of the Long March and restore the tradition of horses and mules."

For a month, a third of the hospital's staff would march four hundred miles through the countryside and camp at villages and small towns. Along the way they would practice treating the wounded and rescuing the dying from the battlefield. Both Lin and Manna joined the training. He was appointed the head of a medical team, which consisted of twenty-eight people. For the first time in his life he became a leader, so he worked conscientiously.

The march went well for the first few days, since the roads were flat and the troops fresh. But it got tougher and tougher as they approached a mountainous area where snow often left no trace of a road. Many of the men and women began to hobble, which often drew the attention of civilians, who would watch them with excitement. Sometimes when the troops entered a town, even the spectators' sincere applause sounded derisive to the limpers and made them hang their heads. As men and women were equal, all the female nurses had to trudge along in the same way as the men did, though they didn't shoulder a rifle and at times were allowed to carry lighter pieces of equipment.

One windless day they marched through a forest toward a

village in the north. They walked for a whole day with only a
lunch break. By seven o'clock they had covered twenty-eight
miles, hungry and exhausted, but five miles still lay ahead.
Then came the orders that they had to reach the village within
an hour—"before the battle gets under way," as they were
told. Instantly a forced march started, the troops running at
full speed.

Manna's feet were severely blistered from bearing a
stretcher for six hours. The "wounded soldier" had been a side
of pork weighing a hundred and twenty pounds. So now she
could barely walk. Lin took the medical box off her shoulder
and slipped its strap over his head, carrying it for her. Then
two soldiers held her upper arms and pulled her along to keep
up with the troops.

Their big-toed boots were throwing up puffs of snow, and
now and then a voice commanded loudly, "Close up!" or
"Don't take off your hat!" In the sky ahead the Big Dipper
was dancing zigzag as though the earth were turning upside
down. Flocks of crows took off from the trees, flapping away
in every direction and cawing like starved ghosts. Time and
again a mug or a canteen dropped on the ice with a sharp
clank. Suddenly a tall man fell; the seventy-pound transmitter
he carried on his back hit the stump of a felled tree. The frightened Jin Tian, who was in charge of communications, helped
him up while saying through his teeth, "Damn! If the
machine's broken, you'll go back to your home village and
eat sweet potatoes the rest of your life!"

All the way Manna was groaning to the men who were
hauling her, "Let go of me . . . Oh so tired. Please let me die
here, in the snow . . ." But they dragged her along. The orders
allowed nobody to be left behind.

Fifty-six minutes later they arrived at the village, which
consisted of about eighty households. Lin Kong's team was
billeted in three farmhouses—the two larger ones were for the

doctors and soldiers, the smaller one for the seven women nurses.

In the pale moonlight, smoke and sparks were spouting out from two chimneys atop the production brigade's office house. The mess squad was busy cooking in there, burning cornstalks and brushwood. Two cleavers were chopping cabbages rhythmically while the cooks were making a soup and baking wheaten cakes. From time to time they larded the field cauldrons with two thick pieces of pork skin. In the yard the horses were drinking warm water and munching fodder, their backs and flanks still steaming with sweat. The mess officer had gone out to look for a stable for the horses, but he hadn't returned yet.

After Lin's men had settled in, Lin went to the "kitchen" with an orderly to fetch dinner. In there he didn't see any of the nurses of his team. It occurred to him that they must have been too exhausted to come. So he let the baby-faced orderly take the wheaten cakes and the cabbage and pork soup back to the men, while he borrowed an aluminum pot from the cooks and carried some soup and a bag of cakes to the nurses.

The wind was rising, and wisps of steam were blown up from the pot, swirling about Lin's chest. Dogs barked at the sentries, who were patrolling the village, toting flashlights and submachine guns. Stars glittered like brass nuggets above the pine woods that were swaying wave after wave in the south. On arrival at the farmhouse, Lin found Manna Wu and Haiyan Niu bathing their feet in a large wooden bowl. An old woman with a weather-beaten face was heating more water in an iron bucket for the other nurses. "Why don't you go fetch dinner?" he asked them.

"We're still drenched in sweat," Nurse Shen answered.

"I'm dog tired," said Manna, whose feet rubbed each other in the warm water with tiny squeaks.

"No matter what, you have to eat," Lin said. "Otherwise how could you walk tomorrow?" He put the soup and the bag of wheaten cakes on a nail-studded chest of drawers. "All right, eat dinner and have a good sleep. We'll have a long way to go tomorrow."

"Doctor Kong, I—I can't walk anymore," Manna said almost in tears, pointing to her feet.

"I can't walk either," the large-eyed Haiyan broke in. "I have blisters too."

"Let me have a look," he said.

The old woman moved an oil lamp closer. Lin squatted down to examine the two pairs of feet resting on the edge of the wooden bowl. Haiyan's feet had three small blisters, one on the ball of her right foot and two on her left heel; but Manna's soles were bloated with blisters that were shiny like tiny balloons. With his forefinger he pressed the red skin around the largest blister, and Manna let out a moan.

"The blisters must be drained," he said to the nurses standing by. "Do you know how to do it?"

"No." They all shook their heads.

Lin sighed, but to their amazement, he rolled up his sleeves and said, "Manna, I need two or three hairs from you, long ones."

"All right," she replied.

He turned to the old woman. "Do you have a needle, Granny?"

"Sure." She went out of the room and called to her daughter-in-law, who was at the other end of the house. "Hey, Rong, bring me some needles."

"Here you are," said Manna, handing Lin a few hairs, each about a foot long. He picked one and put the rest on his knee.

A thirtyish woman stepped in, carrying a large gourd ladle filled with scraps of cloth, balls of white, blue, and black threads, and a small silk pincushion. She said, "I've all the needles here, Mama. What kind you need?"

"A small one will do," Lin put in.

A two-inch needle was placed in his hand. He threaded it with a hair, then said to Manna, "Don't be scared. It won't hurt much."

She nodded. Lin cleaned his hands and the needle with a few cotton balls soaked with alcohol. Then with another cotton ball held with tweezers he wiped the largest blister on Manna's right heel. After patting it gently with his fingertip for a few seconds, he pierced it through. "Ow!" she cried and shut her eyes tight. At once her heel was covered with warm liquid flowing out of the punctured skin.

Lin cut the hair with scissors and left a piece of it inside the blister. "Let the hair stay. It will keep the holes open so the water drains," he said to the nurses gathering around to look.

"Boy, tut-tut-tut," the old woman said, "who'd think you get rid of a blister like this." She shook her wrinkled face, one of her white eyebrows twitching.

Lin went on to pierce and drain the rest of the blisters on Manna's right sole, while the other young women were working on Haiyan's feet and Manna's left foot. The old woman climbed onto the heated brick bed. One by one she turned the seven wet fur hats inside out and placed them at the warmer end of the bed to dry.

When he had finished treating Manna's blisters, Lin washed his hands in a basin, saying to Haiyan, "Don't worry, you should be able to walk tomorrow, but I'm not sure about Manna. It may take a few days for her feet to heal."

At those words, a shadow flitted across Haiyan's face. The other nurses thanked Lin for showing them how to treat blisters and for the dinner he had brought them. "Eat and rest well," he said. "Don't forget to return the pot to the mess squad tomorrow morning."

"We won't," said one of them.

"Doctor Kong, why don't you eat with us?" Nurse Shen asked.

"Yes, eat with us," a few voices said in unison.

"Well, I ate already."

That was a fib, although he felt a sudden warm thrill rising in his chest. Something soft was filling his throat. He was surprised by the invitation and afraid that if he stayed with the nurses for dinner, people would gossip about him and the leaders might criticize him as well. He forced himself to say, "Good night, everybody. Good night, Granny." He raised the thick door curtain made of gunnysacks and went out.

Once outside, he overheard the old woman say, "Good for you, girls. Such a nice man, isn't he? I wish I had blisters too." Laughter rang inside the house.

One of the nurses began singing an opera song:

The wide lake sways wave after wave.
On the other shore lies our hometown.
In the morning we paddle out
To cast nets, and return at night,
Our boats loaded with fish . . .

Lin turned around in the snow, gazing back at the low farmhouse for a long time. Its windows were bronze with the light of oil lamps. If only he could have eaten dinner with the nurses in there. He wouldn't mind walking twenty miles just for that. He wondered whether he had visited them for some unconscious reason other than to deliver the dinner. Then a strange vision came to his mind. He saw himself sitting at the head of a long dining table and eating with all seven young women and the old woman too. No, the old woman turned out to be his wife Shuyu, who was busy passing around a basket of fresh steamed bread. As they were eating, the women were smiling and chattering intimately. Apparently they all enjoyed themselves as his wives living under the same roof. He remembered that in the Old China some rich men had several wives. How lucky those landowners and capitalists must have been, wallowing in polygamous bliss. A scream of the wind brought him back to the snowfield. He shook his head and the vision disappeared. "You're sick," he said to himself. He felt slightly disgusted by his envying those reactionary men, who ought to be condemned as social parasites. Yet the feel of Manna's foot, which seemed to have penetrated his skin, was still lingering and expanding in his palms and fingers. He turned and made his way to his men's billet. His gait was no longer as steady as it had been an hour ago.

Manna couldn't walk the next day. Lin arranged to have her taken by a horse cart, which hauled utensils and provisions, running ahead of the troops. He gave her both his and Haiyan's sheepskin greatcoats, which she wrapped around her legs, so that they wouldn't have to carry them. She traveled in the cart for two full days; then the troops stopped at a commune town for a week. That gave enough time for her feet to heal.

During the remaining days of the training, Lin carried her medical box most of the time. Whenever she thanked him, he would say, "Don't mention it. It's my job."

4

After the troops had returned to Muji, Manna's gratitude to Lin gradually turned into intense curiosity. At work she often stopped by his office to say a word with him. At night, after taps was sounded, she would remain awake thinking about this odd man. Questions rose in her mind one after another. Does he love his wife? What does she look like? Is she really eight years older than he? Why is he so quiet, so kindhearted? Has he ever been angry with anyone? He seems to have no temper.

Silly girl, why do you always wonder about him? He's a good man, all right, but he's already married. Don't be a fool. He's not there for you.

What if he doesn't love his wife and wants to leave her? If so, would you go with him? Stop fantasizing and get some sleep.

Would you marry him?

Hard as she tried, she couldn't stifle the thought of him. Night after night, similar questions kept her awake until the small hours. At times she felt as though his hands still held and touched her right heel; so sensitive and so gentle were his fingers. Her feet couldn't help rubbing each other under the quilt, and she even massaged them now and then. Her heart brimmed with emotions.

From Haiyan she learned that Lin's wife had given birth to a baby girl. This information upset her, because he was bound to his family more than she had thought. Probably you'd better distance yourself from him, she kept reminding herself. You're heading for trouble. No matter what the outcome is, people will blame you. A third party is like a semi-criminal.

Despite all her reasoning, she couldn't help glancing at Lin whenever she caught sight of him. She began to feel as though she were living in a trance.

One evening in June, Manna went to the guinea pigs' house to see a newborn litter. Afterward she returned to her dormitory alone. On the way she saw a man and a woman strolling by the aspen grove west of the mess hall. From the distance she couldn't tell who they were, though from behind the man looked like Lin. The dusk was balmy after a whole day of drizzling, and the trees seemed like a dark fence, against which the two figures in white shirts were moving west.

Manna was eager to find out who they were. There was a footpath going diagonally through the rows of young aspens. Without thinking twice, she turned into the grove so that she might see the man and woman clearly at the other end. As she walked along the path, her heart began galloping. Around her water was dripping pit-a-pat from the broad leaves as if a rain were starting. The indigo sky was drilled with stars.

A shadow appeared ahead of her and paused in the middle of the path. It was a dog. Manna stopped and couldn't tell whether it was the one raised by the cooks or a homeless dog going to the kitchen to steal food. The pair of greenish eyes looking in her direction sent an icy shiver down her back, as she remembered that a boy had been attacked by a rabid dog near the grove a few weeks before. She knew that if she turned back, the dog would chase and snap at her, so she stood still. Then she saw a leafy branch lying nearby, and she picked it up, waving it at the animal menacingly. The dog went on watching her for a while, then skulked away with its nose touching the ground repeatedly.

When Manna reached the far side of the grove, she heard a female voice say, "So he lost the book? I can't believe it." She recognized the voice, which belonged to Pingping Ma, the young woman in charge of the hospital's library.

"Next time I'd better ask him for security," Lin said in a joking tone.

They both laughed. Manna was observing them from behind a few thin aspens. Lin looked very happy. They stopped under a street lamp, saying something Manna couldn't quite hear. Beyond them spread a small pond of rainwater shimmering in the moonlight, from which toads were croaking. Pingping Ma bent down, picked up a stone, and threw it underarm into the pond, the flat stone skipping away on the surface of the water and sending up tiny flashes.

"I made three," she cried in a silvery voice. The stone had silenced the toads for a few seconds, then one of them resumed croaking hesitantly.

"I used to be good at playing ducks and drakes," Lin said. He flung a stone too.

"Wow, five!" the woman said.

They turned around to look for flat stones, but couldn't find a good one. Neither of them made more than three skips in the following attempts thanks to the lumpy stones they had to use. But they obviously enjoyed themselves.

Manna dared not stay too long, because the footpath was often used by others and she was afraid someone might run into her. Also, the dog might appear again. She hurried back, carrying the branch on her shoulder and feeling something pulling her guts. She began to swallow hard as a thirst raged in her mouth. Her sneakers and the bottoms of her trouser legs were soaked through when she reached her dormitory.

That night she stayed awake for hours, thinking about the scene she had just witnessed. What was the true relationship between Lin Kong and Pingping Ma? Were they lovers? They might have been, or they wouldn't have skipped stones together so happily, like small children. No, that was unlikely because Pingping Ma was at least ten years younger than Lin. Besides, she was merely an enlisted soldier, not allowed to have a boyfriend. But she wouldn't give a damn about the rule, would she? No, she wouldn't; otherwise she would not have dated a married man. Was Lin really attracted to her? Probably not. Her face was bumpy and ugly like a pumpkin, and she had gapped teeth. Still, Lin seemed to enjoy being with her very much. He had never looked that natural with others. Again in her mind's eye Manna saw him standing by the pond with arms akimbo as he watched that woman skipping the stones.

The more Manna thought, the more agitated she became. What troubled her the most was that Pingping Ma's father was a vice-commander of the Thirty-ninth Army in Liaoning Province. With such a powerful family background, even a pig could appear attractive in some men's eyes. Was Lin such a snob too?

That thought made Manna more wretched as she remembered the deaths of her parents. Had they been alive, they could have been ranking officials as well. Her aunt had told her that when her father was killed in the traffic accident, he had been an eminent journalist for a large newspaper. For a thirty-one-year-old man, that was remarkable. Her mother had been a college graduate, specializing in French; with that kind of education she could surely have made a lot of progress in her career.

Then another troublesome thought came to Manna's mind. Pingping Ma was well read in classics and worked as the only librarian in the hospital. It was said that she often told legendary tales to her roommates, who would treat her to haw jelly and sodas to keep stories rolling out from her tongue. This might have been what made her attractive to Lin. To some extent they matched each other; both were bookworms. No doubt they would continue to spend time together chatting about books.

What should Manna do? Let that girl take him away? No, she had to do something.

5

Lin had been considerate to Manna, especially after he came to know she had grown up in an orphanage in Tsingtao City. During her first two annual leaves, she had stayed at the hospital, having no place to go. She had neither siblings nor relatives, except for a distant aunt whom she had never felt close to. Lin often advised her to rejoin the volleyball team or take part in the hospital's propaganda and performing arts club, but she said she was too old for them. Instead, she would declare to him half jokingly that she wanted to go into a nunnery. If only she had known of a convent that was still open and would recruit nuns. In reality the Red Guards were smashing temples and abbeys throughout the country, and monks and nuns had been either sent back home or banished far away, so that they could make an honest living like the masses.

Recently Lin was aware of Manna's glances and tried to avoid them. He was unsure whether he was really attracted to her. Since the previous summer when Mai Dong broke the engagement, she had changed a lot. Her face was no longer that youthful. Thin rings appeared around her eyes when she smiled, and her complexion had grown pasty and less firm. He felt bad for her, realizing that a young woman could lose her looks so easily and that however little the loss was, it was always irretrievable. He wanted to be kind to her, but sometimes her smiles and her expressive eyes, which seemed eager to draw him to her, disturbed him.

By the summer of 1967 he had been married for almost four years, and his daughter was ten months old. Whenever he saw a couple walk hand in hand on the street, he couldn't refrain from looking at them furtively and wishing he were able to do the same. As a married man, why did he have to live like a widower? Why couldn't he enjoy the warmth of a family? If only he hadn't agreed to let his parents choose a bride for him. If only his wife were pretty and her feet had not been bound. Or if only she and he had been a generation older, so that people in the city wouldn't laugh at her small feet.

But he was by no means miserable, and his envy for men with presentable wives was always momentary. He held no grudge against Shuyu, who had attended his mother diligently until the old woman died; now she was caring for his bedridden father and their baby. On the whole Lin was content to work in the hospital. He earned enough, more than most of the doctors did because he held a medical school diploma. His life had been simple and peaceful, until one day Manna changed it.

On his desk in the office she left an envelope. It contained an opera ticket and a note in her round handwriting, which said: "This is for *The Navy Battle of 1894* at 8:00 p.m. I hope you will go and enjoy it." He had seen the movie and knew the entire story, so he wondered whether he should return the ticket to her. On second thought he decided to go, because he had nothing else to do that evening and the opera was performed by a well-known troupe from Changchun City. Besides, the seat was good, close to the front.

The hospital's theater was at the southeastern corner of the compound. When Lin arrived, he was surprised to find Manna sitting in the fifth row too, right next to his seat. He hesitated for a second, then went up to her. The moment he sat down, people began throwing glances in his direction. Some of the audience were waving fans and a few were cracking sunflower seeds. Children were chasing one another in the front and through the aisles, holding slingshots, wooden pistols and swords, all of them wearing army caps and Chairman Mao buttons on their chests and a few with canvas belts around their waists. Through the loudspeaker a man was urging people to stub out cigarettes, explaining that smoke would blur the captions projected on the white wall on the right of the stage. A few nurses from the Department of Infectious Diseases were searching about for their patients, who were not allowed to mix with others at such a public place.

Lin was worried, wondering why Manna was so indiscreet, but she didn't seem to care about others' eyes and even stretched out her hand to him, half a dozen candies in her palm. He was nervous but picked one, peeled off the wrapper, and put it into his mouth. It was an orange drop. She smiled, and he felt she looked rather sweet. City girls, they're so bold, he said to himself.

A female announcer came out from behind the curtain and in a melodious voice gave a brief introduction to the historical background of the story. Then the curtain went up. Two actors in golden official robes and black caps with long trembling ears stepped onto the stage, sidling around in their white-soled platform shoes. They were singing to each other about the Japanese inroads on the Korean Peninsula.

One of them sang in a high falsetto:

News just came from the border:
Five thousand dwarf bandits
Emerged from the ocean.
After waiting two days on the sea,
They landed last week,
Now heading toward Pyongyang . . .

The other man chanted "Oh—ah—" from time to time while listening to the report.

Lin couldn't make out all the words and had to turn to read the captions on the wall now and again. Yet like others, soon he was immersed in the opera, in which a top Manchu official was inspecting the North Fleet, twirling a long telescope in his hands. After the inspection, a group of gunners, bare-backed and wearing pigtails, were preparing for the battle with the Japanese navy. Large brass shells were standing on the fore deck of a battleship, around the main cannon. In the background was a seascape on pea-green cloth, white breakers leaping up and falling away.

But before the opera reached the point where the warships engaged the enemy on the Yellow Sea, a hand landed on Lin's left wrist. He wiggled a little but didn't withdraw his hand. He glanced left and right and found everyone enthralled by the send-off party on the stage, drums thundering, horns blaring, gongs clanking, and firecrackers exploding. He looked sideways at Manna, whose eyes narrowed, squinting at him.

Gently her fingertips stroked his palm, as though tracing his heart and head lines. He touched her hand and felt it was warm and smooth, without any callus. How different her palm was from Shuyu's. She pinched the ball of his thumb a little, and in return he held her pinkie, twisting it back and forth for a while. Then she caressed his wrist with her nail. The itch was so tickling that he grabbed her hand and their fingers were entwined. The two hands remained motionless for a moment, then turned over, engaged in a kind of mutual massage for a long time. Lin's heart was thumping.

He didn't pay much attention to the naval battle, which brought the audience to applause and shrieks, although the entire Chinese fleet was sunk to the bottom of the sea. Lin's and Manna's hands remained together throughout the last act. When the curtain fell, all the lights came on and people continued shouting "Down with Japanese Imperialism!" Lin gazed into Manna's eyes, which were gleaming intensely, her pupils radiant like a bird's. Her moist lips curled with a dreamy smile as though she were drunk. Slightly dizzy him-

self, he stood up and hurried away for fear that others might
see his face, which was burning hot.

That night he tossed and turned in his new mosquito net,
taking stock of what Manna had done. Despite not liking what
had happened, he believed she was a decent young woman,
not a coquette at all, unlike the few shameless ones who
would open their pants for their male superiors if the leaders
promised them a promotion or a Party membership. Is this the
beginning of an affair? he asked himself, and was uncertain of
the answer. How come she takes so much interest in me? She
knew I was a married man of course, why did she do that in
the theater? She was so bold. Is she going to be after me from
now on? What should I do?

Questions rose one after another, but he could focus on
none of them. His roommate Ming Chen was annoyed by his
restless movements and said, "Lin, stop making noise. I can't
sleep. I have a train to catch tomorrow morning."

"Sorry." Lin turned on his side and remained still.

Outside, a sentry cried out at someone, "Who's there?
Password?"

"Double Flags," a male voice barked back.

Somewhere in the roof two crickets were exchanging timid
chirps. Moonlight slanted in through the window, casting a
pale lozenge on the cement floor. Lin closed his eyes tight,
counting numbers in order to fall asleep.

He remained awake until midnight. Then in a half-sleeping
state he saw himself and a woman, whose face he didn't see
clearly but whose figure resembled Manna's, working together in an office, both in doctors' white robes and caps.
They were planning to operate on a patient with heart disease,
and a moment later he was chalking words and numerals on a
blackboard and briefing a team of doctors and nurses about
the plan for the operation. Then, falling deeper into his dream,
he saw a spacious home, which had a study full of hardcover

books on oak shelves and several framed pictures on the walls. At the back of the house there was a glassed-in veranda facing an oval green lawn. It was a Saturday evening and several friends and colleagues had come over to talk about operas and movies, while the woman was pouring tea and soda for them and passing around spiced pumpkin seeds, tiger-skinned peas, roasted peanuts, and cigarettes. He still didn't see her face, though obviously she and he were the mistress and master of the house. A few of the guests stayed late, playing cards. In the study there were even two children, whom Lin taught patiently. It seemed that he intended to send them to colleges in Beijing or Shanghai.

The next morning when he woke up, his head ached as if from a hangover, and his tongue and teeth felt fuzzy. He was somewhat bewildered by the scenes in the dream. He had never been interested in having children. Why had he dreamed of having another two and taking their education in hand? Also, cards had been banned and were nowhere to be found nowadays. How could they play them? More bizarre was that he had never desired to be a surgeon. Why were he and the woman planning to operate on a patient in his dream? Many years ago his secret ambition had been to become a three-star general. When he was leaving high school for the army, his language teacher, an old bookish man, had written in the notebook he presented to Lin: "May you some day return as a commander of ten thousand troops!" By bad luck he had later gotten into the medical profession, which most ambitious young men avoided because it did not lead to a top rank.

When he ran into Manna in the department at midday, he felt a little embarrassed, but he managed to greet her as usual. They talked about the condition of a patient dying of gastro-esophageal cancer, as though nothing had happened between them the previous evening. He was amazed that he could talk with a woman so naturally, without his usual diffidence. Outside the window, the sunlight was flickering on the cypress hedge, and four white rabbits were nibbling grass behind an enormous propaganda board. A blue jay landed near a baby rabbit, its head bobbing while its wings fluttered.

"Can we take a walk together Sunday afternoon?" she asked, putting her hand on the window ledge and looking at him expectantly. The same sweet smile appeared on her face.

"Yes, where should we meet?" He couldn't believe his voice.

"How about in front of the grocery store?" Her eyes were shining.

"What time?"

"Two?"

"Sure, I'll be there."

"I have to run. Doctor Liu is waiting for these test results." She waved a sheaf of slips in her hand. "Bye-bye now."

"Bye."

As she was walking away, for the first time he noticed she had a slim back and long, strong legs. She turned around and gave him another smile, then quickened her footsteps toward the Medical Ward. He said to himself, If this leads to an affair, so be it.

6

On Sunday afternoon they met in front of the grocery store and then walked about in the compound. At the beginning Lin felt uneasy, especially when they ran into others. He knew that people, after passing them, were turning around and looking at him and Manna. But soon her carefree manners put him at ease.

They talked about the downfall of the capitalist-roaders on the Central Party Committee—Liu Shaoqi, Deng Xiaoping, and several others who were being denounced by the Red Guards in Beijing. Who could imagine that so many "time bombs" had ticked around Chairman Mao? They also talked about the fighting in large cities, of which they had heard from different sources. Manna told him that in Changchun City two factions of revolutionary rebels had recently shelled each other with tanks and rocket guns installed on locomotives. She heard that the train station at Siping City had been leveled by gunfire.

As they strolled along the path between the turnip and eggplant fields behind the mess hall, they began talking about recent events in the hospital. After the Cultural Revolution had broken out the year before, the medical staff here had divided into two factions. They would argue and quarrel, blaming each other for deviating from the Party's line and for revising genuine Mao Tse-tung Thought. Unlike most people, Lin and Manna had not yet joined either of the organizations, although she was interested in the one called the Red Union.

"Don't join," he told her.

She was taken aback and asked, "Why?"

"None of them really understands Mao Tse-tung Thought.

They just waste their time arguing and fighting. So many people want to be a commander of some sort. We shouldn't join up."

"But don't you want to take part in the Cultural Revolution?"

"You don't have to fight with others to be an active revolutionary, do you?"

She seemed impressed by his candid words and agreed not to become involved with the Red Union. In fact Lin was also surprised by what he had said. Under other circumstances, he wouldn't dare give such advice that might get himself into trouble, but with Manna, the words had just flowed out of his mouth.

On their way back, she said to him as if embarrassed, "Can I ask you something I can't figure out by myself?"

"Sure, anything you think I know."

"What's an angel?"

He was amazed by the question. "Well, I'm not sure. An angel is someone who carries out God's missions, I guess. It's a Christian idea, superstitious stuff."

"Do you know what an angel looks like?"

"I saw a picture once. It's like a chubby baby with three pairs of wings, like a sweet child."

"I see."

"Why did you ask?"

She raised her eyes and gazed at him for a moment, then answered, "An old man once said I looked like an angel."

"Really? Why did he say that?"

"I've no idea. It happened when I was eight. A group of girls in our school performed a dance at an arts center for some heroes of the Korean War. We were all dressed like ducks, wearing white hats and feathers around our waists. When the dance was over, I left the stage for the ladies' room and ran into an old couple at the side entrance to the hall. They both looked shaky with age. The small old man stopped me at the gate and made the sign of a cross over me, saying, 'You look like an angel, child.' For some reason my heart started kicking, although I knew he meant no harm. Some policemen rushed over and dragged the old couple away, while they were shouting, 'Believe in Jesus! Believe in the Lord!' I ran off to change my clothes without going to the bathroom because I was afraid of running into the police. Later I tried to find out what an angel was. I checked the word in some dictionaries, but none of them carried it. I dared not ask anybody. You are the only person that I've ever asked. Now I kind of see what the old man meant, but I was never a chubby child. Why did he call me that?" She said the last sentence as if to herself.

"You must have looked very happy and innocent."

"No, I was never happy in my childhood. I envied those kids who had parents, and even hated some of them. By the way, Lin, don't tell anybody about this angel thing, all right?"

"Sure, I won't."

He peered at her face. The innocent look in her eyes convinced him that her angel story was true.

The next Sunday they met and walked together again; and again the following weekend. In a month they began to meet more often, twice or three times a week before nightfall. By and by Lin grew attached to Manna. Once she couldn't see him as they had planned because she was assigned to accompany a patient to another army hospital; he was so restless that he paced back and forth in his office for two hours that evening. It was the first time that he suffered such a longing to be with a woman.

After August he and Manna didn't need to arrange to meet anymore. They ate at the same table in the mess hall; they went to the hot-water room together, each holding a thermos; they sat next to each other at meetings and political studies; they played table tennis and badminton together; they strolled

about within the compound in the evening whenever the
weather allowed, chatting and sometimes arguing. At times
Lin wondered whether they had become too close, like an engaged couple, although they had never become intimate, not
even touching hands again. He kept reminding himself that he
was a married man.

Neither he nor Manna would join a revolutionary organi-
zation, but they dutifully participated in political activities.
Lin even lectured on three of Chairman Mao's essays, "Serve
the People," "In Memory of Dr. Norman Bethune," and "The
Old Man Moved the Mountain." His talks were so well received that some people borrowed his notes to read. Because
both Lin and Manna were Party members and had a clean
family background, the revolutionaries in the hospital didn't
accuse them of harboring a reactionary motive.

Nevertheless, people began to gossip about them, saying
they were having an affair. The hospital leaders were concerned, but they found no evidence that Lin and Manna had
broken any rule. Never had they been together outside the
compound; nor had their conduct revealed any intimacy,
which lovers usually couldn't help showing, such as patting
each other and signaling with glances. Yet beyond question,
their relationship was more than camaraderie, because no two
mere comrades of different sex would spend so much time together. Even those who were engaged wouldn't have to meet
each other every day, but Lin and Manna were simply inseparable.

At the time Ran Su was the vice-director of the hospital's
Political Department, and Commissar Zhang enjoined him to
handle this case. Ran Su had been on good terms with Lin, because they both loved books and often talked about novels.

He summoned Lin to his office one winter afternoon and
said to him, "My friend, I understand that your marriage was
arranged by your parents, and probably you don't love your

wife, but I want to warn you beforehand that your relationship with Manna Wu may affect your future, no matter what kind of relationship it is, normal or abnormal. In fact you're heading toward trouble."

Lin made no response. He had thought of that, but was unsure whether he could break with Manna, who was actually his first girlfriend. Never had a woman been so close to his heart. He believed that Manna and he, if not lovers in the physical sense, were becoming kindred spirits. These days he almost couldn't refrain from joining her whenever it was possible.

Ran Su combed his dark hair with his fingers, looking at Lin. A pair of little crinkles appeared under his triangular eyes. He smiled and said, "Come on, Lin. I treat you as a friend. Tell me what you think."

Lin managed to say, "I shall keep the relationship normal. Manna Wu and I will remain just comrades."

"Promise me then that you and Manna Wu will have no abnormal relationship unless you have divorced your wife and married her." By "abnormal" he meant "sexual."

For half a minute Lin remained silent. Then he raised his head and muttered, "I promise."

"You know, Lin. I have to do this. If you break any rule, I won't be able to protect you. Now that you've promised, I'm going to assure my superiors that there's nothing unusual between you and Manna Wu. Don't break your word, or else you will get me into trouble as well."

"I understand." A coldness was sinking into his heart. How he regretted having agreed to meet Manna three months ago. Already deep in the relationship, how could he extricate himself without hurting her and filling his own heart with despair? He had his family and shouldn't have gone with a young woman this way.

Ran Su gave him a Peony cigarette and said he would return Lin's novel *How Steel Is Tempered* in two weeks. These hectic days made it impossible for him to finish the book. "I don't understand why the Russians always wrote such fat novels," he said. "They must've had a lot of time. I often skip the first chapters, too many descriptions, passage after passage. The pace is too slow." In fact, it was this little man who had notified Lin the previous year that he ought to close his library without delay to avoid having to forfeit his books.

When Lin told Manna about his talk with Ran Su the next evening on the sports ground, she made a long face and dropped her eyes, her elbow resting on a vaulting horse, which stood between them. Nearby were a set of parallel bars, a horizontal bar, and two jumping pits filled with sand.

After a brief silence, she lifted her head and asked testily, "What are your true feelings about me?"

He was puzzled by the question and asked, "What do you mean?"

"Who am I to you? Are we going to be engaged one day?" She looked him straight in the eye.

He took the question with composure. "If I could, I would propose to you. Actually I've thought about that."

Hearing his words, she melted into tears. Her right hand was holding her side as though she were suffering from a stomachache. Disconcerted, he looked around and saw only a few children playing the game "Catch a Spy" in the dusk. A cluster of tall smokestacks fumed lazily in the south. Fortunately none of their comrades was in sight.

He handed her his handkerchief, murmuring, "Don't be so upset, Manna. I love you, but we cannot be together. I'm sorry."

"It's not your fault. Oh, why is the Lord of Heaven so mean to me? I'm already twenty-eight."

Lin sighed and said no more. I'd be a happy man if she were my wife, he thought.

Manna was also summoned to Director Su's office a few days later and was made to promise the same as Lin had.

At the end of December, for the first time Lin was not elected a model officer. Some people complained about his lifestyle. One officer reported that Lin once had not stood at attention like others when the national anthem was broadcast, even though they had been in the bathhouse, all naked in the pool. A section chief remarked that Lin shouldn't keep his hair so long and parted right down the middle. The hairstyle made him look like a petty intellectual, like those in the movies. Why couldn't he have his hair cropped short like others? What made him so special? His college diploma? Then how come the other three college graduates in the hospital didn't bother so much about their hairstyles? How come one of them didn't mind having his head shaved bald?

Without delay Lin asked his roommate Ming Chen to give him a crew cut. Manna was troubled by his new haircut, which made him look nondescript, saying he now seemed like "neither a drake nor a gander." But he said it didn't matter, since it was winter and he wore his fur hat most of the time.

At political studies Lin often felt that people expected to hear more from him about his inmost thoughts, as though he were supposed to make a self-criticism. He was upset and for months remained gloomy.

7

For over a year Manna wanted to see what Shuyu looked like, but Lin wouldn't give her a chance. Whenever she asked him to show her a photograph of his wife, he would say he didn't have one. Manna was sure he did. In secret she had once searched through the drawers in his desk when she was helping clean the windowpanes of the office he shared with another doctor, but she had found no photograph in them. Her roommates often asked her about Lin's wife, and she felt embarrassed that she could tell them nothing. Without fail they would warn her that Lin might be of two minds about their relationship. So she should be more careful.

At the hospital's annual sports meet in the early fall of 1968, Manna won a third prize for table tennis. She was awarded a perfumed soap wrapped in a white towel. To please her more, that afternoon, in Lin's dormitory, he asked her to make a wish.

"My only wish is to see Shuyu's majestic face," she said, rolling her eyes, which lit up with excitement.

Since his roommates were not in, he picked up his dictionary, *Forest of Words,* took a photograph out of the vellum cover, and handed it to her. It was a new one, black-and-white and four by three inches.

Looking at it, Manna couldn't help tittering. Both Shuyu and Hua were in the photograph. The baby girl, in checkered overalls, stood on the ground with her knees bent, like a dog rising on its hind legs. Her hands were reaching out for the bench on which her mother sat. Shuyu was closer to the camera than Hua, her face gaunt and her forehead grooved by wavy creases. Her flabby mouth spread sideways as though she were about to cry. A small fishtail of wrinkles gathered at the end of her right eye, which was half closed. More surprising, she was dressed like an old woman: a short gown like a dark iron barrel encased her sloping shoulders and short upper body; her thighs were thin, both shanks wrapped in puttees; on the ground her feet were splayed in black shoes like a pair of mice. A fierce-looking goose was flapping its wings on Shuyu's left. In the background were water vats, the thatched adobe house, and half an elm crown over the roof.

"Heavens, oh her tiny feet!" Manna cried. Lin stood up as she went on, "Isn't she your mother?" She broke into laughter, bending forward.

His eyes flashed behind the lenses of his glasses. He picked up his cap and left the bedroom without a word.

"Hey, Lin, come back. I didn't mean to hurt your feelings."

She followed him out, but he didn't turn his head. He was heading toward the back gate of the hospital grounds.

Beyond the wall of the compound stretched an orchard, which had been planted four years before by the local commune members and was now in fruit, the apple-pear trees standing row after row all over the hillside. Hurriedly Lin walked out of the back gate and disappeared in the orchard.

That was the only time Manna saw him in a huff, but he returned to normal the next day. When she again apologized, he told her to forget about it.

The photograph was a great relief to her, because it convinced her that Lin and his wife didn't make a good match, and that sooner or later he would leave Shuyu. At last she had hopes of marrying him one day.

Despite her roommates' plying her with questions, Manna wouldn't reveal anything to them about Shuyu. She still claimed she knew nothing about the country woman. But a month later, unable to contain her excitement, she told her friend Haiyan Niu about the photograph.

They were both on the second shift, which was from 7:00 p.m. to 3:00 a.m. At night when the patients in the ward were asleep, the two nurses had little to do except distribute some medicine in the wee hours and take a few patients' temperatures, so they would chat. Haiyan was pretty and pert, always smiling with neat teeth and often surrounded by young men. She had grown up in Muji City, though she had been born in Harbin. Her paternal grandfather had been a well-known capitalist, but she hadn't suffered much from her family background, because the old man had donated a huge sum of money to the Communist government for a MIG-15 so as to fight the United States in the Korean War. The donation bankrupted his businesses—an oil mill and a tannery—but his family was classified as Open-Minded Gentry, so that later his descendants miraculously remained untouched during political struggles. And his granddaughter Haiyan had even joined the army. In her there was a kind of wildness, which Manna very much admired, and which was probably a residue of the frontier spirit that still possessed some Northeasterners. Sometimes Haiyan reminded Manna of a sleek leopard.

"If I were you, I'd go to bed with Lin Kong," Haiyan said to her one night, her hands crocheting a woolen shawl.

"What? Girl, you're crazy," said Manna. With a pair of large tweezers she was taking some sterilized syringes and needles out of a stainless steel pot that had boiled for half an hour on the electric stove.

Haiyan was working loop after loop of the cream-colored wool. Without raising her head she said, "No, I'm not crazy. You have to find a way to develop your relationship with him, don't you?"

"Well, I'm afraid that might scare him away."

They both laughed, and Manna sneezed. It had grown humid in the office; tiny dewdrops appeared on the metal lid of the trash bin standing by the desk. Haiyan put down the crochet work on her lap and said, "Listen, elder sister, once you've done it with him, he won't abandon you. If he really loves you, if he's a man with a heart, he'll follow you wherever you go. If he doesn't, he isn't the man you want, is he?"

"You think like a little girl. No love is so romantic."

"Don't give me that. What do you know about love?"

"All right, you know everything."

"Of course I know."

"Tell me, how many men have you known?" Manna winked at her. She always doubted if Haiyan was still a virgin. Rumor had it that Haiyan had gone to bed with Vice-Director Chiu of the hospital. That must have been true; otherwise she would have been discharged long ago. Unlike Manna, she had never gone to a nursing school.

"A thousand," Haiyan said teasingly. "The more the better, don't you think?"

"Yes," Manna said matter-of-factly.

They laughed again. Haiyan flung back her braid, whose end was tied with an orange string. Her toe kept tapping the red floor.

Manna had never thought of sleeping with Lin. The fear of being expelled from the army prevented her from conceiving such an idea; she didn't even have a hometown to return to. Furthermore, she was uncertain whether he would continue to love her if she was discharged and banished to a remote place. Even though he wanted to, love would be impossible under such circumstances, because he might be sent back to his home village and they would have to remain apart. Yet Haiyan's suggestion pointed out a possibility. Manna was almost twenty-nine; why should she remain an old maid forever? Once she and Lin made love, he might go about divorcing his wife. For better or worse, she shouldn't just sit and wait without doing anything, or there would be no end to this ambiguous affair. Recently people in the hospital had begun to treat her like Lin's fiancée; young officers would avoid talking with her for longer than a few minutes. She resented this situation, which she was determined to change.

So she decided to act. The next night, after they had distributed medicine to the patients, she said to Haiyan, "Can I ask you a favor?"

Her earnest tone of voice surprised her friend. "Of course, anything you think I can do for you," Haiyan said.

"Do you know some quiet place in town?"

"What do you mean some quiet place?" Haiyan's large eyes sparkled.

"I mean where you can . . ."

"Oh I see, a place where you and he can have a good time together?"

Manna nodded, her face coloring.

"Well, so you agree with me at last. Tell me, what made you change your mind so quickly? You are a bad girl, aren't you? You're planning to seduce a good man, a revolutionary officer, aren't you?"

"Come on, spare me all the questions."

"Comrade Manna Wu, do you understand what you are doing? You've really lost your head, haven't you?" She pointed her forefinger at Manna with her thumb raised, like a pistol.

"Please, just help me!"

Haiyan tittered, then said, "All right, I'll find you a place."

Because hotels and guesthouses in every town demanded an official letter before taking in a guest, it was impossible for an unmarried couple to find lodging in any of them. Manna had to resort to the help of Haiyan, who seemed to have infinite connections. Two of her siblings lived in Muji. That was why she had readily promised to find Manna a place.

On Thursday, at lunch, Haiyan sat down by Manna and nodded to her meaningfully. After others had left the table, she handed her a brass key and a slip of paper with an address on it. She said, "My sister's going to visit her parents-in-law this weekend. You can use her home on Sunday."

"Thanks," Manna whispered.

Haiyan batted her eyes. "But remember to tell me what it's like, all right?"

"What do you mean?"

"You know." Haiyan batted her eyes again.

"Damn you, as if you didn't know."

Chuckling, Haiyan patted her on the shoulder and said with a straight face, "Every man is different."

Since she decided to take this step, Manna had been possessed by a thrill that she had never experienced before. She began to have a faraway look in her eyes and smiled more to herself. At night she often felt as if she were in Lin's arms, her breasts swelling and her tongue licking her lips. She was amazed to find herself having changed into a rather voluptuous woman in a matter of a few days. She enjoyed sleeping without her pajamas on, although she was afraid that her roommates might see her naked legs if she kicked her quilt off in her sleep. The thought of spending an unforgettable day with Lin invigorated her limbs and filled her heart with ecstasy.

The next day when they were walking together in the late afternoon, she told him about the arrangement and even mentioned she would buy a bottle of plum wine and two pounds of smoked sausages. She got so carried away that she didn't notice the shock in his eyes.

"Lin, this is a fabulous opportunity," she said. "We've never had a place for ourselves."

He frowned a little and went on kicking pebbles while walking silently.

The setting sun was like a huge cake sliced in half by the brick wall of the compound. A few patients in blue-striped uniforms were playing soccer with a group of boys on the sports ground. Dried leaves were scuttling about, making tiny noises; bats were twittering and flitting about in the chilly air.

Seeing him unenthusiastic about the arrangement, Manna said peevishly, "I just want to spend some time with you alone, to have a heart-to-heart talk. That's all."

Still he didn't say a word. The look on his face seemed rather distant, although he was blushing a little. Running out of patience, she asked, "Do you think it's easy for me to have gone this far? I've risked losing everything, don't you understand?"

" 'Risk' is the word," he said thoughtfully. "It's too big a risk to take. We shouldn't do this."

"Why?"

"Didn't we promise Ran Su not to break any rule? This would get him into trouble too. I'm a married man; if the secret is out, we'll be dealt with as criminals, don't you think?"

"I don't care."

"Don't lose your head, Manna. Think about this: just a moment's pleasure will ruin our lives for good."

She didn't answer.

He went on, "Besides, you know Haiyan Niu has a loose tongue. Even if she doesn't tell anybody now, what will happen after she gets married someday? For sure she'll tell her husband about this. Then they will have something on us. You know there's no wall without a crack. If we do this, sooner or later people will find out."

"She promised not to tell anybody."

"Do you absolutely trust her?"

"Well, I can't say that." She shook her head. Something stirred in her chest, and tears came to her eyes, but she controlled herself. "What should we do with this?" She waved the key, which glinted in the last sunlight.

"Return it to Haiyan before this weekend. It's crucial to show her that we won't use the place."

His words made her ashamed, and in silence she blamed herself for yielding to her passion. She was overcome with doubtful thoughts. Why did he refuse to spend time with her alone in town? Did he have another woman in his mind? Unlikely. Pingping Ma had left the army the year before, and Lin had treated her merely as a tomboy; he and that girl had just been book pals. Whom was he close to these days? No one except Manna herself. Still, he might've been seeing another woman. No, if so, it couldn't escape her notice since she saw him every day. Then why did he seem to have no desire for her at all?

Manna feared that in his eyes she might be a different woman now. How she regretted having listened to Haiyan.

They passed the medical building, which looked like a green knoll because of its mossy tiles. Two lights flashed on inside. There was a meeting at seven o'clock to study a document recently issued by the Central Committee, which demanded that all the revolutionary rebels fight with words instead of force. Lin would have to attend the meeting, while Manna should get ready for the night shift.

Haiyan was surprised when Manna handed the key back to her. Manna explained that they had to keep their promise made to Ran Su and that they shouldn't break the rule.

Haiyan said, "Hmm, I didn't know Lin Kong was such a loyal friend. A good man indeed. No wonder somebody called him 'a model monk.' "

"Like I said, he isn't a bold man."

"But doesn't he love you? Maybe he's no good in bed."

"Come on, he made a baby with his wife, a very healthy one."

Haiyan sighed feebly and clasped her hands. "To be honest, Manna, perhaps he doesn't love you enough to run the risk. Are you sure you know his heart?"

She didn't respond, still uncertain why Lin wouldn't go to bed with her. She felt that there must have been something more than the reason he had given. Many men broke rules for the women they loved, and some did not regret having done that even when they were punished. How come Lin was so different from others? Did he really love her? Why was he so passionless? Did his refusal mean he was reluctant to get embroiled with her?

Gradually Haiyan's words sank in.

8

In spite of his calm appearance, Lin was quite disturbed by Manna's boldness. That same night, lying in bed, he reviewed the details of their meeting in his mind and felt he was right to ask her to return the key to Haiyan. If he had not opposed her wish, there would definitely be disastrous consequences. Ever since he made his promise to Ran Su, he had tried to cool down his passion for Manna, always reminding himself that he must not fall too deeply in love with her. To his mind, it was still unclear whether their relationship could develop fully and end in marriage, which would require him to divorce his wife first. He had better not rush it.

Outside the window, raindrops were dripping from the eaves, producing a light ding-ding-ding sound. With his eyes closed tight, Lin tried to go to sleep. But a voice rose in his head, asking, Don't you want to make love to Manna?

He was startled by the question, but replied, Not now. Sex is out of the question. It would ruin both of us.

You really don't want to sleep with her? the voice persisted.

No, honestly no. I love her and am attached to her, but that has nothing to do with sex. Our love is not based on the flesh.

Really? You have no desire for her at all?

I can control my desire. At this point of my life I must treat her as a comrade only.

That's a lie. Why don't you talk and walk with another comrade every day? You and she have already formed a special bond, haven't you?

All right, that's true, but the bond doesn't have to be sexual. We love each other. That's enough.

What? You're too rational.

I'm a doctor and an officer. My profession demands that I be a rational man.

Don't you think you might have hurt her feelings by refusing her offer?

I'm not sure. If I did, it couldn't be helped. I didn't hurt her on purpose. She can forgive me, can't she? Can't she see I had her interest in mind as well when I said we shouldn't do this?

The voice fell silent, and soon sleep claimed him. His mind drifted to a distant place reminiscent of the countryside where he had grown up. He then had an extraordinary dream, which would trouble him for weeks. He was walking along the edge of a vast wheat field on a fine summer day. The sun was gentle and the breeze warm. He was whistling at leisure, with a fishing rod on his shoulder. "Lin, Lin, come here," a sugary voice called. He turned and saw a young woman in the field, her head veiled in a red gauze mantilla, but her breasts were naked and full like a pair of white muskmelons. Around her the wheat ears were rustling briskly. Without hesitation he dropped the rod and walked up to her. The luxuriant wheat reached his waist and gave out a sweetish scent. Approaching her, he found a tiny clearing covered by dog-tail grass mixed with dried rice straws. Stark naked, she was lying on the grass with her knees spread open, her hand beckoning him. She no longer had the mantilla on, but her face was concealed by her long glossy hair. He found her midriff a little plump, but her limbs were so youthful that the sight of them made his heart skip a beat. Her pubic hair was thick, a few dewdrops in the downy tuft. Breathing hard, he took off his sweater and shorts and dropped them to the ground.

They began rolling on the grass. Her hands kept caressing his back, rib cage, and thighs while he was wriggling atop her. Then she embraced him firmly against her chest, her belly rocking under him with a rhythmic motion as if she were swaying to some music. She was groaning like an animal; her ecstatic voice was so invigorating to him that he felt his blood seething in his loins. A skein of ducks flew past, calling wildly. Their harsh cries made his arms shudder a little; he held her tightly, like a man incapable of swimming gripping a life buoy in the ocean.

He copulated with her for a long time until exhaustion overcame him and he lay down alongside her. His hand went on massaging her quivering hips, whose size had somehow tripled in the meantime. A moment later she rolled over, raised herself up on her elbow, and hooked her arm around his neck, moaning, "More, more, let's do it again."

He reached for his clothes buried in the grass. The back of his hand hit the iron bedpost, and he woke up, soaked with sweat. He realized he had just had a wet dream. He was deeply stirred by the experience, which was his first time. Who was that woman? he wondered. She had waist-length hair and a shapely body, smelling of fresh peanuts. There was a birthmark on her left forearm, as large as a button. He tried to recall all the women he knew, but couldn't match her with anyone. If only he had caught a glimpse of her face.

Across the dark room Ming Chen was snoring like a bellows. Lin sat up noiselessly, opened his pillowcase, and took out a change of underwear to replace the one he was wearing, which was soiled on the front. For many years he had often heard other men talk about having a wet dream and wondered what it was like. Before his marriage, he had even doubted his manhood, because unlike other men who were crazy about women, he had never fallen in love with a woman. After his daughter was born, he was finally convinced that he was a normal man. Still, what did a wet dream feel like? Why had he never had one? Was there something wrong with him? Those questions would pop up in his mind whenever he heard his comrades bragging about their virility and wild dreams. Now finally he had experienced one, which was quite thrilling to him. Yet the sensation was not unadulterated. Deep in his heart he wished that the woman in the wheat field had been somebody he knew.

He got up at 5:30 when the reveille was sounded on a bugle. Hurriedly he put on his clothes, folded up his quilt, and placed his pillow atop it. Then he saw a yellowish stain on his white sheet. There was no time to wash it off because he had to leave for the morning exercises immediately, so he covered the spot with the current issue of the pictorial *The People's Liberation Army*. Then he rushed out into the cold dawn together with Ming Chen.

The two-mile run was more exhausting to him today, and he sweated a good deal, huffing and puffing all the way. His head was spinning a little.

When Lin returned to his dormitory, Jin Tian, who hadn't gone to the morning exercises because he had been on duty the night before, greeted him with a quizzical grin. "Hey, Lin, you had a wet dream last night, didn't you?" His wide eyes were winking and his stubby nose was wrinkled as though sniffing something delicious in the air.

Flushing to his neck, Lin rushed to his bed, pulled off the sheet, and thrust it into his washbasin, which was half full of water.

"Come on, don't blow off like that. It's a natural thing," said Jin Tian, chuckling.

Ming Chen chimed in, "Of course it's natural. I have it every week. When too much of that stuff has accumulated in you, it will flow out by itself." He turned to Lin. "You don't need to wash your sheet like it caught a virus or something. Look, I don't bother about the splotches on my sheet."

"Me neither," said Jin Tian.

Lin wished they had left him alone, but with a smirk on his

face Jin Tian went on to say to him, "Well, I can guess who you dreamed of."

"I did it with your sister," Lin snapped.

"Oh, that's not a problem. If I had one like Manna Wu, you'd be welcome to ride her like a wild pony as long as you please, but only in your dreams."

His two roommates roared with laughter. Wordlessly Lin took a bar of soap out of his bedside cupboard, picked up his washbasin, and left the room. He was still confused by the dream. In real life he could never imagine lying with an unknown woman in a wheat field and coupling like an animal. He felt a little sick.

9

On Lin's desk lay a sheet of paper, half torn in the middle. It was a telegram from his elder brother, which said, "Father passed away. Return immediately."

Thinking of his father, who had toiled in the fields all his life but grown poorer each year, Lin was tearful again and kept massaging the inner corners of his eyes with his forefinger and thumb. If only he had been able to go home and attend the funeral. He had asked the leaders to allow him to take an early leave, but they hadn't approved, because throughout the spring of 1969 the hospital was in combat readiness. There had been conflicts between the Chinese and the Russian troops on the Amur and the Wusuli rivers in the winter. Though the ice on the rivers could no longer support the Russian tanks and personnel carriers, the Chinese troops would not slacken their alertness until May.

Lin had sent two hundred yuan to his elder brother, Ren Kong, who lived nine miles away from Goose Village, and asked him to give their father a proper burial. Before he died, the old man had bequeathed the farmhouse to Lin because he had been grateful to Shuyu, who had looked after his wife and himself with diligence for so many years.

For months Lin had been in a dark mood. He became taciturn and read more in his free time. When walking with Manna in the evenings, he often looked absentminded. She asked him whether he was gloomy because he couldn't go home for his father's funeral. He said probably. In reality his mind was full of other thoughts. Now that both his parents had died, his need for his wife had changed; now she was only caring for their baby daughter. In his heart he felt for Shuyu, who had never lived an easy day since their marriage, but he didn't love her and was unwilling to spend the rest of his life with her. He wanted a marriage based on love and a wife whose appearance wouldn't embarrass him in the presence of others (to his mind, Manna would be a fine choice). Yet the feelings of guilt, mixed with compassion for Shuyu, were draining him.

In the meantime, Manna began to insinuate that he should seriously consider divorcing his wife. He tried evading the topic whenever she was about to bring it up.

One night in early June, a section chief in the Military Department of the City Administration died of a heart attack. He had been a stalwart man, in his mid-forties. At nightfall he had heartburn and took some medicine, but the symptom persisted. He told his wife that he was going to the hospital to see the doctor. He set out with a flashlight and an umbrella, since it looked like rain. Before he reached the hospital, the heart attack felled him. He lay in a ditch and couldn't climb out to get on the road. When people found him before daybreak, he was dead, his lower lip bitten through and his face smeared with mud and husks of grass seeds. He left a widow and three small children. His death disturbed Manna profoundly, as she had known him by sight.

The next evening when they were walking on the fringe of the sports ground, she sighed and said to Lin, "Life is such a precarious thing. Today we're alive, tomorrow we may be gone. What's the point in trying so hard to live like a human being every day?"

"Don't be so pessimistic. If we think that way all the time, we can't live."

She stopped and leaned against the flaky trunk of a birch. Her right hand held her left wrist, twisting it back and forth, and her eyes dimmed staring at him. She said in a choked voice, "I can't bear this anymore, Lin. This is stifling me. Why don't you do something?"

"What are you talking about?" He looked puzzled.

"We can't continue to be like this. Who am I? Your fiancée or your concubine? You must do something to change this situation."

"What could I do?"

"Ask Shuyu for a divorce." She looked close into his eyes, her lips pursed up.

His head turned away. "I can't rush. I have to figure out a good way. This is not an easy thing to do."

"Why is it so complicated? Tell her you want a divorce and see how she takes it."

"No, you don't understand."

"I don't understand what?"

"I can't just dump her like a pair of outworn shoes. I have to give a good reason, or else everybody will condemn me and I won't be able to get a divorce."

"What's a better reason than that you don't love her?"

"No, no." He gasped.

"Listen, Lin, it's time for you to decide. I'm tired of waiting like this. Who am I to you? I'm not even your mistress." She broke out sobbing and turned around, about to walk away.

"Listen to me, Manna. Wait a moment, please!"

"I've heard enough."

"Please be reasonable!"

"I'm sick of being reasonable. If you do nothing, it's over between us," she said loudly, hurrying away with her palm over her mouth. Her head bent forward and her legs looked shaky while her body kept convulsing a little. A scrap of birch bark was clinging to her hair. She crossed a pile of dried grass and passed the holly hedge.

With a numb heart he watched her disappear at the corner

of the lab building. Around his head a few midges were flitting. A pair of magpies clamored in a tall elm, tossing their mottled tails. In the distant sky a squadron of jet fighters were banking away noiselessly like silver swallows.

From that day on, an emotional tug-of-war was waged between them. Lin was accustomed to being alone, so he didn't go and look for Manna. He wanted peace of mind. Yet whenever she came into sight, he couldn't help looking at her. She seemed aware of his attention and always kept her face away from him. She laughed more than before, especially in the presence of other men, and her neck grew straighter. She wore shirts of bright colors and a pair of new leather shoes. Like some other young nurses, she began using Lily Lotion, the most expensive kind of vanishing cream. In the evening she often played badminton with others in front of the bathhouse, as though all of a sudden she had become a young girl again, full of energy and life.

Never had Lin thought she could be so headstrong. He felt miserable and often breathed with difficulty, as though a weight of lead were jammed into his chest.

He was at a loss, wondering if she really loved him. When his colleagues asked him what had happened between him and Manna, he would say, "I shouldn't keep her waiting. She has to make her choice. I'm a married man."

"So you two broke up?"

"I think so."

For all his calm appearance, Lin felt feverish. Whenever he was reading a book, his mind would wander. He couldn't sleep well at night, sighing and thinking of his life and the women he knew. Some of them were better-looking and tenderer than Manna, but they all seemed beyond the grasp of his mind, which would roam through them one after another and gradually return to Manna. How sorry he felt for her. She had been waiting, waiting, only for a beginning or an ending between them. But his life seemed to have been caught in a circle that he could not escape so as to establish a starting point again. Love did not help. The possibility of love only filled him with despondency and languor, as though he was sick in the soul. If only he had never known Manna; if only he could get back into his old rut again; if only he could return to an undisturbed, contented life.

During the day he tried working harder and even undertook the project of recataloguing all the medical records in his office, just as a way to wear himself out, so that he wouldn't think too much when going to sleep at night. As long as he kept himself busy, he felt in control and self-sufficient. He needed no woman.

10

National Day came. The hospital gave its staff a dinner. In the mess hall, Commissar Zhang, a short paunchy man, spoke before the banquet started. He thanked the nurses who had helped the cooks in the kitchen that morning and talked briefly about the significance of this anniversary to the Chinese nation and to the revolution. Then he spoke about the principle that the Party always commands the gun. After that, with a wave of his hand, he announced, "Now enjoy the meal."

He went to a corner and sat down at the table reserved for the leaders, which had an unlimited supply of dishes and wine.

People began to propose toasts and raise chopsticks to eat. At once the room echoed with laughter, chattering, and the clatter of bowls, plates, ladles, mugs. Eight courses were served. There were smoked flounder, sweet-and-sour ribs, sautéed pork with bamboo shoots, scrambled eggs with tree ears. Each table was given two bottles of red wine, a jar of wheat liquor, and a basin of draft beer.

Lin and Manna didn't sit at the same table, but she was within his view and earshot. Unlike the other men at his table, who were feasting heartily, Lin felt as if his stomach were full, although like most people he too had skipped lunch that day to save his appetite for this banquet. He turned his head and saw Manna's right arm resting on the broad windowsill behind her while her left hand was holding a green enamel mug.

"The wine's divine," she said loudly to Lin's roommate Jin Tian sitting next to her, then she giggled. She removed her arm from the windowsill and touched her nose with her fingertips.

Her words made Lin's cheek muscle twitch. A middle-aged woman doctor at his table said kindly, "Try a meatball, Lin. They're delicious."

He held out his chopsticks absently and picked up a meatball, which, though made of ground pork, tasted like tofu to him. He didn't like the insipid beer either, but he drank some from his white blue-rimmed bowl. Instead of attacking the meaty dishes and the fish like the others, he ate radish salad seasoned with sugar and vinegar. Now and then he let out a small burp.

Meanwhile, at the other table, Manna was laughing jovially, the tops of her cheeks red as if rouged. She lifted her mug and clinked it with others, and with her head tilted back she drained the remaining wine in one gulp.

"You're quite a drinker!" Jin Tian complimented her in a thin voice, then ladled beer into her mug, filling it to the brim.

"Stop," she cried cheerfully. "You want it to overflow?" She laughed again.

"Why not?" Jin Tian said. The head of the beer spilled over.

A ceiling fan chopped away vigorously above Lin's head, yet he was sweating. He didn't feel like eating anymore, so he finished the rice in his bowl, stood up, saying he had forgotten to put out the lights in his office, and made for the door. Passing the table at which Manna was sitting, for some reason he stopped to say, "Manna, don't drink too much. It's bad for your health."

"Am I drinking anything that's yours?" she said, simpering. She raised the mug, whose green surface had peeled off in places, and downed a large gulp of beer. The people at her table paused to watch.

Without a word Lin hurried out, his cap crumpled in his

fist. How he regretted having shown his concern for her! A voice began speaking in his mind. Stupid, you've never learned your lesson. Why can't you forget her? Why not let her drink to death? Leave her alone. Let the alcohol burn up her insides! Serves her right.

The large quadrangle of the compound was quiet. Nobody was in view except for the sentry at the front entrance, holding the muzzle of a rifle that stood beside him with its bayonet raised. Lin went directly to the orchard behind the barracks. The apple-pears had just been harvested, but there was still some fruit left on the trees here and there. Three ponies, one pied and two sorrel, were grazing on the slope. In the depths of the orchard a young man was singing an aria from the revolutionary opera *Taking the Tiger Mountain by Strategy,* "These days I have probed into the enemy's positions / And gotten quite good results. . . ." A flock of wild geese, in the form of a V, appeared passing the tip of the hill, flapping south, honking, and stretching their necks. As they flew past, their wings whistled faintly.

Lin sat down on a boulder and lit a cigarette. The hospital sprawled beneath him, a few windows of the medical building flickering in the setting sun. From the hill slope, the compound looked like a large factory encircled by a thick line of aspens planted along the brick wall. In the east some red rooftops were obscured by wisps of smoke. The humming of the traffic in the city could be heard vaguely. Lin sighed, his heart aching, and he began thinking about what had happened just now. Why had she made a spectacle of him on purpose? Did she hate him so much? She should have appreciated his concern for her health, shouldn't she? A woman's heart was so unpredictable. What a shame it was to be humiliated in front of so many people.

It serves you right, he thought. You're a husband and a father; you shouldn't have started this affair. You asked for trou-

ble and deserve this kind of humiliation. Why can't you wash
your hands of this woman? Why do you allow her to clasp and
yank your heart like an octopus? You are so cheap that the
more distant she is from you, the more you're attracted to her.
Enough of this insanity! You must pluck her out of your chest,
or she'll eat up your insides like a worm.

As he was smoking and thinking, Manna emerged from
behind an apple-pear tree, striding toward him. Her breathing
was heavy and her face carmine. He got to his feet, puzzled,
wondering how he should greet her.

Before he knew what to do, she rushed over and embraced
him. Racked with sobs, she buried her face in his chest.

"I can't stand this anymore!" she moaned. "I can't. I didn't
mean to do that."

"Don't, don't cry."

"I'm bad, so bad," she whimpered. She held him tighter,
her arms trembling with the strain. Her hair smelled of ginger
and scallion; obviously she had worked in the kitchen before
dinner.

"Manna, it's not a big thing," he said. "You see, I haven't
taken it to heart. I forgot it already." He looked around, fearful
of being seen, as the thought came to him that they had broken
the rule that prohibited such a meeting outside the wall.

She raised her eyes, which were radiating an intense light.
Then she lowered her head and giggled hysterically. "I'm an
old maid, a thirty-year-old virgin, do you know?"

"Don't talk like this."

"That's why I'm so cranky, I guess."

"You've drunk too much."

"No, I just had two mugs."

"That's more than you can hold."

"By the way, don't you want to know I'm still a virgin?
Never been touched by any man."

"Manna, you've lost your mind. You shouldn't—"

"Come on, can't you deflower an old maid? Don't you want to do it to me?" She let go of him and broke out laughing, which turned into coughing and more sobbing.

"Let's go back, dear." He slipped his arm under hers.

"Can't you do it to me?" she cried.

"Don't, don't—"

"Are you a man or not? You have a fearful heart like a rabbit's. Come on, do it to me!"

"All right, it's all my fault. I'm a good-for-nothing. Let's go back."

Despite her struggling and sobbing, he pulled her down the slope, holding her upper arm with both hands. All the way down she kept whimpering, "Do it, do it to me. I want to give you a baby."

He dared not take her to the dormitory by the front way, so he pulled her through the neat rows of aspens to the back door of the dormitory house. Coming out of the grove, they ran into a group of nurses who had just left work and were heading for the mess hall. Before the young women could greet them, Lin said, "Manna has drunk too much." Hurriedly he dragged her past. The nurses turned around and watched the couple staggering away.

For a week Manna was the topic of the hospital. She had set a record: For the first time a woman on the staff had gotten drunk at a holiday dinner. The word was that she could easily outdrink most men.

After being shaken by this holiday incident, Lin began to think seriously about getting a divorce. He decided to bring it up with Shuyu the next summer.

11

After telling Lin that she would be back around mid-afternoon, Shuyu left for their family plot with a short rake on her shoulder and a straw hat on her head. She grew pumpkins, taros, corn, and glutinous millet on their squarish half-acre of land, about five hundred yards west of the village. The soil was fertile, and the produce was more than she and Hua could use, so her brother Bensheng would sell the surplus for her in Wujia County and Six Stars, which was a nearby commune town. Shuyu seldom worked in the production brigade's fields, since she had to take care of the child and the home. The money Lin sent back each month helped her make ends meet.

Lin was reading a picture-story book under their eaves with Hua sitting on his lap. The baby girl held a thick scallion leaf, now and again blowing it as a whistle. The toots sounded like a sheep bleating. In front of the house was a deep well walled up with bricks to prevent the child and the poultry from falling into it. Because of her bound feet, Shuyu couldn't fetch water from the communal well with a shoulder pole and a pair of buckets as others did, so Lin had had the well sunk in their yard four years before. To the right of it stretched a footway, paved with bricks, leading to the front gate. Beside the pigpen, a white hen was scraping away dirt and making go-go-go sounds to call a flock of chicks, the smallest of which was dragging a broken leg. It was warm and windless; the air reeked of dried dung.

Without Lin's noticing, Hua opened her mouth. Her cracked lips clamped on the front of his T-shirt and pulled. He lowered his eyes and looked at her in puzzlement. She said,

"Daddy, I'm hungry." Her soiled palm touched his chest, fondling its left side.

He gave a laugh, which baffled her. She looked up at him without blinking. He said, "Hua, a man can't feed a baby like your mom. I have no breasts, see?" He pulled up the T-shirt and showed her his flat chest. A mole like a tiny raisin was under his right nipple. She looked confused, her dark eyes wide open.

"Would you like some cookies?" he asked.

"Uh-huh."

He put aside the book, picked her up, and set her astride his neck. Father and daughter went to the village store to buy cookies.

At dinner that evening Lin described to his wife how Hua had wanted to suck his nipple. Shuyu smiled and said, "Silly girl."

"She's almost four," he said. "You should stop breast-feeding her, shouldn't you?"

"Mother's milk keeps a baby healthy, you know." She took his bowl and refilled it with pumpkin porridge. "Have some more," she said.

"Does Hua often mention me when I'm away?"

"Yes, of course. Sometimes she says, 'I miss Daddy.' It's the blood tie, she doesn't know you that well."

He turned to his daughter. "Did you really miss me?"

"Yeah."

"Can you show how you missed me?"

The baby placed both hands on her stomach, saying, "Miss you here."

He laughed, then tears came to his eyes. He held his daughter up, set her on his lap, and moved her bowl closer so that she could reach it. Before she could go on eating, he smacked a kiss on her chafed face and then wiped her nose clean with a piece of straw paper.

Though Shuyu and Lin slept in different rooms at night, he
enjoyed being at home, especially playing with his daughter.
He liked the home-cooked food, most of which was fresh and
tasty. The multigrain porridge, into which Shuyu always
urged him to put some brown sugar though she wouldn't take
any herself, was so soft and delicious that he could eat three
bowls at a meal without feeling stuffed. The eggs sautéed with
leeks or scallions would make his belches redolent of the dish
even hours later. The steamed string beans seasoned with
sesame oil and mashed garlic gave him a feeling of ease and
freedom, because he would never dare touch such a homely
dish in the hospital for fear of garlicky breath. What is more,
it was so relaxing to be with his family. There was no reveille,
and he didn't have to rise at 5:30 for morning exercises. When
their black rooster announced daybreak, Lin would wake up,
then go back to sleep again. The morning snooze was the
sweetest to him. He had been home four days already. If only
he could stay for a whole month.

His brother-in-law Bensheng came that evening and asked
whether Lin could lend him some money. He was a scrawny
man in his mid-twenties and he had just gotten married; the
wedding had cost him eighteen hundred yuan and thrown him
deeply into debt. As if burdened with thoughts, he sat at the
edge of the brick bed, chain-smoking. His deep-set eyes flickered nervously, and his mustache spread like a tiny swallow.
From time to time he expelled a resounding belch.

While the two men talked, Shuyu sewed a cloth sole with
an awl and a piece of jute thread. She didn't say a word, but
kept glaring at her brother.

"Why do you need money so badly?" Lin asked Bensheng.
His daughter was on his back, her arms around his neck.

"I got in trouble at the marketplace and was fined." Two
tentacles of smoke dangled under Bensheng's nose.

"What happened?"

"Bad luck."

"How bad is it?"

"Come on, elder brother, don't ask so many questions. If you have money, help me!"

Seeing him so anxious, Lin put down Hua, stood up, and went into the inner room where his wallet was. "Serves you right," he heard his wife say to her brother.

He returned with five ten-yuan bills and handed them to his brother-in-law. "I can only lend you fifty."

"Thanks, thanks." Without looking at the money, Bensheng put it into his pants pocket. "I'll pay it back to Shuyu, all right?"

"That's fine." On second thought Lin said, "How about this: you keep the money, but you'll help us thatch our roof this fall when you have time?"

"That's a deal. I'll do it."

"Make sure you use fresh wheat stalks."

"Of course I will."

Bensheng left with his blue duck-billed cap askew on his head, whistling the tune of the folk song "A Little Cowherd Gets Married." Lin was pleased with the arrangement; these days he had been wondering how to get the roof thatched. Although his brother-in-law wasn't always reliable, Lin was certain he would do the job properly. Bensheng had just become the accountant of the production brigade and could easily get fresh wheat stalks.

After his brother-in-law was out of sight, Lin asked Shuyu why he had been fined. She shook her head and smiled, saying, "He asked for it."

"How?"

"He sewed up piglets' buttholes."

"I don't get it. What actually happened?"

She twined the jute thread around the iron handle of the awl and pulled the stitch tight in place. Then she began to tell him the story. "Last week Bensheng went to Wujia Town to sell piglets, a whole litter of them. Before he left, he sewed up four of their buttholes with flaxen thread. He wanted to make them weigh more. When he showed the piglets at the market-place, folks wanted to buy the four fat ones. Fact is those fat ones with their butts blocked up weren't fat at all. They were heavier and worth more, only 'cause they couldn't crap, al-most burst. Bensheng was just about to take the money from a buyer when the guy thought, 'Well, how come these four ras-cals are so clean?' The other piglets all dropped a pile of crap behind them. He looked closer and saw huge bulges on the four fat piglets' butts. He shouted, 'Look, the big suckers all have a sewed-up butthole.' "

Lin burst into laughter, lying down on the brick bed. Im-mediately Hua straddled his belly and began a horse ride with an imaginary whip. "Hee-ya, hee-ya, giddap!"

"Oh whoa—whoa!" he cried.

The girl kept riding him until he held her waist with both hands and raised her up, her feet kicking in the air and her laughter tinkling.

He sat up and asked his wife, "Then what happened?"

"They grabbed him and dragged him to the officials. The officials took his piglets away and fined him ninety yuan. He had to pay on the spot, or they wouldn't let him go home. Lucky for him, Second Donkey was there selling chickens and fish. He loaned Bensheng the money, but he must have it back this week. Second Donkey's building a home, a five-room house, and he needs the money for beams and electric wires."

"It served him right indeed," Lin said. They both laughed, and Shuyu went on licking her lips.

That was a rare moment in the family. The couple seldom talked, and in their home the poultry made more sounds than the human beings. Even Hua was quiet most of the time.

The next afternoon, while working the bellows in the kitchen, Lin came across a scrap of lined paper in the soybean stalks. He looked it over and saw scrawled numerals and drawings in pencil, which included a square, a box, bottles of different sizes, a circle, a jar, a knife. What can these mean? he wondered.

Shuyu was outside in the yard washing clothes, the wooden club in her hand sending out a rhythmic clatter on the stone slab. Hua was playing beside an iron water bucket, into which a mud-flecked goose went on thrusting its bill to drink. Hua washed her hands in the bucket now and then, shouting at the goose, "Shoo!" But it would not be intimidated and kept coming back.

After dinner Lin showed his wife the piece of paper and asked her what it was. Sucking in her lips, she muttered, "A list."

"A list of what?"

"Things."

"What things?"

"Groceries."

She began to explain the list to him. The small bottle stood for vinegar, the big bottle for soy sauce, the jar for cooking oil, the star for salt, the square for soap, the circle for soda ash, the sack for corn flour, the knife for pork, the box for matches, the bulb for electricity.

Behind the jar Lin saw "50" and realized she spent fifty fen on cooking oil. That was less than half a pound each month. Under the knife was "1," which probably meant one yuan's worth of pork, about a pound. He was surprised, because since he was home he had eaten meat or fish every day. He asked, "Shuyu, is the money I send you enough?"

"Yes."

"Do you want me to give you more?"

"No."

She rose to her feet and tottered to the cork-oak chest on the trestle against the back wall. Lifting the lid from a peach-shaped porcelain jar, she took out a sheaf of cash and returned.

"You must need this," she said and handed him the money.

"Where did you get that?"

"Saved."

"How much have you saved?"

"A hundred yuan last year, but spent most of it when Father died."

"How much do you have here?"

"Thirty."

"Keep it, all right? It's yours, Shuyu."

"You don't need?"

"Keep it. It's your money."

Something stirred in Lin's chest, and his breath turned tight. He moved to the wooden edge of the brick bed and put his feet into his suede shoes, which were scuffed and weighted with dried mud on the soles. Hastily he tied the shoelaces and went out for a walk in the gathering dusk alone.

The following afternoon Lin said he would go visit his parents' graves the next morning. His words threw Shuyu into a muddle. She hobbled to the village store and bought two pounds of streaky pork, then went to Second Donkey's home and got a grass carp from his pond. For dinner she boiled ten ears of corn since she didn't have time to bake cakes; but in the evening a small plate of stewed pork was placed beside Lin's bowl on the table. Though he pushed the dish to the center of the tabletop, Shuyu wouldn't touch it, whereas Hua ate with relish, smacking her lips and crying out, "I want fat meat." Her mother stared at her, but Lin smiled and put more pork cubes into her bowl.

Lin got up late the next morning. On the wooden cover of the cauldron sat a bamboo basket. He removed its lid and saw four dishes in it: a fried carp, stewed pork, tomatoes sautéed with eggs, and steamed taros, peeled and sprinkled with white sugar. The last dish had been his mother's favorite. On the chopping board, by the water vat, were a packet of joss sticks and a bunch of paper money. Shuyu had gone with Hua to cut grass for the pigs. Lin touched the bamboo basket, its side still warm.

Quickly he drank two bowls of millet porridge and then set off for the graves, which were at the edge of the larch woods in the valley south of the village, about ten minutes' walk. In recent years most of the dead had to be cremated to save arable land. Lin's elder brother, Ren Kong, had treated the village leaders to a twelve-course dinner and obtained their permission to let their father join their mother on the hillside.

The sun was directly overhead, and Lin was panting slightly when he arrived at the larch woods. Some cocklebur seeds had stuck to his trouser legs, and his shoes were ringed with dark mud. Mosquitoes were humming around hungrily while a few white-breasted swallows were darting back and forth, up and down, catching them. His parents' graves were well kept, covered with fresh earth. Beyond them, wormwood was yellow-green and rushes were reddish, all shiny in the sunlight.

Apparently somebody had cleaned up the place lately. Against the head of either grave leaned a thick bunch of wild lilies, still soaked with dew, but their small yellow flowers had withered long ago. Lin knew that it must have been Shuyu who had gathered the flowers and laid the bouquets, because his elder brother couldn't possibly think of such a thing, he was too deep in the bottle. On one of the headstones was his father's name, "Mingzhi Kong," whereas the other stone carried only "Kong's Wife." His mother had never had her own name. Lin opened the basket and set the dishes in front of the graves. He lit the joss sticks and planted them one by one before the dishes, and then he strewed around the paper coins, each of which was as large as a palm and had a square hole punched in its center. He said softly, "Dad and Mom, take the money and enjoy these dishes Shuyu made for you. May you rest in peace and comfort."

A shotgun popped in the east; a pair of snipes took off, making guttural cries and drifting away toward the lake in the south. A dog broke out yelping. Someone was shooting pheasants and grouse in the marsh.

Unlike the villagers, Lin didn't burn the money. His mind was elsewhere, having neglected the right way of sending cash to the nether world. He was thinking of Manna. He had promised her to start divorcing Shuyu as soon as he got home. Now he had been here for seven days—only three days were left for the leave, but he hadn't mentioned a word of it yet. Whenever the words rose to his throat, they were forced down. Somehow he felt that the idea of divorce was too unseemly to be disclosed. It would make no sense to anybody in the countryside if Lin said he wanted to divorce his wife because he didn't love her. He had to find a real fault in her, which he couldn't. People here would not laugh about her bound feet, and he did not feel ashamed of her in the village.

Having returned from the graves, for a whole day he thought of his predicament. He was certain that if a villager asked him about Shuyu, he would admit she was a perfect wife. Probably had he lived long enough with her, he would have been able to love her, and the two of them would have led a happy life, just as many couples who had gotten married without knowing each other beforehand became perfect husbands and wives later on. Yet how could he and Shuyu have lived together long enough to know each other well? Unless he had left the army and stayed home, which was unthinkable. He had his career in the city.

An ideal solution might be to have two wives: Manna in

the city and Shuyu in the country. But bigamy was illegal and out of the question. He stopped indulging in this kind of fantasy. For some reason he couldn't help imagining what his life would have been like if he had never met Manna. If only he had foreseen this dilemma; if only he could extricate himself from it now.

Two days before he left home, his wife took a pillow into his room at night. He was already in bed and was surprised to see Shuyu come in with her face lowered and twisted a little. She sat down on the bed and sighed. "Can I stay with you tonight?" she asked timidly.

He didn't know what to say, never having thought she could be so bold.

"I'm not a shameless woman," she said. "After Hua was born you never let me share your bed. I wouldn't complain, but these days I'm thinking of giving you a son. Hua's going to be big soon, and she can help me. Don't you want a son?"

For a moment he remained silent. Then he said, "No, I don't need a son. Hua's good enough for me. My brother has three sons. Let them carry on the family line. It's a feudal idea anyway."

"Don't you think of our old age? When we're old and can't move about and work the fields, we'll need a son to help us. You're always away, this home needs a man."

"We are not old yet. Besides, Hua will help us when she grows up. Don't worry."

"A girl isn't a reliable thing. She belongs to someone else after she's married."

He said no more, amazed by a sudden realization that if she were Manna, he might embrace and kiss her, calling her "Little Treasure" or "Sugar Ball," but he did not know what to do with Shuyu, whom he had kissed only in the darkness a long time ago. Now any intimacy with her would be unnatural.

She stood up and walked away, her shoulders drooping

more. He let out a deep sigh. By the door a coil of artemisia was still burning, keeping out mosquitoes. The room was filled with a bitter grassy scent.

Her words made him realize that his wife must have been lonely when he was away. He hadn't thought she had her own ideas and feelings. More worrisome, she never doubted that they would stay together for the rest of their lives. What a simple-hearted woman!

This realization distressed him and foiled his first attempt at a divorce.

12

Why doesn't he want to see me? Manna asked herself time and again.

She was anxious to know how Shuyu had responded to Lin's request for a divorce. He had been back from the country for a week and always said he had too much work to do in the evenings and couldn't walk with her. She sensed that something had gone awry. She talked about it with her friend Haiyan, who advised that she should confront Lin, and if necessary give him an ultimatum. Haiyan said to her, "Without pressure no well will yield oil. You must press him."

On Tuesday, after dinner, Manna went to Lin's office to look for him. Only a reading lamp was on in the room, which was as dark as a movie theater. She was surprised to find he wasn't busy at all. He was lounging in a chair and dozing with his mouth hanging open and his feet on the desk. A hefty book was lying in his lap. She coughed. He woke up with a start and put the book on the desk. Then he rose to his feet, went across the room, and switched all the lights on, so that people passing by in the corridor wouldn't suspect that the two of them might be doing something unusual in the office.

He looked tired and yawned uncomfortably. Manna's temper flared up and her face hardened. She pointed to the book, which she recognized as Marshal Georgi Zhukov's memoir of the Second World War, *Remembrance and Thoughts.* "So you're busy studying military strategy in order to become a general. What an ambitious man."

He grimaced, ill at ease. "Come on, don't be so nasty."

After they both sat down, she asked him bluntly, "Why do you avoid me these days?"

"I—I, what should I say?" He looked her in the face. "It's true that I've avoided you since I came back, because I didn't know how to tell you what had happened. After a few days' brooding, I have a clear idea now."

Manna was amazed by his calm voice, which made her think that he must have worked out a plan for ending his marriage. But to her dismay, he went on to describe how he hadn't been able to divorce his wife this summer, how he couldn't abandon his daughter who was still so young and had hung on his neck all the time calling him Papa, how he had tried to broach the topic with Shuyu but every time his courage had failed him, how he couldn't find any solid reason with which to persuade the local court to grant him a divorce, how the villagers viewed this matter differently from people in the city, how sorry he felt for Manna, who deserved a better man than himself. In short, he was hopeless and couldn't do a thing, at least for the time being.

After he had finished, she asked, "What should we do then? Continue like this?" Her voice was devoid of any emotion.

He said, "I think we'd better break up. No matter how we love each other, there'll be no chance for us. Better to stop before we're trapped too deep. Let's part from each other now and remain friends." He grasped his chest as though suffering from heartburn.

His words drove her mad, and she couldn't keep tears from streaming down her cheeks. She shrieked, "Then what will become of me? It's easy for you to say that—to be so rational. After we break up, where could I find another man? Don't you know the whole hospital treats me like your second wife? Don't you see that all men here shun me as though I were a married woman? Oh, where can I hide my face if you dump me like this?"

"Calm down please. Let's think about—"

"No, I don't want to think anymore! All you can do is think, think, think." She got up and rushed to the door with both hands cupped over her ears. The green door slammed shut behind her.

Her words upset him, but also pleased him slightly. They made him reconsider his suggestion. He had never thought Manna was already bound to him. Now it seemed clear that they ought to stay together, unless she were willing to live as a spinster for good without looking for a husband, which would have been inappropriate and abnormal. Everyone was supposed to marry; even the retarded and the paralyzed were not exempted. Wasn't it a sacred human duty to produce and raise children?

If only Manna could have transferred to another hospital where people would treat her the same as other unmarried women, but that was out of the question because too many nurses were in the service now. In recent years thousands of young women had been demobilized, and there were more to be discharged in the years to come. Those who had left the army were often regarded by civilians as bad women who had lifestyle problems. Many men would refer to them as "used military supplies."

A week later Lin rejoined Manna after admitting the impracticability of his suggestion. He even apologized to her for having considered their relationship only from his point of view. Despite being torn between Manna and his family, he assured her he would try to divorce Shuyu again in the future. But he needed time and could not rush. She agreed to wait with patience.

Before taking his annual leave the next summer, Lin promised Manna that he would definitely broach the topic of divorce with Shuyu this time. To convince her of his determination, he showed her a letter of recommendation issued by the Political Department, which Ran Su had written for him secretly, Lin told her not to breathe a word about the letter to anyone.

During his absence, Manna grew hopeful and was in high spirits. Her colleagues often asked her why she smiled so much. She wouldn't tell them the truth; instead she would quip, "Is it a crime to be happy?" At night when she couldn't sleep, she would think about how to arrange their wedding. How much should they spend? Did a vacuum-tube radio cost more than 120 yuan? What kind of bedclothes should she get? What types of dresser and wardrobe were good and affordable? She should buy Lin a bicycle—a Flying Pigeon. He also needed a pair of leather shoes and a leather jacket, which was currently in fashion. If possible, they should get a wall clock, the kind with a revolving chick inside whose head moved up and down all the time as if pecking at grain. She hoped they would be assigned a decent apartment, ideally with three rooms, so that they could have a living room to hang such a clock. How she wanted to be a mother someday and have a home with a few children.

One afternoon in the hospital grocery store, she saw some gorgeous satin quilt covers for sale. They all had celestial creatures embroidered on them—either a dragon with a fire-ball in its mouth or a phoenix embracing a huge pearl. In the upper left corner of every quilt cover were these words in shiny stitches: "An Unforgettable Night." Unable to restrain herself, Manna bought a pair, which cost almost forty yuan, more than half her monthly salary. But she was pleased with the purchase. One of the saleswomen asked her, "Who's getting married?"

She replied, "A friend of mine in Harbin." She was blushing and left the store in a hurry, carrying under her arm the package wrapped in cellophane.

For several days whenever alone in the bedroom, she would take the saffron quilt covers out of her suitcase, spread them on her bed, and look at the embroidered dragon and phoenix. She dreamed more often now. Most of her dreams were exuberant, full of plants and aquatic animals—sunflowers, watermelons, frogs, lotus flowers, silver pomfrets, giant halibuts. Those signs ought to portend the success of Lin's trip. At times she blamed herself for being too childish, but she couldn't help herself, her heart brimming with hopes and her eyes a little moony.

But when he returned from the countryside, Lin looked dejected. He told her that this time he had talked with his wife about a divorce, but he hadn't been able to go further, not because Shuyu had refused to accept it but because her brother Bensheng had gone berserk, threatening to retaliate if Lin divorced his sister. Moreover, Bensheng turned the whole village against him and spread the rumor that Lin had committed bigamy, taking a concubine in the city. Outraged, Lin showed the official divorce recommendation to him and to the Party secretary of the production brigade, but his brother-in-law declared he would go to the city, talk with the army leaders personally, and ask them why they encouraged their man to abandon his wife.

This frightened Lin. If Bensheng came to the hospital, Ran Su's involvement in the matter would be exposed. Beyond question that would cause a scandal. So to pacify his brother-in-law, Lin gave up pressing for a divorce.

Though heartbroken, Manna was dubious about his account of what had happened. She wouldn't say he was a liar; never had he lied to her; but she felt that his words, despite having some truth, might not be without exaggeration. Perhaps he had purposely retreated from their original agreement. But to her surprise, Lin pointed out another possible consequence, which had never entered her mind and which further justified his decision not to push for a divorce for the time being.

"Everybody knows there'll be a general adjustment of ranks at the end of this year," he said. "If Bensheng comes and makes a scene here, for sure neither you nor I will get a promotion. In fact he doesn't have to come. Just sending a letter to the leaders will be enough to ruin our chance. Don't you think?"

She made no answer, her face getting whiter and whiter. Indeed these days people were talking about the general adjustment enthusiastically, after Commissar Zhang had declared at a meeting that most of the staff would get a promotion in rank at the end of the year. This was a precious opportunity for everybody. For almost a decade there had been no promotion whatsoever in the hospital; people's ranks and salaries had remained frozen in spite of inflation. So now by mentioning the potential damage, Lin persuaded Manna of the correctness of his decision. She agreed that they shouldn't provoke Bensheng for the moment. Lin promised he would figure out some way to obtain a divorce.

In December 1970 Lin and Manna both got promoted and were each given a raise of nine yuan a month. The promotion pleased them, although it had cost them much more than it had other people.

1

In the spring of 1972 Lin Kong received a letter from his cousin Liang Meng, who had grown up in Wujia County and gone to the same middle school as Lin had. Now Liang Meng lived in Hegang, a coal-mining city about eighty miles west of Muji. Since they had not kept up a regular correspondence, his letter came as a surprise to Lin.

He asked Lin to help him find a girlfriend in the army hospital, because he would like to marry a doctor or a nurse. His wife had died two years before, leaving him three children. After long grief, he felt ready to continue with his life. Besides, his family needed a woman to keep the home together. For months he had been looking for a girlfriend in Hegang City, but without success; either the women had disliked the size of his family or he had thought them too vulgar. He was a well-educated man.

Liang Meng's letter brought a ray of hope to the situation that trapped Lin and Manna. The previous summer Lin had returned home and broached the topic of divorce again. To his surprise, Shuyu agreed, but when they arrived at Wujia Town, she couldn't stop her tears in front of the judge and then changed her mind. As a result, the request was declined and Lin was humiliated by the judge, who reprimanded him in harsh language, even calling him "a shameless man." When he returned to the hospital and briefed Manna about the court's rejection, she was disappointed and seemed to have doubts about his effort. She wanted him to promise that he would definitely carry through on the divorce in the near future, but he would not fix a deadline, arguing that all he could do was try his best the next year.

He felt tired and had returned to his former placid state and read more novels and magazines when he had time. His eyes had grown more myopic, and he had to wear a pair of thicker glasses, which made him look gentler. In contrast, Manna had by now become fractious and often quarreled with others. When a few new nurses were assigned to her group, as their head nurse she ordered them around, even telling them to do an orderly's work, such as feeding patients, changing sheets, mopping floors, cleaning bedpans. If an officer's wife looked at her with meaningful eyes, Manna would glare back, as if ready to start a shouting match. When walking with Lin in the evening, if he stopped to talk with a friend or a colleague, she would move away, waiting and watching from a distance, as though she hadn't known them. Behind her back, people called her "a typical old maid." Lin noticed the changes in her, but he didn't know how to help her except to try to get the divorce the next summer. And about that he was uncertain.

Now, his cousin's letter pointed to a possible way for Manna to find a boyfriend. It had never occurred to Lin that unlike the army hospital staff here, civilians in other cities and towns might not regard Manna as his fiancée. So why shouldn't she look for a man elsewhere, outside the army? In any event she must not wait for him passively. Heaven knew when he could succeed in divorcing his wife. In his heart he felt the divorce could easily drag on for five or six years. Probably it would never materialize at all.

Can you really let her go? he asked himself. The question like a pang constricted his chest a little. Though he no longer had the same romantic passion for Manna as he used to have, he was still very much attached to her and could see there was a slight possibility that they might get married someday. She was his woman, the only one he had ever had deep feelings for. Could he give her up? If she and his cousin were married, how would he feel if he ran into them in the future? Wouldn't he hate himself for introducing her to him? If he lost Manna, where could he find another woman as good as she?

Those questions tormented him for several days. Then he made up his mind to mention his cousin to Manna, believing this was a good opportunity for her. She deserved a man who could offer her more than he could. It was a painful decision on his part, but it was necessary. If this static affair between them continued, both his and her careers would be affected or even ruined. In many people's eyes the two of them had already become near-pariahs involved in something illegitimate. It would be too depressing to let the sinister shadows hang on them forever. He had best cut the entangled knot once and for all.

"Look," he said to Manna as they strolled behind the Medical Ward, "I don't mean to upset you, but there's a good way you can find a boyfriend."

Her face fell. "Don't talk about that again. I know you're tired of me."

"Don't be so grumpy. I'm not joking this time."

"Like you didn't mean business before."

"Come on, you know how I feel about you, but we can't get married."

"So? I can wait."

"We don't know how long you may end up waiting."

"I don't care."

"Please listen to me!"

She stopped and looked him in the face. A few gnats were flying around them. The last sunlight fell on the thick aspen leaves, which turned glossy, flickering and rustling in the breeze. A dog burst out barking and prancing behind the steel netting of the kennel, before which gathered a group of small boys and girls watching the animal struggling in vain to get out.

Lin went on, "A cousin of mine wrote me a letter recently.

He asks me to find a girlfriend for him in our hospital. I don't mean you should go with him. It just dawned on me that you might be able to find a boyfriend in another city, where nobody knows about us. The man doesn't have to be an officer." He stopped to catch his breath.

With her lips curled up she said, "I've thought about that a hundred times. It's not so simple."

"How come?" He was amazed by her words, thinking, So you did think about how to dump me.

"Even if I married a man in another city, how could I join him without being discharged? If I remained in the army, he and I would have to live separately. That situation is what I don't want."

"Can't the man move to Muji?"

"Probably he could, but how about us? How would you feel about me marrying another man? Would you be comfortable running into me here every day? Wouldn't the word about our relationship reach the man's ears? Then what would happen to the marriage? Heavens, it gives me a headache to think about this. I feel hopeless."

Her explanation surprised him, as he had never thoroughly understood the complexity of her situation. After a long pause he said, "You shouldn't worry so much. Don't take my feelings into account. Do whatever is good for yourself."

"What could I do?"

"Start to look for a man in another city?"

"Where?"

"Anywhere. For instance, my cousin Liang Meng in Hegang is available. Start looking as soon as you can. Do it step by step, and don't worry in advance. There's always a way out of every situation."

"Okay, tell me about your cousin." She raised her head, and a sly smile curved her lips.

He began to talk about Liang Meng, who was thirty-eight,

a middle school teacher, five feet ten, healthy, intelligent, and reliable, though he was a widower with three children.

Lin produced his cousin's letter from his pants pocket and handed it to her, saying, "You should read this and think about what he says. Take your time to decide. If you want to meet him, I'll be glad to help." Then he added, pointing at the envelope, "His handwriting is very handsome, don't you think?"

"Yes, it looks scholarly."

"When you have thought this through, let me know what you'd like to do, all right?"

"I will."

A week later Manna told him that she wouldn't mind the size of Liang Meng's family since she was fond of children, and that she was more interested in seeing what the man himself was like. Lin was ready to help, but he warned her not to raise her hopes too much in case she might find Liang Meng unsuitable.

Without delay he wrote to his cousin and described Manna as a wonderful match, a woman who was honest and goodhearted and had never been married, without any family ties. Besides, she had strong moral fiber, working hard and living plainly. In a word, she was definitely one in a hundred.

Liang Meng's reply came two weeks later, saying that when school was over in Hegang in June he would come to Muji to attend a wood-engraving class, and that he would be delighted to meet Manna. He thanked Lin profusely for the matchmaking, saying he had been so moved that words almost failed him.

So Lin planned to introduce the two in June.

2

Liang Meng came to Muji as planned. The mail office called Lin and notified him of his cousin's arrival. Lin sauntered to the front entrance to meet him. He and Liang Meng shook hands for a good ten seconds and then waved at the soldier in the sentry box; together they turned and went on into the hospital.

"Did you have a good trip?" Lin asked his cousin.

"Yes. But the train was so crowded I couldn't find a seat."

"Do you have a place to stay in town?"

"Yes, in the Fine Arts Institute."

While walking they glanced at each other continually. Liang Meng's smile reminded Lin of their adventures on the Songhua River twenty-five years before. His cousin had been an excellent swimmer, able to float on his back as if taking a nap, whereas Lin had not dared enter the main channel and had always dog-paddled in the shallows. Life had passed like a dream—twenty-five years were gone in a blink of an eye. Look at his cousin now—he resembled a typical middle-aged man.

"Elder brother, this is a gorgeous place," Liang Meng said sincerely. "It's so clean here, everything's in order."

Lin smiled, amazed by the comment. Yes, he thought, if compared with a coal mine.

He led his cousin to the dormitory. To his surprise, his roommate Jin Tian was there with his fiancée, frying some walleye pollack on a kerosene stove. It was almost three o'clock, so he took Liang Meng directly to Manna, knowing she worked the second shift these days, slept in the morning, and must be up now. He felt bad for his cousin, who looked tired, but he couldn't find a peaceful place where Liang Meng could rest awhile before meeting Manna. Another inconvenience was that if they met in the hospital, Lin had to accompany them like a chaperon; otherwise the intention of Manna's being alone with a male stranger would have been construed by others.

They found Manna in her bedroom, but one of her roommates was still sleeping in there, so together the three of them went out to look for a place where they could talk a little. On their way Lin bought three sodas at a refreshment stand sheltered by a khaki sunshade in front of the grocery store.

Before the medical building they found an unoccupied granite table beneath a grape trellis. They sat down, each drinking a bottle of Tiger Spring soda. The air was intense with camphor, and bumblebees were droning and darting about. A fat larva, hanging from a long strand of silk spat by itself, was wriggling upward in a slanting sunbeam that filtered through the grape leaves. Doctors in white robes were passing by, with either a folded newspaper or a stethoscope in their baggy pockets. Two nurses were pushing a long wheeled oxygen cylinder like a torpedo, giggling, poking fun at each other, and shooting glances at Manna.

Liang Meng, looking troubled, told them he had to give up the wood-engraving class and return home within two days, because his daughter had been struck by inflammation of the brain and was just out of danger in the hospital. He had to phone home in the evening to check on her condition. Manna realized he had come all the way mainly to meet her.

She wondered whether he actually measured five feet ten as his letter claimed. He was a scrawny man and looked older than his age. His appearance was unusual. His hairline had receded almost to the center of his crown, making his shiny forehead bulbous. But his eyebrows were broad and thick, and reached the lids of his deep-socketed eyes. Under his hooked nose was a protruding mouth whose lower lip enfolded the upper. When he spoke, his head would tilt to the right as though there was a pain in his neck.

"What kind of grapes are these?" Liang Meng rose from his seat and plucked a green grape from the vine above his head.

"No idea," Lin said tepidly.

Manna was rather surprised by his terse answer. Just now when they arrived at her dormitory, Lin had been happy. Why did he look rather sullen now? She said to the high-spirited guest, "I don't know either."

Liang Meng put the grape into his mouth and began chewing it. "Bah! it's no good, too sour." He spat its skin and pips to the ground. "We have lots of grapes in our yard."

"Really?" she asked. "Are they good?"

"Of course. Sweet and big."

Despite seeing Lin frown a little, she asked again, "What kind of grapes are they?"

"Mainly Fragrant Rose and Sheep Nipples. We have a bumper harvest this year. The trellises nearly collapsed, and I propped them up with wood stakes. What happened is that we buried some dead animals at the roots of the grapevines in the spring. God, that doubled the yield."

"What animals did you bury?" she asked.

"Well, some dead chickens and ducks, and a mad dog, that was our neighbor's. The dog bit a schoolgirl and was shot by the police." He turned to Lin. "Elder brother, I meant to ask your professional opinion. Do you think it safe to eat grapes fattened up by a rabid dog?"

"I have no professional opinion," Lin said curtly. Then he caught himself and added, "What a question! By common sense that should not be a problem."

Manna was intrigued by Liang Meng's talking of grapes. Evidently he was a family man; he even raised poultry, although he was a sort of intellectual. Perhaps she should find out more about him.

Since the hospital was an inconvenient place for more conversation, Lin suggested that the next day his cousin and Manna meet and talk by themselves somewhere in the city. They agreed to rendezvous at Victory Park. Perhaps the Songhua River was a more pleasant place, but there were always so many people on the bank that they might miss each other.

Victory Park lies at the southern end of the city. It was built in 1946, in memory of the Russian soldiers who had fallen while fighting Japanese troops in Manchuria toward the end of the Second World War. At the main entrance to the park, a stout statue of a fully equipped Russian soldier stood against an obelisk; his helmet and the barrel and round magazine of his submachine gun were missing, chopped off by the Red Guards at the outset of the Cultural Revolution. But currently the statue was under repair, surrounded by scaffolding. On the ground, in front of the monument, a slogan was still legible: "Down with Russian Chauvinism!" Those words had been scraped off, but the dark strokes remained distinguishable on the grayish concrete.

Manna arrived at ten o'clock. Inside the park, Victory Lake was greened by drooping willows. Two young men, apparently college students, were laughing heartily and paddling a dinghy, whose bow carried a line of words in red paint: "Long Live Chairman —!" The word "Mao" had washed off. A few pairs of white ducks and wild geese were swimming near the bank. Manna leaned over the railing on a stone bridge and observed carps gliding in the water beneath, most of them about a foot long. She had on a yellow poplin shirt, which together with the army skirt made her look younger and more curvaceous. She was sweating a little because of the long walk, so she remained in the shade of a willow, which sheltered almost a third of the bridge. A sudden breeze blew a few candy wrappers into the air, and a brown plastic bag was flapping on the blossoms of a cherry tree. She remembered meeting her first love, Mai Dong, at this place. That had been eight years before. How time had passed. The park was different now, almost unrecognizable; it had become a zoo, noisy and crowded, with hundreds of animals kept in iron cages and deep concrete pits. On the opposite shore, behind rows of trees, stood several new buildings.

Her memory of Mai Dong feeding mallards with popped rice on this very bridge brought a slight contraction to her chest. Where is he now? she wondered. What a heartless man he was. Does he really love his cousin? What does he do for a living? Is he still in Shanghai? Does he often think of me?

Her thoughts were interrupted by a male voice speaking from behind her. "Hey, Comrade Manna Wu." Liang Meng appeared, carrying a large manila envelope under his arm and waving at her.

She waved back, but didn't move toward him.

Coming over, he smiled and shook hands with her. "How is your daughter?" asked Manna.

"She's doing all right. She returned home yesterday afternoon. My sister-in-law is with her now. The doctor said there wouldn't be any aftereffects."

"That's good news. Is she your oldest child?"

"No, she's the youngest and she has two brothers. One is eleven and the other nine. She's seven."

They turned to go farther into the park. Before they stepped off the bridge, Liang Meng cleared his throat and spat into the water. Immediately a red carp, about two feet long, rushed over and swallowed the blob of phlegm. Manna made a mental note that Lin wouldn't do that. They bore left, walking along the bank clockwise.

He told her that he had heard a great deal about her from Lin and was impressed by her work as a head nurse. Then, without a transition, he began talking about himself. He had graduated from Harbin Teachers School in 1965, specializing in the fine arts. The graduation year was significant, meaning that his education had not been disrupted by the Cultural Revolution. Unfortunately his wife had died two years ago; people used to call them "a pair of mandarin ducks," meaning an affectionate couple. True, the two of them had spent some peaceful, loving years together and had never fought or quarreled. His children were well disciplined and sensible, the boys being model students at school. Though approaching middle age, he was in good health and only had a cold sometimes in winter when the air in Hegang was heavy with coal dust. He earned seventy-two yuan a month; since they had no debt, the family managed fine.

Manna was afraid he would ask about her rank and salary. If he did, their relationship would end here, because she hated that kind of materialistic attitude. But he had the decency not to raise the question, and instead he switched to the topic of his teaching.

When they reached the opposite shore, the dome of a concrete building emerged on their left, partly blocked from view by poplar crowns. That was the city's Children's Palace. A row of sedans—Warsaws, Volgas, and Red Flags—were parked in a lot encircled by hawthorn hedges. Children's singing, accompanied on the organ, could be heard.

Manna and Liang Meng sat down on a long bench facing the lake. The blue paint on the bench was flaky in places, and the wooden slats forming its back felt scaly. On their left a cartridge box sat on the ground, filled with snow crocuses.

Liang Meng put the large envelope on his lap and pulled out a few small drawings. "These are my work. I hope you like them," he said and handed them to her. She noticed he had stubby fingers.

She looked through the drawings. They were all illustrations of a battle in which the Vietcong wiped out the American invaders. In one of the pieces, two enemy men—a black soldier and a white officer—were impaled upon the bamboo stakes in a trap, yelling "Help!" Manna wasn't interested in the illustrations. She had come here to see the man, not his work. She handed them back and said blandly, "Good pictures."

"They are for a children's book. You like them?"

"Yes. When will the book come out?"

He knit his brows and muttered, "It was supposed to be out this year, but the publishing house wants to wait."

"How's that?"

"There're too many books of this kind on the market. I'm told that the United States is no longer our chief enemy. So they don't want to publish the book now."

"What are they publishing?"

"Anything related to criticizing Confucius."

"Then why not draw something they want?"

"It's so hard to predict the wind. If I take up a project now, by the time I'm done with it, it will probably be out of fashion."

"I'm sorry." She truly felt for him.

He put the drawings back into the envelope. "It's all right. I just did these pieces as an exercise. But God knows how hard I worked on them."

"I can tell you did."

A pause set in, and Manna looked across the lake for a view of the other shore. She was struck by the sight of the massive mountain in the southeast. It suddenly brightened as sunlight penetrated the clouds and fell on its craggy shoulders. She said to Liang Meng, "Wow, look at that mountain!"

"It's really pretty," he echoed.

In the distance, beyond the train station where locomotives were chugging past and puffing dark smoke, the immense mountain rose, tall, rugged, indigo. The jagged rocks on its ridges pierced the mist surrounding it; a footpath could be seen winding up the precipitous slope and disappearing in the clouds. A few birds were soaring almost motionlessly along the middle of a cliff; an air-raid cave beside the path was visible owing to the yellowish fresh earth dumped at its mouth, which formed a gigantic triangle spreading down the slope. The sun cast a few colorful streaks of light above the pine woods that stretched on the western shoulder of the mountain. Suddenly a dusty cloud arose from a ridge; the birds swerved in the air, soaring higher. A few seconds later came the sound of an explosion. Apparently people were quarrying rocks up there.

"I never thought the mountain looked so awesome," Manna said to him.

"Yes, it's lovely."

"We can hardly see it from the hospital."

"Because of the smog or too many buildings blocking the view, I guess."

"No, not because of those things only. You just forget that the mountain is there and so awesome. You're too mindful of things and people around you."

She grew thoughtful as he straightened his neck and recited loudly, "The mountains and rivers are so enchanting / They have inspired innumerable heroes to compete for them." He was quoting from Chairman Mao's poem "Snow."

Manna tittered. He turned, looking at her in some perplexity. "What's so funny?" he asked.

"Nothing." She took out her cambric handkerchief and dabbed the sweat from her cheeks.

Two boys ran by, each with an iron bar in his hand rolling a steel hoop that was the rim of a bicycle wheel. The harsh, metallic noise jarred on Manna's nerves.

She stood up and said she had to leave now because she had to sleep a few hours before her night shift. He got to his feet, and together they went back the way they had come.

Passing the bridge, she caught sight of a bus waiting at the entrance to the park, so she promptly took her leave without saying whether she would like to meet him again. She hurried through the crowd, striding toward the bus. He followed her a few steps, then stood on a stone bench and watched her disappear among the passengers. He waved at the bus as it rolled away with popping coughs. His upper body rose above the pedestrians' heads bobbing around him. His neck stretched so long that Manna covered her mouth with her palm to keep from laughing.

When she told Lin about his cousin's drawings and his reciting Chairman Mao's poetry, he shook his head and said, "What a bookworm. But Manna, he's a trustworthy man, don't you think?"

"I don't know. He's so strange."

"Look, you don't have to decide now. Think about him. If you want to meet him again, let me know."

"Again? Not for a thousand."

A week later Lin received a letter and a parcel from his cousin, which contained a pound of dried oyster mushrooms. Liang Meng wrote that he was very interested in Manna and that she seemed to him very "mature and unaffected." He hoped they could hit it off when they saw each other next time. Since Lin didn't cook, he gave the mushrooms to Ming Chen, the new director of the Personnel Section, who had treated Lin's arthritis with acupuncture and always cut his hair.

Showing Liang Meng's letter to Manna, Lin said, "You see, he has good sense. You should write him back."

"What should I say?"

"Just tell him what you think."

"Lin, he made me feel like a moron. He really is a character."

"Why is that?"

"I wasn't attracted to him at all. Why did I bother to meet with him in the park?"

"I'm sorry to hear that." He felt a surge of delight in his chest, which to some degree embarrassed him. He turned his face away.

She went on, "In the matter of love, I ought to follow my heart. Even birds may not become mates if you put them together in a cage, not to speak of us human beings. So don't talk about looking for another man again."

"All right." He heaved a sigh of relief. "So you think I'm a better man?" he asked half-jokingly.

"If only I didn't love you so much," she said. Two or three wrinkles appeared at the left corner her mouth, revealing a shadow of sadness.

Manna wrote to Liang Meng the next week, saying that she didn't feel well these days and had to inform him candidly that she suffered from serious rheumatic heart disease. This misinformation must have scared the man. After her letter, Lin never heard from his cousin again.

3

The next summer Lin and Shuyu went to the divorce court again. The day before setting out for Wujia Town, he had talked with her, promising to take good care of her and their daughter after the divorce, so she had agreed to it. He told her that all he wanted was a home in the city.

They waited almost an hour in the courtroom before the judge appeared. He was a tall police officer who had just been promoted to the position; he was so corpulent that he had no neck. Having sat down on a scarlet leatherette chair, the judge licked his buck teeth, then peered at the couple with one eye open and the other shut, as though aiming a gun. His broad, greasy face reminded Lin of the clay statue of a local god in the Divine Horse Shrine west of Goose Village. With his left hand picking a wart under his nostril and with his right forefinger pointing at Lin, the judge ordered, "Now, present your case."

Lin began with a slight stammer: "Respectable Judge, I—I came here today to beg you to allow me to divorce my wife. We have been separated for six years, and there's no love between us anymore. According to the Marriage Law, every citizen has the freedom to choose a wife or a hus—"

"Excuse me," the judge cut him short. "May I remind you that the law does not say every married man is entitled to a divorce? Go on."

Lin was flustered. He remained silent for a moment while his face was burning. Then he resumed warily, "I understand that, Comrade Judge, but my wife has already agreed to a divorce. We have worked out an arrangement between us, and I shall financially support her and our child afterward. Believe me, I'm a responsible man."

As he was speaking, Shuyu covered her mouth with a crumpled piece of paper. Her eyes were closed as though her scalp were smarting.

The judge turned to her after Lin was finished. "Comrade Shuyu Liu, I have a few questions for you. Now promise me you will think about them carefully before you answer me."

"I will." She nodded.

"What's the true reason that your husband wants a divorce?"

"Don't have a clue."

"Is there a third party involved?"

"What that mean?"

The young scribe, sitting behind the judge and taking notes, shook his head, blinking his round eyes. The judge went on, "I mean, has he been seeing another woman?"

"I reckon there must be lots of them around him in the army. He's a handsome man, you know."

The scribe chuckled, but the judge kept a stern face. "Answer me, do you know if he's having an affair with another woman?"

"I'm not sure. He said he needs a family in the city."

"A family with another woman?"

"Probably true."

"I have a final question for you. Do you still have feelings for him?"

"Oh yes, of course," she moaned, then broke out sobbing, as the last question had touched her heart.

"Do you still love him?"

"Yes." She nodded, wiping her tears, too moved to say more.

The judge turned to her husband. "Well, Officer Lin Kong,

you must confess to the court whether you have a mistress in the city."

"I don't have a mistress, Comrade Judge," he said in a shaking voice, realizing that the judge meant to drag Manna into the case.

"Even if you have no mistress, there must be an illicit love affair."

"I've never had an affair."

"Then with whom will you form a new family in Muji? Another man?"

"Oh no. With a friend of mine."

"What's her name?"

"Is that relevant to this case, Comrade Judge?"

"Of course it is. We have to investigate and find out your true relationship with her before we can decide how to handle your request for a divorce."

"She has nothing to do with this. We have a relationship of pure comradeship."

"Then why are you so reluctant to tell me her name and work unit? Do you feel too ashamed, or do you want to cover something up?"

"I . . . I . . ." Sweat was breaking out on Lin's face.

The judge folded a yellow booklet and with it swatted at a hornet fluttering on the table. He missed the insect, which took off buzzing as if catapulted. He was waiting for the husband to answer the question, but Lin remained speechless, unsure about the consequences if he revealed Manna's name. He glanced at the judge, whose thick-lidded eyes were half closed as though he were about to doze off. Uncertainty kept Lin from saying anything.

Having waited almost two minutes, the judge cleared his throat and concluded, "All right. If you had not done anything to be ashamed of, you would not be afraid of a ghost knocking at your door. We cannot proceed with this case unless you provide us with that woman's name, age, workplace, and marital status. Go home and come again when you have the needed information ready. In the meantime, you must treat your wife decently, like a friend and comrade. The court will check on that." He smiled with one eye screwed up.

Lin knew it was no use to argue, so he said diffidently, "All right, we'll come again."

As if in a trance, he rose to his feet and turned to the door, Shuyu following. His right leg had gone to sleep and made him limp a little.

While the couple were inside the courthouse, Bensheng and a dozen men from Goose Village had stood outside, waving spades, flails, hoes, shoulder poles. They threatened to create a disturbance if the judge granted Lin a divorce. A large crowd gathered on the street, believing the maddened villagers were going to beat up the unfaithful husband. Nobody wanted to miss such a spectacle. The judge called the county's Military Department, which immediately dispatched a militia platoon to keep order outside the courthouse.

"So he's a big officer or something? Still he mustn't be bigger than the law," a middle-aged woman said to others.

"Even an emperor isn't free to divorce his wife," a toothless crone put in.

"Men are all alike, beasts."

An old man in bifocals retorted, "A woman shouldn't be allowed to divorce either, or else there'll be disorder everywhere. The order of the world is rooted in every family, as Confucius said."

"What a heartless animal!"

"He has no reason to do this to her."

"The army should send him back and let him scratch a living out of the earth."

"I heard he's a doctor."

"Small wonder he has no heart. Doctors are butchers."

To the dismay of some of them, the judge had turned down Lin's petition and therefore precluded the anticipated spectacle. Seeing the husband and wife come out of the courthouse, some spectators whispered that the couple indeed didn't match. The husband looked quite gentle, in no way like an evil, abusive man, whereas the wife was as thin as a chicken whose flesh, if cooked, couldn't fill a plate. If they were so different, they might not be able to avoid conflicts. But that should provide no grounds for divorce, because it was normal for a married couple to have a quarrel or even a fist fight once in a while. A good marriage was full of moments of cats and dogs. It was the uneventful marriage that was headed toward disaster. In a word, the differences between the husband and the wife should only help stabilize their marriage.

Lin's face turned bloodless when he saw so many eyes in the crowd glaring at him. Hurriedly he and Shuyu left the courthouse for the bus stop. All the way home he didn't say a word.

After the couple had left, the militia was withdrawn from the courthouse. But it took half an hour for the crowd to disperse completely. The ground was littered with popsicle wrappers and sticks, bottle caps, cucumber ends, patches of melon seeds.

That evening Lin bolted the door of his room and remained inside alone, smoking, thinking, and sighing. He felt lucky that the angry villagers hadn't done any physical harm to him, and that only two women had spat on the ground and balled their fists when he came out of the courtroom. Had he won a divorce, he might not have gotten home unharmed. Maybe he shouldn't have tried to divorce his wife this year. Evidently his brother-in-law had been prepared to deal with him, and he had played right into Bensheng's hands.

The next day, after lunch, Shuyu stepped in with a copy of the county newspaper, *Country Constructs,* which was merely a handwritten, mimeographed affair at the time. "This just came," she said and handed it to Lin.

"Where did you get it?" he asked without taking the paper.

"Bensheng gave it to me. He said there was a pile of it in the commune opera house."

She left the newspaper on the short-legged table. On the brick bed Hua was napping, her thick lips puffing up a little when she exhaled. Shuyu unfolded a yellow toweling coverlet and drew it over the child, then went out to wash dishes in the cauldron.

Lin picked up the newspaper and began looking through it. On page three he saw a short article about his attempted divorce. It stated:

> *The County Court declined a divorce case yesterday af-*
> *ternoon. Lin Kong, an army doctor in Muji City of eigh-*
> *teenth rank, appealed to the court for a divorce on the*
> *grounds that he and his wife Shuyu Liu no longer loved*
> *each other. But Shuyu Liu insisted that she still had*
> *deep feelings for him. Hundreds of people sympathetic*
> *to the wife gathered outside the courthouse, criticizing*
> *the husband for his change of heart and demanding that*
> *the authorities protect the woman. The experienced*
> *judge, Comrade Jianping Zhou, reprimanded Lin Kong*
> *and reminded him that he was a revolutionary officer*
> *and a son of a poor peasant. He said to him, "You have*
> *forgotten your class origin and tried to imitate the*
> *lifestyle of the exploiting class. The court advises you to*
> *wake up before you fall into the abyss of misfortune and*
> *cannot get out."*

*Everyone was relieved to see the couple come out of
the court still married. Some applauded.*

Having read the article, Lin was wretchedly disappointed.
He suspected his brother-in-law might have been behind its
publication. The author, who had not signed his name, using
"Defender of Morality" instead, must have been Bensheng's
friend. Lin clearly remembered that there had been no applause at all when he and Shuyu came out of the courthouse.
Obviously this article was meant to shame him and prevent
him from seeking to divorce his wife again.

How he hated Bensheng! He decided not to speak to him
during the remaining days of his leave.

"Hello, is somebody home?" a throaty voice shouted from the
front yard the next afternoon.

Shuyu went out to see who it was. At the sight of the tall
man with a massive scar on his left cheek, she beamed and
said, "Come on in, elder brother."

The man dropped on a sawhorse a bundle of sweet
sorghum canes, each of which was about an inch thick and
two feet long. "These are for Hua, from our field," he said.

"You shouldn't have carried them all the way here," Shuyu
said. Yet she was happy to see the sweet canes.

"Is Lin home?"

"Yes."

The visitor was Lin's elder brother, Ren Kong. He wore a
blue jacket with brass buttons and a pair of rubber-toed
loafers. He had heard of Lin's court appearance, so he came to
intercede for Shuyu, whom he regarded almost as a sister because she had done so much for the Kongs. Also, a few
months ago he had written to Lin, asking him to bring home
some Tower Candy for his children, to get rid of roundworms

in their bellies. His three sons had all looked sallow for months; lately his youngest son had a stomachache every afternoon, and worms like thick noodles had been found in the boy's stool. Tower Candy was a sugary pill in the form of a tiny solid cone with spiral grooves on its side. Children in the country loved it and would eat it as a treat.

The army hospital had several drugs for roundworms, but it didn't stock Tower Candy. In spite of the regulation that allowed no one to appropriate drugs for personal use, many of the hospital staff got what they needed from the pharmacy. That was why the three pharmacists each had a good number of friends in the hospital and would receive a lot of gifts on holidays. But Lin was too shy to ask the pharmacists for any medicine without a prescription. He had decided to buy some Tower Candy at a department store, but before taking the leave, he had become so engrossed in completing an article on the topic of becoming "Red and Expert" that he totally forgot his promise to Ren to bring some back. Now, his brother's appearance reminded him of his word. What should he do? He worried, wondering how to come up with an excuse.

The two brothers were chatting and drinking tea while Shuyu was cooking in the kitchen. Hua was with her mother, working the bellows by the cauldron. Lin overheard his wife order the child, "Girl, don't suck that cane while you're working."

"I didn't. I just keep it here," Hua said.

"I say put the cane away."

"No, I want to have it here."

"Give me it!"

Lin shouted to his wife in the kitchen, "Let Hua have it her own way, okay?" That stopped the exchange between mother and daughter.

Lin had never felt attached to Ren because they had not grown up together. In their adolescent years, Lin had gone to school most of the time while Ren worked in the fields. Yet he was grateful to his elder brother, who had never complained about the arrangement made by their parents, which deprived him of the opportunity of education. Ren hadn't even finished elementary school. Looking at his brother's scarred face, which had been hurt by a rock twenty years ago at a construction site, Lin felt bad for him. Because of the injury Ren had married on condition that he live under the roof of his parents-in-law, who were unwilling to let their only daughter leave home. That was why Lin's wife later had to take care of his parents. Ren was merely forty-five now, but he looked about sixty and had already lost three front teeth. His mouth was sunken.

"Brother, you should've talked to me before going to the court with Shuyu," Ren said, placing his teacup on the wooden edge of the brick bed after taking a sip.

"This is my personal matter," Lin said tersely.

"But our parents chose Shuyu for you. Shouldn't you respect their wish?"

"It's their wish that messed up my life."

"Why so?" Ren dragged on his pipe, the tobacco in the bronze bowl glowing red and sizzling faintly. He would never take the cigarettes Lin gave him, saying they were too mild. Seeing that Lin was reluctant to reply, he added, "A man ought to have a conscience. I can't see where Shuyu is not worthy of you. She's given everything to our family. We should take—"

"Like I said, this is my personal matter."

"Maybe not. A divorce will affect everybody in our family. Kids in my village have already started calling your nephews names, saying, 'Your uncle has two wives,' or, 'Your uncle is a womanizer.' How can you say a divorce is just your own affair?"

Lin was shocked by the question. How ridiculous people are, he thought. How far-fetched their ideas can be. What does my marriage have to do with my nephews' lives? Why should the boys feel ashamed of me?

The bellows stopped in the kitchen. He overheard his wife say to Hua, "Go tell your uncle."

He wondered why Shuyu had sent their daughter to Bensheng. As he was thinking, the door curtain made of strings of glass beads opened and in came his wife with a plate of fried pork. "Time to eat," she said and smiled at Ren.

Lin took out two wine cups. His brother always enjoyed drinking and was famous in the commune for his ability to hold alcohol. Once chosen to accompany some official guests, Ren had outdrunk the county vice-magistrate, who had gone to the village to present medals but ended up lying under a dining table. "What would you like?" Lin asked Ren, though he had only two kinds of liquor.

"Anything. I really don't feel like drinking today."

"Drink some to refresh yourself," Shuyu said. "You must be tired out, such a long way."

Lin opened a bottle of sorghum liquor called White Flame and poured a full cup for his brother and half a cup for himself. Meanwhile Shuyu placed another three dishes on the table—scrambled eggs with onions, sautéed pole beans, and fried peanuts mixed with a pinch of salt.

As they were eating, Hua returned, announcing with a cry, "Uncle's coming."

Lin frowned when his brother-in-law entered. In Bensheng's left hand was a package wrapped in straw paper. He grinned at Ren, saying in a familiar tone of voice, "Welcome, elder brother, you came at the right time." He stretched out his hand to Ren.

After they shook hands, Bensheng turned and called to his sister in the kitchen, "Shuyu, get me a plate."

Lin was amazed that Bensheng seemed to know Ren quite well. Did he arrange my brother's visit? he asked himself.

Shuyu brought an empty plate and put it on the table.

"My goodness, what are these?" she said as her brother opened the package.

"Big worms," said Hua.

"Are these some sort of insects?" Ren asked, pointing at the red creatures on the plate, each about three inches long.

"Shrimp," Bensheng told them proudly. "Haven't you heard of shrimp?"

"I have, but I never saw one," said Ren.

"This is my first time too," Bensheng confessed. "I bought them in the county town this morning. When I saw them for sale, I thought, 'Damn, a man must try new things, or he'll die with regret.' So I bought two pounds. Boy, they're expensive, seven yuan a pound. I was told they came from the South and used to be a kind of export stuff that only foreigners could eat."

Lin was surprised by their ignorance. Then he recalled that he had never seen shrimp at the market in Wujia Town, though it was on the river. Doesn't the Songhua have shrimp in it? he wondered. Probably not.

As Lin was thinking, his brother asked, "Are they still alive?"

Both Bensheng and Lin were amused by the question. Lin tried hard to keep back his laughter, but he blurted out, "Yes, alive."

Ren picked one up. "I'm going to sample it anyway, alive or dead. You know, Hua, I eat anything that has more than four legs except for a table." He put the shrimp into this mouth and began munching. "Ouch, it bit my tongue!" He grimaced and covered his mouth with his hand.

"Uncle, is your mouth bleeding inside?" Hua asked innocently. "Can I see it?"

Lin burst out laughing. "Hua, he knew they were cooked. He just wanted to be funny."

"I don't think that's the right way to eat shrimp, though," Bensheng said. "Am I right, Lin?"

All eyes turned to Lin, who, still laughing, was making a kind of bubbling sound in his nose. He stopped to reply, "Yes, you're right. You should get rid of the shell, the claws, and the head first. Like this, use your hand." He stripped the shell from a shrimp and removed the dark dorsal vein, then put it into his mouth. "Umm, it's good, very fresh."

Following his example, the others, except Hua, started to eat the shrimp with relish. The girl was frightened by the crimson creatures and refused to touch one.

Lin put a shelled shrimp in her bowl, but Hua tried to get it out. Bensheng took a sip of White Flame from his cup and said, "Hua, you must try it. It's delicious."

"I don't want to."

"Haven't you eaten silkworm pupas?"

"Yes."

"This is ten times more delicious. Come, give it a try."

Timidly the girl nibbled the tail of the shrimp. "Tastes good, eh?" Bensheng asked.

Hua nodded and went on eating it, while the grown-ups were laughing. "This girl only listens to her uncle," her mother said.

After Hua finished the shrimp, Bensheng put another into her bowl, but she wouldn't eat more, however hard they tried to persuade her. Her father picked it out of her bowl and ate it himself.

Ren Kong had to leave before eight o'clock because he had to walk nine miles home. Bensheng was on his way to give an account of the annual balance to the production brigade's leaders, so he couldn't stay longer either. After dinner, Lin took out a ten-yuan bill and put it into Ren's hand, saying, "Brother, my hospital doesn't stock Tower Candy, so I couldn't bring any back. Please use this money to buy some at the commune department store for my nephews."

"You don't have to give me money. I just thought we might get Tower Candy free."

"Take it, please."

Ren put the money into his breast pocket. Without drinking tea, the men all got to their feet. As they were leaving the house, Ren stretched up his arms and said, "Ah, I've eaten shrimp at last!" He wouldn't take a small bag of taros Shuyu wanted him to carry back for his wife, explaining it would be too heavy for the long way. Shuyu didn't insist.

At the front gate, they parted company, Bensheng heading in the opposite direction while Lin walked Ren out of the village. Lin was moved and even happy as it crossed his mind that he had not laughed so much in many years. He felt a tenderness toward Ren, who was breathing rather heavily thanks to the liquor he had drunk and carrying his blue jacket in the crook of his left arm. Ren's footsteps were long and firm.

"Brother," Lin said, "can I ask you something?"

"Sure." Ren paused and turned his head.

"Did Bensheng invite you to come?"

"No, I came of my own free will. He and I are friends of a sort, but we've had no direct contact. To be fair, he isn't that fine a man, but he's always been good to Shuyu and Hua. That's why I like him."

"I know that, brother. Have a safe trip back. Give my greetings to your wife and kids."

"I will. Take good care of yourself, Lin. You're thinner than last year."

As Ren was climbing the bulging slope, on which a few cattle were still grazing, Lin stood under an elm tree, watching his brother moving away. His mind returned to the shrimp dinner. He remembered that he had decided not to speak to Bensheng again, but somehow he had forgotten his decision.

Now he and Bensheng seemed to have remained in-laws. If only he could have put on a hard face. If only he could have cut all his ties with that crafty man.

The still moon hung like a gold sickle. Ren's white shirt was wavering on the hill, getting smaller and smaller. Three minutes later it disappeared into the darkness.

4

A week after Lin returned to his army post, Ran Su, who was now the director of the hospital's Political Department, wanted to talk with him. Lin feared that the county court must have reported him to the hospital's Party Committee. Now he seemed to be in trouble.

After lunch, Director Su and Lin went out of the compound, walking toward the middle school, which was three hundred yards southeast of the hospital. Ran Su's splayed feet were very large in comparison with his small stature and slight build. He wore shoes of black cloth, one of which had a hole in the toe. But it was patched up in dense stitches, obviously by his wife, who had recently come to live with him in the army so that their son could start elementary school here.

"How did the divorce go?" he asked Lin.

"The court didn't approve it."

"Why?"

"My brother-in-law and his buddies made a scene outside the courthouse."

Ran Su moistened his cracked lower lip with his tongue and said, "Take heart—it will work out."

In silence they continued walking. Lin was puzzled that Ran Su didn't ask more about the divorce. It seemed that the director had something else on his mind.

They sat down in the shade of an acacia tree. In the distance the gray school building appeared whitish in the blazing sun, most of its windows open and a dozen furled flags standing atop the slate-blue roof. To Lin's right, a group of students were pulling up grass on the edge of the soccer field. They were all squatting on their haunches, a few in topees but most of them bareheaded. They looked like a herd of grazing sheep, and their slow motion was almost invisible. "Stupid," Director Su said. "Why are they getting rid of all the grass? It will be dustier in the fall."

Lin smiled and handed him a cigarette.

Ran Su lit it and asked, "Lin, do you know of Vice-Commissar Wei of the Provincial Military Command?"

"I've heard of him."

"He's a well-educated man, an eloquent speaker, and has a remarkable memory for words."

"What happened to him?"

"He divorced his wife two months ago, and now he's looking for a fiancée."

Lin looked at him fixedly. Ran Su went on, "I want to tell you something, but you musn't lose your temper."

"Okay, I won't."

"Commissar Wei asked our hospital to recommend to him a suitable woman. I guess he wants to marry a nurse or a doctor because he needs a wife to take care of his health. He's in his fifties, and most girls here are too young for him, so the Party Committee has been considering Manna Wu as a candidate. Among all the old maids she's the best-looking." He paused to observe Lin's face, which showed little change. He went on, "But we haven't made the final decision yet. If you're seriously opposed to this, I may be able to say a word on your behalf when we discuss it at the next meeting."

Lin remained silent for a long while, his eyes fixed on a scarlet butterfly fluttering on a leaf of a baby fern. Nearby was a troop of large ants busy transporting the dried hulk of a beetle back toward an anthill four or five feet away. Lin plucked a blade of wild buckwheat and put it between his white teeth. A numb feeling stirred in his chest.

Ran Su said again, "Come on, Lin, tell me what you think."

"Does Manna know of this?"

"Yes. We talked to her when you were away. She said she'd consider it."

"She hasn't given you her answer yet?"

"No."

Lin spat the blade of buckwheat to the ground and said, "Perhaps this will do her good. If Commissar Wei agrees to marry her, that will be fine with me."

Director Su looked at him in amazement. After a pause he said, "You're a kindhearted man, Lin. Few men would give up their woman so willingly. Some would go berserk if such a thing happened to them."

Lin cleared his throat. "I haven't said everything yet. I have two conditions, if Commissar Wei really wants her."

"What are they?"

"First, he must raise her rank two rungs up. Second, he must promise to send her to college in the near future."

Ran Su looked astonished, then burst out into a roar of laughter. Lin was puzzled by his reaction and asked, "What are you laughing at? You think I'm crazy?"

"You are so earnest, my brother. I can see you really love her." Ran Su held his nose with his thumb and forefinger and blew it on the grass. He went on, "But who are you? You've forgotten you're neither her fiancé nor her bridegroom. In fact, it's inappropriate for any one of us to tell Commissar Wei what to do. Even our Party Committee can't do that."

Lin knit his thick eyebrows without saying a word. Ran Su kept on, "Don't worry yourself about the conditions. If he marries Manna Wu, of course he'll try to have her promoted and improve her status. My question to you is whether you would let her go."

After long silence, Lin muttered as though to himself, "I'm a married man and shouldn't hold her back. It's entirely up to her."

"Lin, you have a big heart."

They got up, dusting themselves off. By accident, Lin had sat on a yellow mushroom. Touching the wet spot on the seat of his pants, he turned around and asked Ran Su, "How big is the stain?"

"Just the size of an egg."

"Damn, is it very obvious?"

"No problem. If it was on the front, it would leave a small map there and make you more attractive to girls." Ran Su laughed.

"I don't know if Manna can wash it off," Lin muttered. Since the year before last Manna had been doing laundry for him, as most fiancées would do for their men.

They turned back to the barracks. Director Su asked Lin not to reveal their talk to Manna, because he didn't want her to feel he was interfering with her personal affairs. Lin promised he wouldn't say a word.

Manna talked with Lin about Commissar Wei three days later. They both believed this was an opportunity she shouldn't miss. The man was a top officer in the province—if her relationship with him developed successfully, he could arrange for her to be transferred to Harbin. That would open a bright future for her. Possibly the commissar could place her in a crash program for training doctors or in a college to earn a diploma.

In his heart Lin was quite upset about the possibility of losing Manna. He was also angry with the commissar, who could choose any woman simply because he had power and rank. As a man, he was as smart as that old bastard, probably more handsome. Why couldn't he keep Manna? The commissar must have plenty of women already, but he had only one woman. How true the saying was: A well-fed man can never feel a beggar's hunger pangs. Lin was unhappy with Manna too, who, in his eyes, seemed eager to jump at such an opportunity. He said to himself, See how she loves power. She can't wait to drop me.

At the same time, a feeling of relief had been settling in him, because this new development meant that he might not have to push for a divorce every summer—to stir up that hornet's nest in the countryside. If he tried to divorce Shuyu again, heaven knew what kind of tricks his brother-in-law would devise against him. If this state of affairs dragged on, sooner or later Bensheng would come to the hospital to nab him. A few days ago he had told Manna about the judge's demand, and she had said she was unsure whether Lin should give out her name to the court in the future.

Bad-tempered and sarcastic, he began to make fun of Manna whenever he could. At the end of their table tennis game one evening, seeing no one else in the room, Lin said to her, "When you become that big officer's wife, don't forget me, a small powerless doctor who used to play Ping-Pong with you every week. I'll appreciate that."

"For pity's sake, stop it!" she snapped, scowling.

"It's just a joke."

"You think I enjoy going through this thing? I feel like I'm trying to sell myself."

"Don't take that to heart. I mean—"

"I hate it! You're so happy because finally you can get rid of me."

Her eyes were flashing with anger. She put her Double Happiness paddle into its green canvas case and zipped it up. Without another word she walked out of the room.

Lin was speechless and closed his eyes as though suffering a fit of vertigo. He regretted having made the remark, but he did not follow her out. He wiped the sweat off his face with his cap. After picking up his shirt and the other paddle and turning off the lights, he went back to his dormitory alone.

Later he promised Manna that he wouldn't banter about the subject again.

5

It happened that Commissar Wei was going to stay for a night at Muji City on his way to the border, where he was to negotiate with the Russians for the sovereign rights to a small fortress. The fortress, constructed by the Japanese Guandong Army in the 1930s, was intersected by the boundary line between China and the Soviet Union, and both countries now claimed it. Skirmishes had broken out when soldiers of both sides ran into each other at the fortress, but so far no guns had been fired. Instead, the patrols had used rocks, sticks, and steel whips to strike each other, because neither the Russians nor the Chinese wanted to open fire first—to be blamed for violating the cease-fire agreement.

Before departing for the border, Commissar Wei had the hospital informed that he would be delighted to meet Manna Wu on Tuesday evening at the army's hotel in Muji City. The hospital leaders told Manna to get ready as soon as possible, since it was already Monday.

She was granted leave the next day. Because she would have to wear her uniform, there wasn't much to prepare. All she did was take a hot bath in the bathhouse and lie in bed for almost the whole afternoon, trying to get some sleep. She felt nervous, as if she were going to sit for the exam on the history of international proletarian revolutions that the hospital gave its staff annually. Yet there was neither the pounding of the heart nor the tightening of the chest as she had experienced long ago with Mai Dong and Lin Kong.

Despite making an effort to rest, she could not set her mind at ease, because she didn't know how she would get downtown in the evening after the bus service had stopped. She could walk but it would take at least an hour, and she might be sweating on arrival at the hotel. She didn't know how to ride a bicycle. If only she had dared to ask the leaders to assign an automobile to drive her there. She regretted not having listened to Lin the previous summer when he had offered to teach her how to bicycle.

After dinner, she put on a pair of patent-leather sandals. They were the only thing she could add to the uniform, but the shoes did make her appear taller and gave a touch of elegance to her carriage. She remembered that when she was a little girl, she had often dreamed of wearing a flowered blouse, fluffy and flossy, which made her look like a butterfly fairy and enabled her to soar into the clouds whenever she ordered, "Fly." In her heart of hearts she still cared very much for colorful clothes, though she understood it was inappropriate to wear them at her age.

She was wondering whether she should set out on foot, wearing a pair of sneakers and carrying the sandals in her satchel so that she could wear them for the meeting. As she was brushing her teeth, a jeep with a large fog light on its front arrived. The leaders had made arrangements for her transportation, but they hadn't told her.

With Manna on board, the jeep rolled out of the front gate and turned townward. The army hotel was at the west end of Glory Street, an area that used to be a red-light district. It occupied a black brick building that fifty years ago had been a Japanese brothel whose owner wouldn't take Russian rubles, which were in circulation together with Chinese yuan at the time. He would charge a Chinese customer double the price, even though most of the prostitutes were Korean women pretending to be Japanese ladies. It was the rush hour, and the street was crowded with bicycles. At a crossroads a beefy policeman was shouting at the cyclers through a megaphone and wielding a white zebra-striped truncheon to direct the traffic.

The smell of roast mutton and stewed turnip hovered in the air.

The jeep dropped Manna at the front entrance to the hotel and pulled away. For a moment she worried about how to return to the hospital, then she dismissed the thought, feeling certain she could walk back. She wasn't afraid of dark streets, though the sandals might not give her an easy time. A soldier at the front desk told her that the commissar was expecting her in Suite 6 on the second floor. She thanked him and turned to the stairs. Somehow she felt unusually calm.

An orderly answered the door and led her into the living room. She was struck by his young face, his upper lip not downy yet. He couldn't be older than sixteen. After pouring her a cup of jasmine tea, he said, "Commissar Wei will be with you in a minute." Then he quietly withdrew.

Sitting on a sofa with her legs crossed at the knees, she looked up at the whitewashed wall, on which hung a portrait of Chairman Mao—a tall, thirtyish man in a blue cotton robe and with an umbrella under his arm, trudging up a mountain trail toward a coal mine to mobilize workers. She looked around and noticed that the room was much smaller than a living room in a modern hotel. Then she heard a noise and turned. In came a tall man, smiling and nodding as he walked up to her.

"You must be Comrade Manna Wu," he said and stretched out his hand.

She stood up and said, "Yes." They shook hands; his palm was as soft as though gloved in silk.

He told her, "I'm Guohong Wei. Very happy to see you. Sit down please."

The commissar's natural manners put her at ease. After he sat down, he began asking about her work and the city. He made no inquiries about her family and hometown. She realized that he must have read her file and knew she had grown up as an orphan. Wearing a white shirt, he looked more like a professor than an officer, smiling kindly all the time. Half of his hair was gray, and his face was round and flabby, somewhat incongruous on his large, sturdy body. She noticed one of his eyes was larger than the other one. He reminded her of a gentle giant cat.

Though she dared not ask any questions and had to answer him all the while, she didn't feel uncomfortable with this man, who was amiable, without any superior airs. More amazing, he listened to her attentively and nodded his head now and then. Never had she met a man who was such a good listener. She couldn't help wondering why he and his wife had gotten divorced. It seemed he must have been a considerate husband.

He took out a gilt cigarette case from his pocket and asked, "May I?"

She was surprised because no man had ever been so polite to her. "Of course. I like the smell of tobacco." She told him the truth. In fact she herself would smoke one or two cigarettes when she was depressed. In her bedside cupboard there was always a pack, which would last a year.

"Do you smoke?" he asked.

"Not really."

"That means you smoke?"

"No . . . yes," she said, hesitating over her words. "I smoke only on some occasions." His cigarette gave off a minty, sweetish scent. She wondered what brand he was smoking.

He said, "I see, you smoke when you are bored?"

"Yes, a few times a year."

"What can you do for fun in the hospital?"

"I go to the movies sometimes and also read magazines."

"Do you like reading books?"

"I read books sometimes."

"What have you read lately?" He flicked the burned tip of the cigarette over an ashtray. His hand was large and pinkish, with swollen veins.

The question caught her off guard. For a moment she didn't know how to answer, because she hadn't read a book from cover to cover in recent years. Then she remembered those novels from Lin's library she had looked through long ago. She managed to reply, "I don't read a lot now, I'm too busy. But I used to read fiction."

"Such as?"

"*Reg Crag, And Quiet Flows the Don, Anna Karenina, The Vanguards . . .*" She paused and regretted having blurted out those titles, particularly the two Russian novels, which were no longer popular and probably unhealthy or pernicious.

"Good, those are excellent books." His eyes brightened as a thrill surged in his voice. "I can see you have good taste. I wish more people read those great Russian novels nowadays. How I used to devour them when I was a young man."

She was pleased by his praise, but too shy to say more.

"Let me show you what I've been reading." He turned and drew a yellowish book from his leather briefcase. "Have you heard of *Leaves of Grass*?" He raised the book to display the front cover, on which a lean foreign man in a tilted hat stood with one arm akimbo, the hand almost invisible, while his other hand was in his trouser pocket, as though he were trying to conceal his hands.

"No, I've never heard of it. Who wrote it?"

"Walt Whitman, an American poet. This is a remarkable book of poetry, and the poems are so robust and brave they include everything. In a way they form a universe. I've read this book four times."

With amazement she looked at his animated face.

He realized he had gotten carried away by his enthusiasm and added, "Of course it was written last century when American capitalism was still developing. In fact the optimism in the poetry reflects the confidence and progress of the time. Nowadays no American poet can write like this. They have all degenerated in the rotten capitalist society, without the rising spirit anymore."

She was impressed by his knowledge and eloquence, although she didn't understand his view completely. "I'll go to the City Library and see if I can find a copy," she said.

"No, they may not have it. I got this copy twenty years ago, from the translator himself. He was my teacher at Nankai University when I was a student."

"You studied English?"

"No, I majored in philosophy and minored in Chinese literature. My teacher knew English well because he had been educated in a missionary school. He was a well-read man, a true scholar, but he died of pneumonia in 1957. Perhaps it was good for him to die young. With his problematic family background, he could hardly have escaped becoming a target for political movements." The commissar's face turned grave and he kept his head low, as though recollecting something.

"So this is a rare book?" Manna said a moment later.

"Not exactly." His face turned vivacious again. "In some university libraries you probably can find a copy, but it has been out of print since the early fifties."

"I see."

"How about this? I'll lend you the book for a month. After you read it, you tell me what you think of it. Would you like to do that?"

"Sure, I'll be glad to read it."

She took the book from him. Though she agreed, a shade of doubt came over her mind because she was uncertain whether she could understand the poems, not to mention report to him her appreciation of them. She might make a fool of herself.

As she was putting the book into her satchel, the orderly stepped in and announced, "The car is ready, sir."

"Would you like to go to the movies with us, Comrade Manna Wu?" asked the commissar.

Hesitating for a moment, she said, "Yes, I'll be happy to if I haven't seen it."

"Have you seen *The Flower Girl?*"

"No."

"Neither have I. It was made by North Korea. Come along with us, I've heard it's very good."

Together they went out. At the front entrance to the hotel, a young officer was waiting for them beside a cream-colored Volga sedan. Commissar Wei introduced him to Manna. "This is Comrade Geng Yang, from the Third Border Division."

"Very glad to meet you. I'm Manna Wu." She held out her hand.

As they were shaking hands, she almost cried out—the officer's hand was so powerful that it felt like a vise gripping her fingers, though he apparently didn't notice her wince. He was a stern-faced man, not very tall but of heavy build. He held his body straight, a dark-reddish belt cinching up his jacket. At his flank he wore a 1959 pistol, which was much smaller than those earlier Russian models. Seven squat bullets were sheathed on the flap of his holster.

They all got into the car, including the orderly. The movie was to be shown in the Workers' Cultural Palace, which was just a mile away.

The theater was almost full. As they were walking to their seats, Manna noticed several of her colleagues sitting among the audience and turning their eyes toward her. Haiyan was there, talking in different directions. At the sight of Manna, she stood up and signaled that she should join her. Manna waved back and shook her head, reddening a little.

Before they reached their seats, a fat official in a blue Mao suit appeared and stretched out both hands to the commissar, saying in a booming voice, "How are you, Old Wei? How I miss you!"

Commissar Wei looked startled, then smiled. "I'm well. How about you, Old Zhao?" he said delightedly.

"Fine, fine," the man said.

"Please join us."

The two men were still holding each other's hands while walking toward Row 14, talking about the condition of the municipal Party secretary, who had just broken his leg on a fishing trip. Manna recognized the official, who was a vice-major of Muji City.

They all took their seats. On her right sat the commissar and the vice-mayor; on her left were seated Geng Yang and the orderly. A few minutes later the lights went off and the movie started. Commissar Wei dropped his half-smoked cigarette on the terrazzo floor and stamped it out.

The movie told a sad story about a poor Korean family. Strange to say, it had almost no plot. A little girl was eager to have a fresh chestnut, so she went under a large tree, on which two boys, whose father was the richest landowner in the village, were plucking nuts and throwing them down at the children in rags. One of the brothers aimed at the poor girl and hit her with a thorny nut, which injured her eyeball. Then her elder sister had to sell flowers on the streets to support the blind girl and the family. The sisters went on weeping from the beginning of the movie until the very end. Their tears had a tremendous impact on the audience. As the girls cried on screen, many people in the theater could not hold back their tears.

Manna heard people sobbing and sniveling around her.

Their weeping was so contagious that soon almost everybody in the theater began to mist up. Manna couldn't keep her tears back, but she didn't raise her hand to wipe them, just letting them trickle down her face. On her right, Commissar Wei dabbed his eyes again and again with a handkerchief, while the vice-mayor lowered his head sobbing and at times gasping for breath. Commissar Wei squeezed her hand and whispered, "I'm really sorry about this."

"It's a good movie," she said earnestly.

Then she noticed that Geng Yang on her left didn't show any emotion. Unlike others, he was sitting stock-still, making no noise at all. Doesn't he feel sad? she wondered. Time and again, out of the corner of her eye she glimpsed his stony face, which looked distant and detached. He seemed aware of her observation and exhaled a sigh, which betrayed more impatience than sadness.

At long last the movie was over and all lights came on. Many people had red eyes, but nobody looked ashamed. Some were still wiping their faces and blowing their noses with grimy handkerchiefs or scraps of newspaper. "Comrade Manna Wu," the commissar said in a miserable voice, "I didn't know it was such a sad picture. Otherwise I wouldn't have invited you."

"It was good and I was very touched."

"I have to stay with Old Zhao for a while. Do you mind if I let Comrade Geng Yang take you back to the hospital?"

"No, not at all."

"Please write to me and tell me what you think of *Leaves of Grass,* will you?"

"Yes, I will."

Commissar Wei shook her hand and said good-bye. He gave instructions to Geng Yang, then moved away to join the vice-mayor.

The Volga was waiting for them in front of the building.

They got into the car, which started heading north toward the hospital. Because the night had grown quiet, Manna noticed how little noise the car made. Only a small whirring sound could be heard as they drove along the asphalt road partly sheltered by sycamore leaves. The chauffeur had also seen the movie just now, and he was so affected by it that he began talking to the two passengers. "What a sad picture!" he said.

Manna entered into conversation with him, but meanwhile Geng Yang, seated in the front, didn't say a word. She was curious and wondered why he was so cold. "Geng Yang, what did you think of the movie?" she asked.

"It was all right."

"So you were not moved by it?"

"Actually not."

"Why not? Everybody was crying in the theater. Why were you so calm?"

"I don't cry. I've seen things more terrible than that."

The chauffeur seemed irritated by his answer and said, "Tell us what you've seen."

"Oh, I've seen a lot."

"Like what?"

"For instance, last fall we dug a large vegetable cellar. As we were laying bricks to build its wall, a landslip happened and buried twelve men in the pit. In less than a second they all disappeared from sight, buried right under my nose. When we dug them out, nine men had no breath left in them. Then their parents came to my battalion from different provinces. You should've seen how they cried their hearts out; it twisted my entrails to hear them. But I had to remain coolheaded in order to maintain discipline among my men. One by one I turned down the parents' unreasonable demands, even though they called me names and made terrible scenes. If you were on the front, you'd see deaths and injuries quite often and grow used to them. So many men die in accidents; a man's life is worth nothing. In military exercises there are casualties all the time."

As he was talking, the car rolled to a stop. Both he and Manna got off, but instead of holding out her hand to him, she just waved good-bye.

She turned and walked away toward the dormitory house, feeling his eyes following her for a long time. Then came the sound of the car door being shut, and the Volga pulled away quietly. To some extent she found Geng Yang interesting; he was so manly and so different from the others.

6

Sitting at his desk, Lin kept saying to himself, I must see her today.

For a whole morning whenever he was not with a patient, his mind would wander to Manna's meeting with Commissar Wei. He was anxious, because he had heard horrible stories about the top officers' private lives and was afraid Manna might become a victim. There was this general of a field army, Commander Pengfan Hong, who had changed wives every three or four years because he was too savage in bed for a regular woman to last longer than that. Every one of his wives would fall ill within a year of the wedding and soon die of kidney disease. Again and again the Party arranged a new wife for him, but after the deaths of several women he was finally persuaded to marry a large Russian woman, the only one who remained unbroken after living with him for seven years. Lin was fearful, since he had been told that Commissar Wei was a bulky man.

From Ran Su he had heard that Commissar Wei had called the hospital the morning after meeting Manna, saying that he had been very pleased to see her in person, and that he would like to keep contact with her and see where the relationship would go. Also from Director Su, Lin had found out that the commissar had divorced his wife not because of any marital problem but because she had written a booklet criticizing some member in the Political Bureau in Beijing and had been turned into a counter-revolutionary. Now she was being reformed on a remote farm north of Tsitsihar. Fortunately they had only one child, a daughter, who had already grown up and was a fledgling actress at Changchun Film Studio.

So Lin went to see Manna after lunch. He was relieved when she said the commissar was more like a scholar than a warrior. They were standing in the corridor of her dormitory, his hips against the windowsill. She seemed to be in a cheerful frame of mind and told him, "He's rather avuncular, a very cultured man."

"That's good. I was so worried."

"About what?"

"I was afraid he might take advantage of you."

Behind him, a horsefly suddenly started rasping on the wire screen, struggling in vain to get outside.

"I'll be right back." Manna returned to her bedroom.

In no time she came back with a plastic flyswatter and a book. Slapping the horsefly twice, she killed it, the screen ringing feebly. She put the yellow swatter on the windowsill and said, "Lin, have you read *Leaves of Grass?*"

"No, I haven't. Is it a novel?"

"No, a book of poems."

"I've never heard of it. Why do you ask?"

She showed him the book. "Commissar Wei wants me to read it and report to him my understanding of it. I really don't know how to do that. I read a few pages this morning, but the poems didn't make sense to me."

"You must take the report seriously."

"Can you help me with it?"

"Well . . ."

"Please!"

He agreed to see what he could do and took the book back with him. That evening he looked through it. Then for three nights in a row he worked at the poems, which he enjoyed reading but couldn't understand assuredly.

In the meantime, a kind of serenity settled in him. He was somewhat bemused by his peace of mind, wondering why he no longer felt angry with Commissar Wei and why he didn't act like most men in love, who would try every means to keep their women. He remembered that two years ago there had been a murder case in an artillery regiment—a soldier blew up himself and his platoon commander with a grenade, because both of them had been running after the same girl, who was an announcer at a commune broadcasting station. After the murder, people had criticized the platoon leader instead of the soldier, who stood no chance against his rival; they said the officer ought to have expected the soldier's violent act. Now, though Manna might part from Lin for good, why didn't he feel any deep resentment? How come he was so benign and so largehearted? True, he was afraid of having to try to divorce his wife again. Yet normally he should have felt more reluctant to let Manna go, shouldn't he?

His answer to the questions and doubts was that he was a better-educated man, reasonable and gentle, different from those animal-like men driven by lust and selfishness.

He read *Leaves of Grass* once more, still unable to understand it well enough to write about it. To him, this was a bizarre, wild book of poetry that had so many bold lines about sexuality that it could be interpreted either as obscenity or as praise of human vitality. Moreover, the celebration of the poet's self seemed to verge on a kind of megalomania that ought to be condemned. But on the whole this must be a good, healthy book; otherwise the commissar wouldn't have let Manna read it.

After considering several aspects of the poetry for another day, he decided to avoid dealing with the subjects of sexuality and self-celebration, and instead focus on the symbol of grass and on those poems praising the working class, particularly the one called "A Song for Occupations." To his mind, Manna's response to the book didn't have to be long and comprehensive, but it should be thoughtful and to the point.

So he began to write the report at night. The part on the

working class was not difficult, because there was a pattern to follow. He just listed what these brave and diligent people did in the poems and emphasized that workers and farmers were basically the same everywhere—whether they were Americans or Europeans or Chinese: they all loved working and had their own "strong and divine life." But the symbol of grass was hard to elaborate, because he did not have a ready-prepared language for it and had to come up with his own ideas and sentences. He rewrote the passages about the symbol of grass three times. Finally he was satisfied with saying that the grass gathered the essence of heaven and earth, yin and yang, and the material and the spiritual, and that it unified the body and the soul, the living and the dead, celebrating the infinity and abundance of life. In brief, it was a very progressive symbol, charged with the proletarian spirit.

When he gave Manna the five pages he had ghostwritten, he told her to add something of her own. He also wanted to advise her to use good paper and write every word carefully in her best handwriting, but on second thought he refrained from saying anything, because she was not a little girl and understood the importance of this report.

Without delay she copied his essay verbatim in a six-page letter, and mailed it to Commissar Wei together with his book.

Then began the long wait.

Manna and Lin thought the commissar would answer the letter immediately, but three weeks passed and no word came from him. They were both anxious.

Meanwhile, Manna was aware that people began treating her differently. The hospital leaders became very considerate to her. Every now and then a nurse would fasten meaningful eyes on her, as if to say, "Lucky girl." Once Manna overheard a young woman whisper to others behind her back, "I don't see anything special in her." As for the officers' wives, one of them asked her, "When are you going to Harbin?" Another reminded her, "Don't forget to send us wedding candies." Some said about the commissar, "What a lucky old man." A few repeated, "Poor Lin."

On such an occasion Manna just kept silent, not knowing what to say. Their words unnerved her, because she had no idea how serious the commissar was about their relationship. Furthermore, even if he offered to marry her eventually, the marriage wouldn't be an ideal one, not based on love or made in her heart. As she had often told Lin, she felt Commissar Wei was more like an uncle than a boyfriend. Probably he was too old to be able to give her a baby. At times she wondered whether she should ask Lin to father a child with her before she left Muji, but she was too ashamed to mention this idea to him. Besides, she was sure he would not do it. It would be too great a risk for her as well—if Commissar Wei found out she was already pregnant, he might have her sent back to the hospital or demobilized.

The week after she mailed the book report, Manna began to learn how to cycle, which would be an indispensable skill if she lived in Harbin in the future. Neither she nor Lin owned a bicycle. Fortunately Lin's roommate Jin Tian had a Little Golden Deer, which stood idle in the bedroom because its owner had been away with a family planning team in the country for the summer. So they could use the bicycle, provided they didn't do any damage to it. There was another problem: they could not practice cycling outside the hospital grounds. But within the compound, in the presence of their comrades, it would be embarrassing for Manna to ride a bicycle with Lin holding its carrier constantly so as to keep her in balance. Few adults were unable to pedal. Manna couldn't only because she had grown up as an orphan, never having had an opportunity to learn.

She and Lin set about practicing on the sports ground at nightfall when they would be less visible. While she was pedaling unsteadily, he kept saying, "Look ahead. Don't think of the wheel."

"I can't," she cried.

"The wheel goes where your eyes go. Try to look at something faraway."

"Like this?"

"Yes, that's good."

She wasn't a slow learner. In just two hours, she could cycle zigzag by herself. But she could not get on or off the bicycle on her own, and he had to run to keep up with her all the time. Whenever she wanted to dismount, he had to bring the bicycle to a stop for her. Another trouble was that she often ran into objects she tried to avoid—once she hit the pole of the soccer goal, and another time a wooden box filled with dummy grenades. The drive chain slipped off several times; Lin managed to loop it back around the sprockets.

Though she was sweating copiously, Manna was having a wonderful time. She was so happy that at the end of the night she wanted to pedal back to the dormitory by herself.

Since it was already dark, Lin let her do that after telling her to be very careful. She cycled away on the dirt road while he followed, jogging and striding alternately. The night was smoky, full of the smell of charred wood. Moths and gnats were swarming around the street lamps, beyond which tree leaves had grown black. Manna turned her head and cried over her shoulder at Lin, "I can ride a bicycle now."

The moment Manna made a right turn, a woman in dark civilian clothes appeared ahead of her, walking in the same direction, her left hand holding a basin against her waist. Manna wanted to keep as clear of her as possible. Yet coming close to her, somehow the bicycle intractably headed for the woman. Manna tried to turn away, but the handlebars seemed to have their own will. In a flash the front wheel hit the woman from behind and got in between her legs. Manna gripped both brake levers and the bicycle leaped with a screech; the pedestrian was tossed up a little and landed on the front fender. Manna let go of the brakes. The woman, astride the front wheel, was carried along on the bicycle for two or three seconds, as if she were an acrobat riding a unicycle. "Oh Mama!" she cried. Her hand was still clutching the yellow basin containing a bundle of laundry and a cake of soap.

Then the bicycle clattered to the ground.

"Are you hurt, Aunt?" Manna asked, having picked herself up.

The woman, remaining on her feet, grumbled, "My goodness, were you aiming for my behind?"

"I'm sorry. I didn't mean to—"

Suddenly Manna panicked as she recognized the woman was Director Su's wife. She didn't know what to say.

Lin arrived, saying between gasps, "Look at this, look at this! I told you not to ride . . ." He paused, as he too recognized the woman.

He said to Mrs. Su; "I'm terribly sorry. Are you injured?"

"I'm all right," the woman said, still patting her buttocks. "She was so accurate, man. Caught me right between the legs."

Despite trying hard to restrain herself, Manna burst out laughing. For a moment Mrs. Su and Lin were bewildered, then they both joined her in full-throated laughter. A bicycle whizzed by, its rider whistling loudly, and disappeared in the darkness with the bell still jingling. "Crazy dolt," said Lin under his breath.

Mrs. Su found herself bareheaded, without the hat she had been wearing, her hair still wet from the bathhouse. Lin walked back a few steps and retrieved the hat for her. It was made of black velvet, a standard piece of headgear for a country woman. Once put back on her head, it turned Mrs. Su into a withered crone, since her dark hair had all disappeared from

sight. Surprised, Lin looked down at her feet, which were
large and manly, in a pair of army sneakers.

They accompanied her all the way to Director Su's apartment, feeling lucky that Manna had not hit a different person.
Mrs. Su complained that the bathhouse wouldn't allow her
seven-year-old son to bathe with her in the women's area, and
that as a result she had asked their neighbor to take the boy
home. "What an odd rule. He's just a little kid," she muttered.

Though they were more careful the next evening, Manna
rode into a weeping willow. A branch scraped her jaw and left
a purple welt there. The bruise was so eye-catching that the
following day many people knew what had happened; yet
Manna didn't care, eager to continue to practice until she
could bicycle with confidence on the streets downtown. But
the bruise caught the attention of the hospital leaders, who
were alarmed. Manna Wu now was a girlfriend of Commissar
Wei. If anything bad happened to her, the top officer might
hold them responsible. So they ordered Manna and Lin to
stop the practice sessions in case she might hurt herself more.

Finally the hospital leaders heard from Commissar Wei's
office. To their disappointment, the commissar had decided to
discontinue his relationship with Manna. His aide explained
on the phone that the leader had been impressed by her understanding and literary cultivation, but he was not satisfied with
her handwriting. Commissar Wei had been a published author
for twenty years, and at the moment he was preparing a book
manuscript, so he needed someone whose handwriting was
handsome to help him with secretarial work.

The truth was, as Ran Su heard afterward, that Commissar
Wei had dated half a dozen women at the same time. After
careful consideration, he had decided to marry a young lecturer in world history at Harbin University.

Lin was not very upset, although he regretted not having
reminded Manna that she should be careful with her hand-

writing. To some extent he was pleased that she could remain with him again.

Instantly Manna became a new topic in the hospital. The word spread that because of her ugly handwriting she was jilted by the top officer. People began talking about her. What a useless woman she was. How come she had blown such a rare opportunity so carelessly? How could she let a caged bird fly away? Indeed, an old maid couldn't hold a man. Even the jeep driver who had driven Manna to the hotel would say, "She wasted our gas."

Manna was humiliated, though she knew she did not love the commissar. But what was more fearful than being surrounded by gossiping tongues? It seemed to her that most people were just eager to ridicule her, to get some fun out of her misfortune and suffering. She was so hurt she declared to Lin that he must never try to persuade her to look for another man. She said tearfully, "I won't shame myself like that again!"

Now, for better or worse, she preferred to wait for him. Probably it was already too late not to wait. So with rekindled passion and a heavier heart she returned to Lin.

7

The following spring Lin fell ill. Tuberculosis was diagnosed and he was quarantined in the hospital. Every afternoon, at about two, his face would glow with pink patches and his temperature would go up. He often trembled during the day, weak in the limbs. When coughing, he sometimes brought up phlegm with traces of blood in it. At night, sweat often soaked his underclothes. Because he had lost over twenty pounds, his Adam's apple stuck out and his cheekbones became prominent. He could not return to his home village that summer.

Since Shuyu was illiterate, he wrote to his brother-in-law Bensheng, saying he would not be coming home, having too much work to do in the hospital. He didn't tell him the truth for fear of making his wife worry.

The Department of Infectious Diseases was at the northeastern corner of the hospital, behind a tall cypress hedge. It occupied two brick buildings, one of which was mainly for tuberculous patients and the other for those suffering from hepatitis. In the space between the two buildings stood a brick house with a massive chimney. That was the kitchen. The quarantined patients ate better food than those in the regular wards.

Manna often came to see Lin in the evening. Because Lin was a doctor, the nurses in charge of the tuberculosis building didn't prevent him from going out. Lin and Manna would stroll around the sports ground, along a section of the brick wall that encircled the hospital, and sometimes by the guinea pigs' house, the wire-fenced kennels, the tofu mill, and the vegetable fields that were irrigated in the evening by water pumped out from a deep well. Ever since he got sick, she had been more considerate and spent more time with him, though she was unhappy at heart because he couldn't go home to divorce his wife this year. Meanwhile, most of the hospital leaders pretended they hadn't seen Lin and Manna walking together in the evenings; as long as the two of them didn't break the rules—staying within the compound and not making love—the leaders would leave them alone.

In early September the patient who had shared Lin's room left, and another patient, who had been transferred from another hospital, moved in. Lin liked the new arrival a lot. He was an officer in a border division, of medium height and with the build of a weight lifter. According to the gossip among the nurses, this man was known as a Tiger General despite his lower rank of battalion commander. It was said that he had once made his troops run seven miles in an hour with their full equipment—as a result, a dozen soldiers had fainted from dehydration and been hospitalized. For some years he had held the divisional championships in both bayonet charge and machine-gun marksmanship. Then he contracted tuberculosis; his right lung had a hole the size of a peanut kernel, which had almost healed when he came to share the room with Lin. On the very first day he said to Lin, "Heaven knows why I landed here, a total wreck, no use to anybody." He also told him that he was going to be discharged from the army soon.

The next evening Lin mentioned his new roommate to Manna.

"What's his name?" she asked.

"Geng Yang."

"Really? I think I know him." She explained how she had met him the previous year when he came to Muji to accompany Commissar Wei to the border. "As I remember, he was very healthy, as rugged as a horse. How come he's here?"

"He has TB, but he's all right now."

"Maybe I should go say hello to him."

"Yes, why not?"

Then she regretted having suggested that, as a pang stung her heart and reminded her of the humiliation inflicted by Commissar Wei.

"You should go see him," Lin insisted.

It was getting more overcast, so they turned back to the building. The ground was dusty, as it hadn't rained for weeks. Dark clouds were gathering in the distance, blocking out the city's skyline; now and then a flashing fork zigzagged across the heavy nimbuses. As Manna and Lin were approaching the building, a peal of thunder rumbled in the south; then rain-drops began pitter-pattering on the roofs and the aspen leaves. A line of waterfowl was drifting in the northwest toward the Songhua River, where sunlight was still visible. Because Lin shouldn't strain his lungs, he and Manna didn't run and merely hastened their footsteps toward the front entrance.

Lin's room, on the third floor, had a single window and pale-blue walls. Two beds and a pair of small cabinets almost filled the room. Geng Yang was peeling an apple when Lin and Manna arrived. At the sight of them, he stood up in sur-prise. "Aha, Manna Wu, I'm so happy to see you again."

He put down the apple and the jackknife, wiped his hands on a towel, and extended his hand, which she shook gingerly.

"How long have you been here?" she asked after they all sat down.

"Almost two weeks."

"Really? Why didn't we run into each other?"

"I don't know. Still, this is a small universe, isn't it?" He laughed and resumed peeling the apple. He looked thinner than the previous year, but still very robust. He now wore a thick mustache, which made his face look rather Mongolian. Manna noticed his sinewy hands and felt that they were not made to handle fruit.

Lin said to him, "I mentioned your name just now, and she said she knew you, so we came in to see you."

Geng Yang looked at Manna and then at Lin with a questioning smile. Lin said, "Oh, I forgot to mention Manna was my girlfriend."

"You're a lucky man," he said firmly, then looked at her again. His eyes were doubtful, as though asking, Really? How about Commissar Wei?

She realized the meaning in his eyes, but without flinching she said, "How are you now?"

"I'm okay, almost cured." He stuck the knife into the peeled apple and handed it to her. "Have this please."

"Oh, I just had dinner." She hesitated for a second as she remembered he had tuberculosis. "Can we share? I can't eat the whole apple."

"All right." He cut it in two and gave Lin and her each a half.

The wind roared outside and the rain was falling, soon mixed with tiny hailstones. White pellets were jumping about on the window ledge and striking the panes. Geng Yang said, "God, what weather we have here! It hardly ever rains. But when it does, it shits and pisses without stopping like all the latrines in heaven have lost their bottoms."

Manna looked at Lin, who too seemed surprised by his roommate's language. She wanted to laugh but checked the impulse.

Then Geng Yang began telling them what the weather was like on the Russian border, where thunderstorms or showers were rare in summer. When it rained, it would drizzle for days on end and everywhere were mud and puddles. No vehicles could reach their barracks until at least a week later, so for days they had to eat mainly salted soybeans as vegetable. But the rainy season was short, as snow began in early October. By comparison, the short fall was the best season, when the dry weather would enable them to gather mushrooms, day lilies, tree ears, nuts, wild pears and grapes. Also, boars were fat before winter.

After finishing the apple, Manna had to leave for her night shift in the Medical Ward. She put on Lin's trench coat and went out into the torrential rain.

Because Lin was well read in chivalric novels, the two roommates often talked about legendary heroes, knights, swordsmen, beauties, kung fu masters. Sometimes Geng Yang would comment on the young nurses who worked in the building: this one walked like a married woman; that one looked so dainty; another was handsome but not pretty, her face was too manly; the tallest one, whose behind was too wide, wouldn't make you a good wife—she was a girl a man should play with only. On such occasions, Lin could say little because he didn't know how to talk about women. He couldn't help wondering why his roommate was so knowledgeable about female charms.

In the beginning Geng Yang mistook Manna for Lin's fiancée, since the word "girlfriend" could be understood in different ways, but later he came to know Lin had a wife in the countryside. "Boy, you're in trouble," he would say to him. "How can one horse pull two carts?"

Seeing him too shy to answer, Geng Yang would add, "You're such a lucky man. Tell me, which one of them is better?" He was winking at him.

Lin wouldn't talk to him about his wife and Manna, though Geng Yang pressed him. Tired of his questions, one morning Lin said to him, "Stop being so nosy. To tell you the truth, Manna and I never went to bed together. We're just friends."

"Well, does this mean she's still a virgin?" His broad eyes were squinting at Lin.

"Heavens, you're hopeless."

"Yes, I am hopeless where women are concerned. Tell me if she's a virgin."

"She is. All right?"

"Doctor Kong, how could you be so sure? Did you check her out?"

"Stop it. Don't talk like this."

"Okay, I believe you. No wonder she has a slim butt."

Despite being annoyed by his unrestrained way of talking, Lin was somehow fond of this man, who was so different from anyone he knew, straightforward and carefree. What is more, Geng Yang seemed to always speak his mind. As they got to know each other better, Lin began to reveal to him his predicament—he had tried to divorce his wife, but hadn't succeeded. He was eager to seek advice from him, because apparently Geng Yang was a man full of certainty and capable of decisive action, a real go-getter.

One afternoon, after a two-hour nap, Lin told Geng Yang that in the past summers he had asked his wife for a divorce, and she had agreed, but later she had changed her mind in the court, saying she still loved him.

"What did she want, do you know?" Geng Yang asked.

"Nothing."

"Why did she say that after she had agreed?"

"I have no idea."

"There must've been some reason."

"I think my brother-in-law was behind everything. He's the source of the trouble." Lin was too ashamed to tell him about the scene outside the courthouse.

"If so, you should keep him out of it next time."

"How could I do that?"

"There must be a way." Geng Yang lifted a honey jar he used as his drinking glass and took a sip of tea.

Lin went on, "You know, in the villagers' eyes my wife is perfect. I can't do anything too awful."

"I know." Geng Yang chuckled.

"What's so funny?"

"Divorces are of course rare in the countryside. I heard of only one divorce in my hometown—the woman was caught in bed with the master of the elementary school by her husband. The husband took both the adulterer and adulteress to the commune administration. The militia broke the schoolmaster's leg, and he was jailed for three months. So the husband divorced his wife. If you're really concerned about losing face, you shouldn't try to divorce your wife."

"But I've already started it."

"To be honest, if I were you, I wouldn't think of leaving my family. I'd just keep Manna as my woman here. A man always has more needs, you know." He grinned meaningfully.

"You mean I should have her as a mistress?"

"Good, you're learning fast."

Lin sighed and said, "I can't do that to her. It would hurt her badly. Also, it's illegal."

Geng Yang smiled thoughtfully. A trace of disdain crossed his face, which Lin didn't notice. Outside in the corridor, an orderly was wiping the floor, the mop knocking the baseboards with a rhythmic thumping.

"Forgive me for my candid words," Geng Yang said. "We're army men and shouldn't talk and think too much about a decision that has already been made. If you've decided to divorce your wife, you must carry it out by hook or by crook. What's the good of being a good man? You can't be nice to everybody, can you? In this case, damage is unavoidable. You have to choose which one of them to hurt."

"I can't."

"To be honest, Lin, I don't think the divorce is that hard, but you've made it hard for yourself."

Lin sighed again. "I really don't know what to do."

"You've been shilly-shallying and made yourself miserable. I've handled hundreds of men for many years. I know your type. You're always afraid that people will call you a bad man. You strive to have a good heart. But what is a heart? Just a chunk of flesh that a dog can eat. Your problem originates in your own character, and you must first change yourself. Who said 'Character is fate'?"

"Beethoven?"

"Yes. You know so much, but you can't act decisively." He closed his eyes and recited another quotation. " 'Materialist dialectics holds that external causes are merely the condition of change whereas internal causes are the basis of change.' Who said that?"

"Chairman Mao in *On Contradiction.*"

"See, you know everything, but nothing can make you steel yourself. If you really have the will to change, you can create the condition for change."

"But my case is not so simple."

"Chairman Mao also said, 'If you want to know the taste of a pear, you must change the pear by eating it yourself.' Trust me, my friend, sleep with Manna. If you find her good in bed, you'll be more determined to get a divorce."

"No, that's crazy!"

Although the talk didn't help Lin find a solution, by chance Geng Yang confirmed to Manna that Lin was still trying to leave his wife. One evening the three of them ate muskmelons together, sitting on the stone curb at the front entrance to the hospital, where vendors from the suburban villages were selling fruits and other foods. Geng Yang would not chip in for the melons, insisting that since he wouldn't be able to attend their wedding after Lin divorced his wife, the future bride and groom ought to give him a treat in advance.

He said to Lin, "I know your wife will say yes in the court next year. Don't worry about that. I'll help you figure out a way to end your marriage. Be a generous bridegroom now."

Both Lin and Manna were pleased with this accidental rev-
elation, which corroborated Lin's claim that he was still looking for a way to obtain a divorce. The previous year, when he
showed Manna the article in the county newspaper about the
attempted divorce, she had been heartbroken, wondering
whether Lin would give up his effort altogether. After three
months' consideration she had decided to let the judge have
her name if necessary. Lin was touched by her determination
and courage, saying he would do everything he could. Still,
sometimes she couldn't help feeling that he had been using
her—just to keep a woman around and make her work for
him, although afterward she would check her thoughts and remind herself that he was a good-hearted man and wouldn't
hurt her purposely. Now, she was so glad he had been seeking
advice from his roommate that she bought a pound of strawberries from a fruit vendor.

"Help yourself," Manna said to Geng Yang pleasantly, and
placed the paper bag containing the strawberries on the curb.

"Your treat?" He grinned at her.

"Yes."

8

Lin's condition improved rapidly. His face returned to its normal paleness. After two months' treatment, the spot on the upper lobe of his left lung had shrunk to the size of an almond. The prognosis was that it would calcify soon. His recovery was mainly due to the newly invented herbal drug named Baibu, with which the hospital had treated some of its tuberculous patients. Whereas streptomycin remained more effective on most of the patients, some of them reacted to the herbal drug miraculously. To Lin's amazement, the injections he had received, along with cod-liver oil and vitamins, had cured his arthritis as well, although both sides of his hips were now covered with painful swellings, which gave him a slight limp.

Toward the end of November, when he had entirely recuperated, Lin was ordered to go to Shenyang to attend a program designed for officers, studying Marx's *Theories of Surplus Value*. He was eager to go, not because he was interested in the book but because his alma mater was in that city. He wanted to revisit some places he remembered.

Officially Geng Yang was already discharged from the army, but he was still waiting to be released from the hospital, which had to make sure his tuberculosis was fully cured. His departure for home was imminent. So a few days before Lin left for Shenyang, he and Manna decided to treat Geng Yang to dinner in a restaurant. They asked Ran Su for permission to go to town, which the commissar granted them, but the *three* of them had to be together outside the hospital.

They took a bus downtown. It was Sunday and the streets were crowded, vendors shouting and greasy smoke rising

here and there on the sidewalks. They arrived at Four Seas
Garden at about noon. After entering the restaurant, they
climbed the dingy concrete stairs and found an octagonal
table on the second floor, where diners were fewer and less
noisy than those eating and drinking downstairs. Geng Yang
removed his fur hat and hung it on the ear of an iron chair. So
did Lin and Manna. The moment they sat down, a middle-
aged waitress in a red apron came and took their orders. They
would have a few cold dishes—pork head, pickled mushrooms, baby eggplants, and salted duck eggs. As for the entrée
they ordered dumplings stuffed with pork, dried shrimps, cabbage, and scallions. In spite of Manna's admonition, Geng
Yang added a liter of stout.

First came the beer in a huge mug, fizzing faintly. Geng
Yang lifted it up and said with a smile, "Cheers!" Lin and
Manna raised their smaller mugs containing merely hot water.

"You don't want your lungs anymore?" Manna said to
their guest as he swallowed a gulp.

Geng Yang grinned, displaying his square teeth. "My lungs
are rotten already." He dashed a lot of chili oil onto his plate,
while Lin and Manna spooned some mustard onto theirs,
waiting for the dumplings. Outside, four sparrows perched on
the window ledge, which was coated with soot that looked
like rat droppings. The birds were chittering and shivering
with the blasting horns of the automobiles passing on the
street. One of them had a blind eye, whose corner carried a
drop of frozen blood. It was snowing lightly, a few snowflakes
swirling beyond a pair of power lines slanting across the window. The sky had grown overcast, shimmering a little. A male
voice cried below the windows, "Fresh pike, just out of the
river this morning." A woman chanted, "Fried dough twists,
sweet and warm, fifteen fen apiece."

The cold dishes and the dumplings came together; for a
moment steam obscured the tabletop. Lin was glad they

didn't have to wait long. Geng Yang picked up a chunk of pork ear and put it into his mouth. Munching it, he said, "This is delicious!"

With chopsticks Lin and Manna raked a few dumplings onto their plates. They exchanged glances, and he realized she was thinking the same thought—this was the first time they had eaten together in a restaurant. A miserable emotion surged in him, but he remembered they had company and made an effort to take hold of himself. Meanwhile, Manna kept her eyes on the table, as though not daring to look at either man. Lin tried to be cheerful, urging their guest to eat to his heart's content. That was hardly necessary, since Geng Yang was helping himself comfortably.

Halfway through dinner, the guest claimed that it was too bad he wouldn't be able to drink their wedding wine. At the word "wedding," Lin and Manna fell silent, their faces gloomy.

"Come on," Geng Yang said, "don't be so sad. We're still alive and should enjoy ourselves."

"If only I knew what to do." Lin massaged his forehead with his fingertips while chewing a garlic leaf that served as garnish for the sliced pork head.

"Try again next year," Geng Yang said. "If I had a beautiful woman like Manna with me, I'd do anything. Cheer up, Lin, remember you're lucky and you should be grateful."

"Grateful for what?"

"For everything you have."

Lin shook his head while Manna's eyes were moving back and forth between the two men's faces.

A moment later she asked Geng Yang, "Can you give us some advice?"

"To tell you the truth, I don't like the idea of divorce. But if you two really want to live together as husband and wife, you'll have to go through this thing."

"We know that, but how can I bring about the divorce?" Lin asked, cutting a dumpling in half with his chopsticks.

"There must be a way. Even if a goose has an iron neck, it must have a spot where you can plunge a knife in."

"Tut-tut," Manna said, "don't brag. Say something specific."

"I'm not in your shoes. But one thing I know for sure: if you spend some money, it will work. Say, give Shuyu two thousand yuan."

"No, no, you don't understand," Lin said. "She doesn't want any money. She's a plain, simple-hearted woman."

"I don't believe that. If you spend money on the right person, I'm sure it will help. With money you can hire the devil to grind grain and cook dinner for you."

Neither Lin nor Manna said another word, surprised by his assertion.

Geng Yang continued, "Come on, don't look at me like I was a zombie or something. I can prove what I said is true." He pointed his chopsticks at Lin's chest. "For example, three years ago a regimental commander in my division had a young woman, a journalist from Beijing, detained in his barracks and wanted to spend a week with her. Then her colleagues sent a telegram to the Shenyang headquarters, and the officer was ordered to release the woman immediately. He had no choice but to let her go. Afterward we all thought this man would be either demoted or discharged. There was an internal report criticizing him severely, and we all believed he was a goner. Do you remember that bulletin?"

"Yes, I do," Lin said. "What happened to him?"

"Last year he was promoted to divisional chief of staff."

"How could that happen?" Lin and Manna asked in unison.

"Well, according to what I heard, he spent fifteen hundred yuan for two pairs of gold bracelets and presented them to our divisional commander and commissar, one pair for each, saying the bracelets were his hometown's local product. Everybody knew it was a damn lie, but it helped him. So he was promoted. You see, with money he reversed his fortune. If I had money, I'd have done something and would not have been discharged like this. Even though I may no longer be good enough to lead troops on the front, I can still be a useful officer at headquarters, at least more useful than many others. Don't you think?"

"Yes, of course," said Lin. With a spoon he removed the mashed garlic from within a pickled baby eggplant. He cut it in two and put a piece into his mouth.

For a minute Lin and Manna ate quietly, not knowing how to respond to their guest's advice.

Then Lin asked Geng Yang, "Can we do something for you before you leave?"

With that, they began talking about how to have Geng Yang's belongings shipped economically by rail. He had recently purchased some thick pine boards through a back-door deal, because timber was scarce and expensive in his hometown in Anhui Province. He had also bought thirty pounds of linden honey and six sheepskins, from which he would have a few overcoats made once he was home.

That evening Lin thought about Geng Yang's advice, which gradually began to make sense to him. Shuyu might not want money, but there were others who could be bought off, particularly his brother-in-law. No doubt his wife would listen to her brother. If Bensheng told her to accept a divorce, she might not go back on her word again. If so, the case surely wouldn't fall through the next summer. By now Lin was convinced that Bensheng was the key to a solution.

On second thought, he felt uncertain about his brother-in-law, who might just pocket the money without helping him. A bribe offered to such a man was always a dangerous investment. Two thousand yuan was a huge sum, more than the amount of his one and a half years' salary. It might be too much of a risk, although Bensheng was undoubtedly a greedy fellow who could sell his parents for that amount.

The more Lin reasoned, the more dubious he became. The next evening he went to the Medical Ward and found Manna alone in the office. At the sight of him, she stopped reading the daily record left by the nurses of the previous shift, and drew up a chair for him.

He explained to her what was on his mind. To his surprise, she asked calmly, "Do you have the money?"

"No, I only have six hundred in the bank. Don't you have some savings?"

"Yes, a little." She didn't tell him the amount, which he was eager to know.

"Maybe we can borrow some from others if we decide to do it," he said. "What do you think?"

After a pause, she said, "If you don't have the money, don't think about it." She frowned and her lips tightened. Apparently she must have thought this matter over as well; he was amazed by her definitive answer.

He realized she was unwilling to share the cost if they decided to spend the money. This realization daunted him. Never had he thought that he could save such an amount by himself, not to mention borrow the money and pay back the debt alone. He asked her, "So what should we do? Just wait?"

"I don't know," she said despairingly. "I'm afraid that giving Bensheng money will be like hitting a dog with a meatball—nothing will come back. But I thought you must've saved that much, haven't you?"

"No, I only have six hundred."

"If you had the money, we might think of doing it."

"So we shouldn't try?"

"No." She turned away and resumed checking the daily record.

Silence filled the room. He felt ashamed, because by custom it was the man who should pay all the expenses to take his bride home. It was unreasonable for him to ask her for help. Perhaps he should never have talked with her about this matter.

9

On Tuesday morning, Manna ran into Geng Yang at the bus stop in front of the hospital's theater. These days he had been busy packing up, sending his belongings to the train station, and paying farewell visits to his friends and fellow townsmen in the city. He told her, "I still have two of Lin's books with me. Can you come and take them back?"

"When will you be in?"

"Anytime this evening. I'll leave tomorrow afternoon."

She said she would come at around eight, since she worked the day shift now. He grinned, his eyes shining with a gleam which unnerved her slightly, as if some gnats were flying in his irises and yellowing the black. She turned and walked away, sure that he was observing her from behind. What hungry eyes he has, she thought.

Though often disturbed by Geng Yang's eyes, she rather liked him. In many ways he was more like a man to her, strong, straightforward, fearless, and even coarse. She wished that Lin could be a little more like him, or that the two men could exchange some of their traits so that both their characters would be more balanced. Lin was too much of a gentleman, good-tempered and studious, with little manly passion.

Lin had left for Shenyang City a week ago. After his departure, a feeling of peace had settled in Manna. She found herself not missing him very much. To some extent she enjoyed being alone, at least for a few weeks, during which she didn't need to wash laundry for Lin or have him on her mind constantly. But whenever she bickered with a colleague or something went awry at work, she wished Lin were around so that she could talk to him. This feeling made her realize that, in addition to forming a family and having children, a marriage might also provide an opportunity for a couple to talk and listen to each other, since they wouldn't dare speak their minds in public.

Having more time now, she registered in the hospital's night school to learn English, which had become popular after Richard Nixon's visit to China in 1972. Recently it was said that a foreign language exam would be required for a nurse to be promoted to assistant doctor. Before the 1960s Latin had been the only foreign language acceptable for the medical profession, but now both English and Japanese could fulfill the requirement. As a result, more than forty nurses enrolled for the night class. At the time English dictionaries were difficult to come by, and Haiyan helped Manna buy a pocket copy through a relation of hers in town. Haiyan had married the previous summer and was also a head nurse now. Because she was pregnant, she wouldn't be attending the night school. The class would start in a few days, on December 8. A woman lecturer from Muji Teachers College was to teach it.

In the evening, Manna set off for the Department of Infectious Diseases to fetch Lin's books. It was so cold that she could see the wisps of her breath. The moon was round and silvery, cleaving the clouds which were swaying like waves. Moonlight filtered through the naked branches and scattered dappled patches on the snowcovered ground. A few birds flew up in the darkness, their wings twanging and phosphorescent. Ahead of her, skeins of snow dust, blown up by the wind, were slithering and twisting. Under her feet the snow was crunchy while the wind was crying like a baby.

She raised the leatherette door curtain and entered the building, which was dim and quiet inside, as though deserted. Climbing the stairs, she couldn't help envying the nurses in charge of this building. Apparently they had fewer patients here and much less work to do.

Geng Yang, in gray pajamas, answered the door and let her in. The room reeked of alcohol, and the air was damp because of the steam rising from a wet jacket on the radiator beneath the window. The frosted panes were purplish against the night. She turned and looked at him; he grinned with blood-shot eyes as if to acknowledge his drunken state. His face was sallow in the fluorescent light, which rendered his cheeks concave and his mustache spiky. On the bed that Lin had once occupied lay an opened suitcase, partly filled with clothes and pillow towels of various colors—pink, orange, yellow, saffron. Obviously they were gifts from his men. Two thick novels, *The Golden Broad Road* and *The Chronicle of the Red Flag,* were on a bedside cabinet; next to the books stood a liquor bottle, short-necked and half empty. A picture of an ear of golden corn curved along the side of the bottle.

"You're drowning yourself in this stuff again?" she said, pointing at the liquor. She took off her fur hat and put it under her arm.

"He-he-he," he chuckled. "Sit down, Manna. Let me ask you something." He went to the door and locked it.

"What?" she asked with a start, putting Lin's books into her satchel.

"Why are you so concerned about me?" His eyes were leering at her as he put both hands on her shoulders to make her sit down on the bed. She blushed and turned her head, facing the wall.

"Come on, look at me," he said. "Don't you have some good feelings about me?"

She was too flustered to reply, her heart throbbing. He went on, "Tell me, why did you buy me the strawberries?"

She was shocked. For a second she wanted to laugh, but she controlled herself.

Hearing no answer, he grasped her arm with his right hand. The grip was so forceful that she cried, "Take your hands off me!" Her hat dropped on the floor, but she couldn't bend down to pick it up.

"Listen to me, my little virgin. Am I not a better man than Lin Kong? Why are you so devoted to that sissy?"

"Who told you that about me?" she exclaimed. "Shameless, all men are shameless."

"Yes, I am a shameless man where pretty women are concerned."

"Geng Yang, you're drunk and out of your mind, or you wouldn't talk like this."

"No, my mind isn't drunk although my face is red. I know you are always interested in me. I saw that in your eyes. In fact I can smell that in a woman." He began coughing, covering his mouth with his palm. His breath was hot and sour.

"Let me go please."

"No, you can't."

"You're Lin's friend. How could you treat his fiancée this way? Don't you know the saying, 'A good man must never take liberties with his friend's wife'?"

He threw his head back and let out a laugh, which shook her heart. "How could a virgin be thought of as a wife?" he asked. "Do you believe Lin Kong will marry you? You aren't even his mistress, are you? He's no good and doesn't know how to handle a woman."

"Stop it. Let me go." She bent down and picked up her hat, but he grasped her shoulder and blocked her way.

He went on, "Wait, let me finish. He told me that he had never slept with you. How could he do that? I saw his dick when we bathed together in the bathhouse. I've wondered ever since if he's a bisexual."

His last sentence threw her into a daze. She held out her hand and grasped the bedpost to support herself. Then she thought, This cannot be true. Lin had a baby with Shuyu and his Adam's apple always juts out. If he weren't normal, he couldn't have passed the recruitment physical. "Don't slander my man!" she cried out. "Let me go, or I'll scream."

Before she could say more, his large hand seized her throat. "Shut up!" he rasped. "If you shout again, I'll strangle you."

"Don't, don't hurt me. Geng Yang, you're a revolutionary officer and shouldn't do this. Please—"

"No, I'm not an officer anymore, so I don't care. Why should I? Now, you delivered yourself to me, didn't you? Didn't you come here of your own free will? Everybody will take you to be a slut."

"You told me to come and pick up the books!"

"How can you prove that?"

He forced her down on the bed and began kissing and licking her face and neck while she struggled, begged, and wept. She tried wriggling her legs loose, but they were gripped between his. His right hand held both of her wrists, while his free hand went beneath her shirt and grasped her right breast and then her left. "Ah, you smell so good, delicious, but your breasts are small, you know?" His nose kept thrusting into her hair, beads of sweat glistening on his forehead.

She tried pushing him away, but his body and his legs pinned her to the bed. Meanwhile, his left hand was unbuckling her belt and pulling down her pants. "Let go of me!" she groaned.

"My, you have a nice butt."

"Geng Yang, spare me just this once, please! I'll come back to you tomorrow, I promise. You can do anything you want with me. I'm not ready now. Please—" She choked, feeling dizzy, her temples pounding and sparks splashing in the air. His head looked twice the size it was.

"No. You think I don't know you're lying?" He pulled her over on her stomach and forcefully pressed his thumb on her spine at the small of her back. The pressure nearly made her black out. Her lower body turned numb; she felt injured. He spat on his fingertips and began rubbing her anal cleft. She tried to hold her legs tight, but they felt no longer her own. She was sobbing, unable to fight back, her arms flailing helplessly on the bed.

"Look at this." He grabbed her hair and pulled her head around. She had never expected that the male organ could be so large; his was like a donkey's and terrified her.

"See how big my cock is," he said, panting. "It's like a rolling pin, no, it's a little mortar."

"Please, don't. Don't do this to me! Oh—"

He pushed her face down on the bed. "Shut up! My cock is designed to blast into an old virgin like you." As he was speaking, he pressed his organ into her, thrusting away like a dog.

She felt totally paralyzed, a numbing pain contracting her limbs, as though she were struggling for life in dark, freezing water. The white sheet turned black under her eyes, and a bloody taste sprang into her mouth. Suddenly rage flamed up in her chest and words gushed out of her throat. "I curse your whole clan! Damn you, you'll be childless. Your parents will drop dead next year."

"Say whatever you want. My parents are dead and I already have two sons."

"They'll die like homeless dogs!"

"Oh . . . ah . . . ah!" He came, still rocking on her.

"Damn you, your sons will be run over by trucks!"

He pushed her face into the bed and instantly her voice was smothered. She tried to twist her head aside so that she could breathe, but his hand nailed her neck down. Meanwhile his body was still wriggling on her. She was choking and had to use all her strength to breathe in a little air through the stinking sheet and cotton mattress.

As he stopped writhing, he released his grip of her neck.

The moment he got up from her, she coughed and gasped, then resumed swearing.

"What did you say, bitch?" He pulled her up by the collar.

"You'll be the last of your father's line!" she said through her clenched teeth, her eyes flashing.

"Shut up!" He slapped her, and she fell on the bed again. Her hands were trembling, holding up her pants and buckling the belt.

He moved away and lay down on his back on the other bed and closed his eyes. "I've got what I wanted." He chuckled. "You can go tell anyone you want to. Let the leaders have me arrested or expelled from the Party. I don't care. They can punish me in any way they like. But think twice before you do that. Who will believe you?" He lit a cigarette, then grabbed the liquor bottle by its neck and took a gulp. "You know, if you weren't a virgin, I would've given you this." He waved the bottle, chuckling again. Then he began a hacking cough.

Without a word she snatched up her hat, unlocked the door and rushed out. As she was running toward the stairwell, the corridor echoed with the thud of her heavy boots. She stumbled at the landing but grasped the iron gooseneck of the handrail. She bolted down the stairs and reached the front entrance, where the black door curtain faced her like a huge mouth. She pushed it aside and dashed out. Once outside, she began having double vision. Houses and trees were swimming around, and the white road seemed like a cloud under her feet, while the wind was howling from behind as though chasing her. A hundred yards later she slipped and fell into the snow. Unable to get up, she threw a few handfuls of snow on her face and swallowed two mouthfuls. The icy water, which had a rusty flavor, went down her throat and stung her esophagus and stomach, but it cleared her head a little. She climbed to her feet and staggered back to the dormitory.

Fortunately none of her roommates was in, two having

gone to the movies and one to work. Lying on her bed, Manna wept for half an hour while wondering what to do. She thought about reporting the rape to the leaders, but wondered if it was wise to do that. Will they believe me? she asked herself. I went to his room of my own accord. Won't they say I offered myself to him? For sure Geng Yang will deny he forced me. He'll say I tried to seduce him, then I won't be able to clear myself. I have no witness and can't prove my innocence, let alone my being a rape victim. Heavens, what should I do? If only Lin were here. No, he couldn't help me either. How I hate Lin! It was he who told that man I was a virgin. Without him, this would never have happened to me. Why did he make friends with that wolf?

Then the thought came that she should let Geng Yang's semen drain out of her in order to prevent pregnancy. She opened her pants and saw a wet, reddish patch on her panties, as large as a palm. She felt sure there must be more semen left in her, so she placed her washbasin on the floor and squatted over it, waiting for the remaining semen to drip out. Meanwhile she couldn't help sobbing. Her thighs, sprained, were aching and shaking, and not only her pants but the entire room smelled fishy. She felt as though all her clothes had been soaked with that man's semen, which seemed to be giving her stomach spasms. She started retching and moved her bottom aside to vomit into the basin.

Having squatted in the corner for almost twenty minutes, she was terrified to realize that not a drop of semen had drained out. She remembered the burning moment of his ejaculation, which had lasted for almost half a minute. Does this mean that his sperm has already gone deep into my uterus and found an ovum? she wondered. No, it can't be so quick, can it?

She stood up, put on a fresh pair of pajamas, and picked up the basin. With a towel over her shoulder, she went out to

fetch some water. Once she was out of the bedroom, the cold
air in the drafty corridor made her wince, and she felt her face
prickling and clammy, as though it were swollen. This
couldn't have been inflicted by the slap, which had landed on
her jaw. Soon her entire face began smarting. Apparently
Geng Yang's saliva was still stinging her skin. In the washroom, she emptied the basin and filled it with cold water,
scrubbing her face with the towel again and again. She
changed water three times, but the reek of his saliva seemed to
cling to her skin. She remembered when she was a child, a
yellow-banded caterpillar had once stung her neck; now the
same kind of prickle was all over her face and throat.

Back in the bedroom, she took off her clothes and began
washing herself in hopes of getting rid of the fishy odor and
the remaining semen in her. The odor, however, didn't disappear; it was as if everything in the room were impregnated
with it. She thought of burning her panties, but it occurred to
her that they might be useful as evidence, so she wrapped
them up in a shirt and put the bundle on the wooden board
under her bed. As for the semen, even after she had jumped up
and down thirty times, not a drop of it came out. She had no
idea how much of it had entered her uterus. This uncertainty
frightened her.

That night, not daring to arouse her roommates' suspicion,
she covered her head with her quilt and wept noiselessly, unable to decide whether she should tell somebody about the
rape. How she was longing to cry in a pair of warm, reliable
arms and let out everything bottled up in her. Or if only she
had had a house for herself, where she could cry to her heart's
content and yell at the top of her lungs without being heard by
others. But in this small room shared by four people, she kept
her left hand around her throat all the while, until the weeping
exhausted her and she fell asleep.

10

Manna's eyes became blue-lidded the next morning. The nurses in the Medical Ward asked her why she looked so pallid, and they advised her to take a day off. She told them that she was allergic to the fried beltfish they had eaten the day before, but she felt much better now. She was amazed by her ability to come up with such an answer. For the whole morning, whenever the telephone rang, she would rush to answer it. Despite having a tearing headache and intense hatred for Geng Yang, she was expecting to hear from him, because she fancied that he might apologize to her and blame alcohol for what had happened. It seemed to her that the whole thing wasn't over yet. If he called and begged her for forgiveness, she wouldn't forgive him, and instead she would give him a round of blood-curdling curses.

Not having heard from him by midday, she phoned the Department of Infectious Diseases and was told that Geng Yang had checked out early in the morning, that a new patient had just moved into the room, and that a satchel containing some books had been left in the nurses' office for her to pick up. This information brought a flood of tears from her. Evidently Geng Yang had planned the rape. But it was too late to have him detained, as he had left Muji and the crime scene had been transformed.

What should she do? She was at a loss.

In the afternoon she tried keeping herself busy by doing whatever she could—wiping clean all the tables and chairs in the office, fetching boiled water for some patients, sorting and listing the sacks of holiday gifts donated by civilians—shoe pads, tobacco pouches, notebooks, preserved fruits, woolen gloves, candies. Hard as she tried, she couldn't concentrate on anything. Geng Yang's ghostly face would thrust itself into her view from time to time. Lacking an appetite, she didn't eat dinner that evening.

She had no friend except for Haiyan. Unable to hold back her feelings any longer, she went the next evening to Haiyan's home, which was in a dormitory house at the east end of the hospital compound. Haiyan's husband, Honggan, was an officer in charge of recreational activities in the Propaganda Section. Haiyan had married him mainly because he could write and speak well; she had once revealed to Manna that she would never marry a doctor, who in her eyes was no more than a well-trained technician. She wanted an abler man.

"Come on in, Manna," Haiyan said, pleased to see her.

Her husband was clearing the dining table. At the sight of Manna, he nodded and turned off the radio. He was a tall man with a carbuncular face and two gold teeth. Although Haiyan was happy with her marriage, many people would comment behind her back, "A fresh rose is planted on a cowpat."

"Haiyan," Manna whispered, "I want to talk to you. This is something just between us, very personal."

Haiyan took her into the bedroom. "What is it?" she asked, placing both hands on her protruding belly. She had been pregnant for five months.

"I—I was raped."

"What?"

"I was raped by Geng Yang."

"How did it happen?"

"He lured me into his room and raped me."

"Slow down. Say it clearly. What do you mean he lured you into his room?"

In a shaky voice Manna described how he had invited her to the ward and what he had done to her. Tears were trickling down her face. Now and then her tongue stuck out licking the tears from her upper lip.

Honggan cried from the other room, "Haiyan, I've left some hot water on the stove. If you want tea, you can use it. I'm leaving now."

"Where are you going?"

"To my office."

"All right, come back early." She turned to Manna and asked, "Have you reported him to the Security Section?"

"No. I don't know what to do."

"Where's Geng Yang now?"

"He left for his home yesterday morning. Should I report it?"

"Let me think." Haiyan frowned, a slanting wrinkle on either side of her nose.

"I'm afraid nobody will believe me," Manna added, and wiped her cheeks with the back of her hand.

"Manna, I think it may be too late now. It will be very hard to prove that you didn't have a date with him unless Geng Yang admits the crime himself. You know a date rape is rarely treated as a rape."

"Oh, what should I do?" She began sobbing. "So it was all my fault, wasn't it?"

"My dear, I'm not blaming you." Haiyan put her arm around Manna and said, "Come, don't treat yourself like you were in the wrong. This has happened to a lot of women. In fact, my elder sister was raped by a friend of hers some years ago, and she couldn't do anything about it. Some men are animals in human clothes."

"So I should keep quiet about this?"

"What else can you do?"

After a pause, Manna asked, "Do you think I should tell Lin?"

"Not right now. But you should tell him sometime in the

future. He loves you and he'll understand. My sister told her husband about the rape. For a few months it was hard for him to accept it. You know, most men assume their brides are virgins. I'm sure Lin is different. He's a kind man, and married. Besides, you two have been together for so many years. He'll understand."

The advice sounded sensible to Manna. Before leaving, she asked her friend not to divulge the rape to anyone.

"Of course I won't breathe a word," Haiyan promised.

Manna was terribly depressed during the following days. Sometimes her face still felt clammy, smarting from Geng Yang's foul saliva. At night she prayed to the Lord of Heaven that she would have her next period on time in mid-December. What if I'm pregnant? she kept asking herself. For sure that will cause a scandal. What would I do then? Have an abortion? No, that's impossible. There has to be a male partner who signs all the papers for you, or else no hospital would perform the operation. But by signing the papers, the man would have to take the punishment and all the responsibilities. Who would do that? Even Lin might not be willing to help me that way.

Lin wouldn't be back for two months. What should she do if she was pregnant? This question almost drove her out of her mind. There was no way out. She decided that if she was pregnant, she would kill herself. In her office a line of stout, amber bottles sat inside the medicine cabinet, two of which contained soporific drugs. She began to pilfer five tablets from each bottle every day.

The night school had already started three days ago, but she was too distracted to go to the class. She sold the English dictionary to Yuying Du, a pharmacist who was also an old maid, and she told others that she had severe menstrual pains and had to rest in the evening.

A week later she received a letter from Lin, who told her

that he was well in Shenyang and asked how she was getting along. She didn't write back immediately, still waiting for her period, which was already several days late.

At long last, on December 23, she began to feel the usual swelling in her breasts and the cramps in her abdomen. The next evening came the belated menstrual flow, which scared her—the period was so heavy she felt that some blood vessels might have broken in her. That bastard Geng Yang must have done her an internal injury.

11

Lin returned six weeks later, just before the February Spring Festival. He was surprised to find that Manna had aged so much. Her eyes had dimmed with a depth of sadness, and her lips were bloodless; the skin on her face, which looked grief-stricken most of the time, had become slack and dry, and two vertical creases grooved her forehead. Sometimes by the end of the day her hair was unkempt, but she didn't seem to care. She was often absentminded when he was talking with her, as though she took no interest in what he said. In her voice there were some edgy inflections he hadn't noticed before. Even her breathing seemed difficult, often dilating her nostrils. She reminded him of a pregnant woman tormented by morning sickness, miserable and about to break into tears.

Something must have happened to her during his absence. What was it? He asked her many times, but she would assure him that nothing was wrong and that she felt fine. In secret she had been taking a few kinds of herbal boluses, which she hoped would strengthen her body, nourish her yin, and help her recover.

Throughout the Spring Festival she eluded Lin, saying she was too exhausted to walk and wanted to be alone. A few times she shouted at night, startling her roommates, who jumped out of their beds and thought there was an emergency muster. She slept more now. During the holiday period she remained in bed more than fourteen hours a day.

However, two weeks after the festival she told Lin the truth. They were standing near a concrete electrical pole as she spoke to him. Overhead the power lines were swaying in the wind with a fierce whistle. Her words widened his eyes, riveted on her face. His chin kept shaking, his lips were quivering, and his complexion was dead pale. Beads of sweat appeared on his nose.

After she finished the story, he said between his teeth, "Beast! Such a beast!" His face was contorted, his left cheek twitching.

She wanted to say, "Remember, he was a friend of yours," but she repressed the impulse.

Strangely enough, Lin turned speechless as if lost in thought. His hands were twisting a pamphlet, a document he was supposed to read.

"Lin, I shouldn't have gone to his room. Can you forgive me?" she managed to ask. She shifted her weight from one leg to the other while her lace-up boots went on knocking each other to prevent her feet from freezing.

He didn't answer, as though he had not heard her question; his eyebrows furrowed. She thrust her hands into her jacket pockets and said again, "Lin, don't be too upset. It's all over and I'm on the mend now. The herbal pills really help."

A crosswind veered and threw up a few coils of coal dust, which were winding away into the snow-covered space between the smokestack and the bathhouse. A swarm of sparrows drifted past like a floating net and then disappeared in the leafless branches of a willow. An air gun cracked from the other side of the boiler house, and a flock of pigeons blasted into the air, scattering puffs of snow. They were the old boiler man's pet birds.

Still, Lin didn't say a word and looked more pensive. Anger was surging in Manna as she remembered that Lin had revealed to Geng Yang that she had been a virgin. She said almost in a yell, "So you think I'm a cheap woman now because I lost my virginity? Come on, speak. Tell me what's on your mind. Don't torture me like this. Remember, it was you who told him I was a virgin. You're a part of this too."

"Oh, I'm so sorry. If only I had known him better. I should've taken precautions after he said a heart was just a chunk of flesh." He touched his forehead with his palm and turned silent again.

She knew what he referred to, expecting him to say more, but again he fell wordless. His reticence unnerved her, because she felt he might have been incredulous. She was frightened by this thought. What if your own man doesn't believe you? she asked herself. What if he too thinks you are a slut? Her jaw began shivering as she was suddenly gripped by a desire to weep. But she restrained herself.

At last he seemed to recognize the resentment and suffering in her eyes. He said, "I was so dazed that I lost my presence of mind. Are you sure you're okay now?"

"Yes." Tears came to her eyes.

He wanted to hold her in his arms and comfort her, but they were in the presence of seven or eight soldiers, who were whistling deliberately while shoveling snow on the sidewalk thirty yards away. Remaining where he was, Lin managed to say, "I'm afraid you may need medical help. You look very ill, Manna."

"Where can I get that? I have to take care of myself."

"We should be able to figure out a way. Let me think about it. Can we talk it over this evening?"

"Sure, but don't worry about me. I'm really fine now."

He signaled with his eyes and hand that they should not stay within others' sight too long. They turned and went into the office building together.

For the rest of the afternoon, whenever free, Lin thought about the rape. The more he thought, the angrier he grew with himself. He realized that Geng Yang had taken advantage of his inability to develop his relationship with Manna. If he had married her, or if they had been engaged, that devil wouldn't have known so much about her or been given the opportunity to perpetrate the crime. Obviously his indecisiveness had opened the door to the wolf. Manna was right that he was responsible for the rape too, at least partially. How he hated himself! He was a man incapable of protecting his woman and irresolute in taking action. "Such a wimp!" he cursed himself in an undertone and clutched at his hair.

"What did you say?" asked the young doctor who shared the office with him.

"Oh, nothing."

For some reason Lin felt the case was not over yet. He worried about Manna's health, not only her physical condition but also her emotional state. But what should he do? He dared not even arrange a checkup for her, which would undoubtedly reveal the rape to the rest of the world. Even though he himself was a doctor, all he could do was get some antiphlogistic for Manna. He was unsure what kind of medical treatment a rape victim needed, because the textbooks he had studied in medical school had not touched on this topic. Somehow the more upset he felt about the situation, the more he resented Haiyan's role in covering up the rape without offering Manna any other help.

He and Manna had a talk in his office after dinner. He said to her, "I think we should tell Ran Su what happened."

"Why? You're crazy. That's equal to broadcasting the secret."

"I'm afraid we'd better let the leaders know before it's too late, or there will be more troubles waiting for us."

"What do you mean, Lin?"

"If they know of the case, at least you can officially get medical or psychological help when you need it. For us, this is more important than anything else."

"I'm really well and have no need for any treatment."

"Please listen to me just once!"

"No, we can't do that. Let me tell you why: if people know of the rape, I'll become cheaper in everyone's eyes, and I'll belong to a different category, lower than a widow."

Lin sighed, but he didn't give up. He continued, "There's another reason that I believe we should let Ran Su know."

"What's that?"

"You told Haiyan Niu everything. She's not that reliable. We should take measures against a leak now."

"She promised me she wouldn't tell anybody."

"I dare not trust her."

"Why?"

"I can't say exactly; just by instinct I know we dare not count on her promise. You've put too much in her hands. If this gets out, you'll have a personal catastrophe. People can kill you with their tongues. It will be better to report it to Ran Su now."

She began weeping, her face buried in her arms on the edge of his desk. Softening, he said, "Don't cry, dear. If you don't want to let others know, I won't tell anybody."

"I want to keep it secret."

"All right, but you should talk to Haiyan and remind her of her promise."

"I'll do that tomorrow."

After their talk, Lin became more considerate to Manna. He bought her fruits—oranges, frozen pears, sugar-coated hawthorns, and dried persimmons. From a medicinal herb store he bought a small fork of deer antler, which cost him fifty-two yuan, over forty percent of his monthly salary. Though Manna couldn't use the antler, because it would generate too much yang in her body, it pleased her. She was grateful, and her heart began absorbing warmth again. At last she felt she could leave the rape behind; she was on her way to recovery.

12

One morning in April, Manna ran into Ran Su at the entrance to the lab building. Although he greeted her kindly, his heavy-lidded eyes were observing her oddly, as if sizing her up. She turned to face him, and his eyes slipped away. Then he turned his head back and gave a smile, which was so forced that it resembled a grimace.

Suddenly it flashed through her mind that Ran Su must have found out about the rape. A flush rose on her face as a pang seized her heart and rendered her speechless. She was sure of her conjecture and later told Lin about it. He said she might be wrong, though he was agitated too. He swore he had never revealed the secret to anyone.

She guessed right. The next afternoon, as she and Lin were going to the hot-water house, each holding a thermos bottle, they saw Mrs. Su coming from the opposite direction. Passing them, the skinny little woman spat to the ground and said out loud, "Self-delivery." She wore black clothes and a mink hat, and one of her eyes was swollen. Both Manna and Lin, despite being shocked, pretended they had heard nothing. When the woman was out of earshot, Manna began cursing Ran Su. But Lin was certain that it wasn't Ran Su who had told his wife about the rape, because Mrs. Su was deranged and unreliable and her husband seldom talked to her. It must have been those officers' wives, who always enjoyed gossiping, that had spread the word.

From then on, whenever the little woman saw Manna she would call her "Self-delivery" or shout, "Poked by a man!" The curses often made Manna feel as though she had lost a limb or a vital organ and become handicapped. How she re-

gretted having divulged the secret to Haiyan. She hated the
telltale's bone marrow. If only she had listened to Lin and reported the rape to Ran Su two months ago.

Lin was deeply disappointed by the leak and felt ashamed
as well, because sometimes the little woman would call him
"a green-hatted cuckold" in front of others. Ran Su was a
friend of his, but there was no way Lin could ask him to dissuade his wife from calling Manna and himself names. Mrs.
Su had suffered from dementia since the Sus lost their only
child the summer before. The boy had drowned in the
Songhua River one afternoon when he went to the bank with
his pals to net tiny water insects for his goldfish. It was ru-
mored that Ran Su had to give his wife all the money left in
his wallet every night; otherwise she would curse his ances-
tors without stopping, or smash dishes and bowls, or wail like
a child, or turn on him with a steel poker. As a result, he always kept banknotes inside the plastic cover of a diary. Because he was so good-tempered and had never thought of
sending his demented wife to a mental asylum, Ran Su had
gained a lot of respect and sympathy in the hospital. People
said he deserved his recent promotion. He was the vice-
commissar of the hospital now.

Naturally Manna was furious with Haiyan and would not
speak to her. She didn't go and see her baby, a nine-pound
boy, when she heard of the birth. Haiyan, after her maternity
leave was over, tried to explain to Manna how the secret had
come out. But whenever Haiyan got close to her, Manna
would move away and would not listen to the tattletale. Having no way to approach her, Haiyan went to Lin one afternoon
and made him listen to her story.

"I never meant to tell on Manna," she said, sitting before
Lin in his office. "You know, a couple in bed will chat about
anything, especially when you are bored. I told Honggan not

to breathe a word about Manna to anyone. He promised he wouldn't, but on Spring Festival Eve he got drunk with his buddies and spilled it out. I went to their homes and tried to stop them from spreading the word, but it got out of hand. Lin, I never meant to hurt Manna. She's been my best friend for many years, why should I sell her out? What could I gain from doing that? Oh, this makes me feel like hell." She looked tearful.

"I understand," he said damply.

"You know how I hate that ass of a husband. I almost cracked his skull with a broomstick when I found out what he had done to Manna. If you don't believe me, go ask him."

"I believe you, but it's too late."

"Oh, how can I make it up to Manna?"

"I don't see there's a way now."

"Can you tell her I am very, very sorry?"

"I can do that."

He smelled a soapy odor exuding from Haiyan. After she left, he wondered if she had just washed diapers before coming to his office.

Though he passed Haiyan's explanation and apology on to Manna, Manna was inconsolable and unforgiving. And she had her reason for being so. After the rape became known to everyone, people at the hospital began to treat Lin and her like husband and wife. Their food coupons and salaries sometimes arrived at his desk together at the end of a month; without second thoughts the soldier in charge of mail would leave with Manna letters for Lin; by accident, a clerk once sent them a booklet on family planning, which should have gone to married couples only. Some new nurses would mention Dr. Kong to Manna as if he were her husband, though they would feel embarrassed later when she told them that she was unmarried. All these occurrences hurt her, but she had grown timid now, not daring to fight back or quarrel with others as often as before. She was afraid that anybody might shame her just by referring to the rape.

At last it was clear that she had no choice but to wait for Lin wholeheartedly, as though the two of them had been predestined to be inseparable.

Thus continued their long "courtship," which gradually became steady and uneventful during the following years. Summer after summer, Lin and Shuyu went to the divorce court in Wujia Town and returned home as man and wife. Year after year, he and Manna hoped that the requirement of eighteen years' separation before he could end his marriage would be revised or revoked, but the rule remained intact. Ran Su, after Lin had bought him a used copy of *Around the World in Eighty Days,* a rare book at the time, proposed to the Party Committee to have the rule loosened a little, but the majority of the leaders were opposed to the idea, uncertain about the repercussions. As time slipped by, people grew oblivious to the origin of the rule, as though it were a sacred decree whose authenticity no one would dare question. Year after year, more gray hair appeared on Lin's and Manna's heads; their bodies grew thicker and their limbs heavier; more little wrinkles marked their faces. But Shuyu remained almost the same, no longer looking like an old aunt of Lin's but more like an elder sister.

During these years, most of Lin's and Manna's colleagues were promoted to higher positions or left the army, but the two of them remained in the same offices doing the same work, although they got raises. Ran Su, after another promotion, became the commissar of the hospital in 1980. Lin heard that his cousin Liang Meng had married a model worker, a nationally known operator who had memorized over eleven thousand telephone numbers. In 1981 Commissar Wei died in prison, where he had been incarcerated for his connections with the Gang of Four.

Finally, in 1983, Lin asked Shuyu to come to the hospital. This time he would take her to People's Court in Muji City. After eighteen years' separation, he was going to divorce her, with or without her consent.

1

Bensheng accompanied his sister Shuyu to the army hospital in July 1983, but he stayed only a day, having to return home to attend to his business. The year before, the commune had been disbanded and he had opened a small grocery in a neighboring village, mainly selling candies, liquor, cigarettes, soy sauce, vinegar, and spiced pumpkin seeds. During his absence, Hua was taking care of the store, but he couldn't set his mind at rest and was unwilling to be away for long. Hua hadn't passed the entrance exams the previous summer, and fortunately she could work for her uncle instead of going to the fields.

At the hospital, nurses, doctors, officers, and their wives were all amazed to see Shuyu totter about with bound feet, which only a woman of over seventy should have. She always walked alone, since Lin wouldn't be with her in the presence of others. Whenever she crossed the square before the medical building, young nurses would gather at the windows to watch her. They had heard that a woman with bound feet usually had thick thighs and full buttocks, but Shuyu's legs were so thin that she didn't seem to have any hips.

A few days after she arrived, a pain developed in her lower back. It troubled her a lot, and she couldn't sit on a chair for longer than half an hour. It also hurt her whenever she coughed or sneezed. Lin talked to Doctor Ning about Shuyu's symptom and then told his wife to go see the doctor. She went to the office the next morning; the diagnosis was sciatica, at its early stage. She needed electrotherapy.

So she began to receive the treatment. The nurses were exceptionally kind to her, knowing Lin was going to divorce her soon. After the diathermic light was set, they would chitchat with her. Lying facedown on a leather couch, Shuyu would answer their questions without looking up at them. She liked the lysol smell in the air, which somehow reminded her of fresh almonds. She had never been in a room so clean, with cream-colored walls and sunshine streaming in through the windows and falling on the glass-topped tables and the red wooden floors. There was not a speck of dust anywhere. Outside, cicadas buzzed softly in the treetops; even sparrows here didn't chirp furiously like those back home. How come all the animals and people seemed much tamer in the army?

In the beginning, she was rather embarrassed to loosen her pants and move them down below the small of her back, and the infrared heat on her skin frightened her a little, but soon she felt at ease, realizing the lamp wouldn't burn her. She enjoyed lying on the clean sheet and having her lower back soothed by the heat. A sky-blue screen shielded her from people passing by. When nobody was around, she would close her eyes and let her mind wander back to the countryside, where it was time to harvest garlic and crab apples and to sow winter vegetables—turnips, cabbages, carrots, rutabagas. She was amazed that people in the city could have so many comforts, and that the young nurses always worked indoors, well sheltered from wind and rain. They were never in a hurry to finish work. What a wonderful life the girls had here. They all looked nice in their white caps and robes, though some were sickly pale. When they gave her an injection, they would massage her backside for a few seconds; then with a gentle slap they plunged the needle in. They would ask her whether it hurt while their pinkies kept caressing her skin near the needle. The tickle made her want to laugh.

A nurse once asked her if Lin had bullied her. Shuyu said, "No, he's a kind man, always good to me."

"Does he buy you enough food to eat?" another nurse put

in. She was holding a syringe, its needle connected to a phial filled with pinkish powder.

Shuyu replied, "Yeah, always white steamed bread, or sugar buns, or twisted rolls. I eat meat or fish every day. Here every day's like a holiday. Only it's too hot at noon."

The nurses looked at each other. One giggled, then a few followed suit. "What does he eat?" asked the nurse holding the syringe.

"I don't know. We don't eat together. He brings everything back for me."

"He's a good provider, eh?"

"Yeah, he is."

They all tittered. They were somewhat puzzled by Shuyu's words. Even though Lin held a rank equal to a battalion commander, his wheat coupons couldn't exceed twelve pounds a month. How could he feed his wife with such fine foods the whole time? Where had he gotten all the coupons? From Manna? It was unlikely, because she had overtly declared she would have nothing to do with Shuyu. What did Lin eat then? Did he eat corn flour and sorghum himself? What a weird man. He must have saved a lot of wheat coupons for Shuyu's visit. It seemed he still had some affection for his wife, or he wouldn't have treated her so well.

Shuyu liked the nurses. Yet however hard they begged her, she would not take off her small shoes, of which they often sang praises. They were all eager to see her feet.

One day, after the treatment, Nurse Li, a bony girl from Hangzhou who had never seen a bound foot, said she would give Shuyu a yuan if she showed them her feet. Shuyu said, "No, can't do that."

"Why? One yuan just for a look. How come your feet are so expensive?"

"You know, girls, only my man's allowed to see them."

"Why?"

"That's the rule."

"Show us just once, please," a tall nurse begged with a suave smile. "We won't tell others about it."

"No, I won't do that. You know, take off your shoes and socks is like open your pants."

"Why?" the tall woman exclaimed.

" 'Cause you bound your feet only for your future husband, not for other men, to make your feet more precious to your man. By the way, do you know what this was called in the old days?" She patted her left foot, whose instep bulged like a tiny knoll.

They all shook their heads. She continued, "It's called Golden Lotus, like a treasure."

They looked at her with amazement, winking at one another. Nurse Ma asked, "Wasn't it painful to have your feet bound?"

"Of course it hurt. Don't tell me about pain. I started to bind my feet when I was seven. My heavens, for two years I'd weep in pain every night. In the summer my toes swelled up, filled with pus, and the flesh rotted, but I dared not loosen the binding. My mother'd whack me with a big bamboo slat if she found me doing that. Whenever I ate fish, the pus in my heels dripped out. There's the saying goes, 'Every pair of lotus feet come from a bucket of tears.' "

"Why did you bind them then?" a ruddy-cheeked girl asked.

"Mother said it's my second chance to marry good, 'cause my face ugly. You know, men are crazy about lotus feet in those days. The smaller your feet are, the better looking you are to them."

"How about Doctor Kong?" Nurse Li asked earnestly. "Does he like your small feet?"

The question puzzled Shuyu, and she mumbled, "I don't know. He never saw them."

The girls looked at one another, simpering, their eyes full of amusement. One of them sneezed loudly, and they all laughed.

Because the divorce wouldn't fail this time, Lin had been trying to have Shuyu's rural residential status changed to urban. The army would sponsor such a change only if the officer had served longer than fifteen years or held a rank higher than a battalion commander. Lin was qualified, having been in the service for twenty-one years; so the office in charge of this matter was cooperative. He wanted Shuyu to have a residency card, which would enable her to live in any city legally. Besides, their daughter Hua needed such a certificate as well; according to the law, she would follow her mother and automatically become a city dweller if Shuyu's residential status was changed. With such a card in hand, Hua would have a better chance for employment in Muji. Since she couldn't go to college now, this was her only chance to leave the countryside.

By no means could Lin make Shuyu understand the necessity and complexity of the process, but she complied with whatever he said. If he told her, "Don't fetch hot water—I'll do that," she would never take either of the thermos bottles out of the room. If he handed her some pills and said, "Take these, good for you," she would swallow them without thinking twice. To her, his words were like orders, which she couldn't imagine would do her any harm.

One morning he gave her a one-yuan note and told her to have her hair cut at the barbershop, which was behind the hospital's tofu mill and was run by three officers' wives. The moment he left for work, she set off for the shop.

Unlike back home where Hua would cut her hair with a long comb and scissors, here a haircut cost thirty fen. When a plump young woman in the shop told her the price, Shuyu felt uneasy, as though they were overcharging her. She had never spent money so lavishly; for thirty fen she could buy half a cake of Glossy soap, which would last at least two weeks. Nevertheless, she agreed and sat down on a leather chair.

A large kettle began whining from the coal stove outside the door. The middle-aged woman with bobbed hair went out, removed the seething water, and banked the fire with three shovels of anthracite mixed with yellow mud. Then with a poker she drilled a hole through the wet coal. She came back into the room, threw a white sheet over Shuyu, and fastened its ends at the nape of her neck with a wooden clothespin.

"What hairstyle do you want, sister?" she asked Shuyu, raising a red plastic comb.

"I don't know."

Two male customers laughed, sitting on the other adjustable chairs.

"How about a crew cut like mine? It feels cool in the heat," said one of them, who was the swineherd, the most famous man in the hospital. He had raised a pig weighing over twelve hundred pounds; several major newspapers had reported his accomplishment. Children called him Pigman.

"Come on," the woman said to Shuyu, "it's your hair. You must tell me how to cut it."

"Well, how about like yours?" She pointed at the hairdresser's bobbed hair.

The plump young woman chimed in, "She'll look nice with that."

"Are you sure you want my kind of hairdo?" the middle-aged woman asked Shuyu. "You'll lose your bun."

"Sure, cut it as much as you can." She wanted her hair to be short, so that she wouldn't have to come to the barbershop too often and waste money.

The woman untied her bun and began combing the tangled hair while Shuyu sucked her lips noisily. The initial strokes of the comb pulled her scalp and hurt her a little, but in a moment she got used to it. She began to wonder how come the hairdresser could click the scissors so rhythmically, without stopping. In the right corner of the room a tailless cat was sleeping, now and then stretching out its limbs; its ear went on twitching to shake off flies. Shuyu was impressed by the bowl of sorghum porridge near the door. City people were so rich, feeding a cat like a human. No mice could live in this room with a cement floor, why did they need to keep a cat?

While trimming the ends of her hair, the woman asked Shuyu, "Is Lin Kong good to you?"

"Yeah."

"Do you two live in the same room?"

"Yeah."

"How do you sleep?"

"What you mean?"

"Do you and Lin Kong sleep in the same bed?" The hairdresser smiled, while the two younger women stopped their scissors and clippers.

"No, he sleeps in his bed and me in my own bed."

"Do you know he's going to divorce you?"

"Yeah."

"Do you want a divorce?"

"I don't know."

"Tell you what, climb into his bed when he's sleeping at night."

"No, I won't do that."

Everyone laughed. Shuyu looked at them with confused eyes.

The haircut made her look almost ten years younger. Her face appeared egg-shaped now, and her eyebrows seemed like two tiny crescents.

The hairdresser poured some hot water from the kettle into a bronze bucket hanging on the wall and added three scoops of cold water. Then she had Shuyu sit over the sink and put her head under a rubber hose attached to the bucket. While soaping Shuyu's hair, she said to her again, "Don't be a fool, sister. Sneak into Lin Kong's bed at night. If you do that, he can't divorce you anymore."

"I won't do that."

They laughed again.

"Oh my eyes," Shuyu cried, "stinging from the soap."

"Keep them shut. I'll be done in a second." The woman let the remaining water run over her head, then wiped her eyes and face with a dry towel, which smelled clean and delicious, still warm with sunlight.

"How are your eyes now?"

"They're okay."

Shuyu returned to the barber chair. The woman combed her hair to one side and praised its fine texture. She even applied a few drops of sweetish perfume to the hair.

When Shuyu took out the one-yuan note, the woman said, "No, elder sister, you don't pay for the first visit. You pay next time, all right?"

Shuyu thanked her and put the money back into her pocket. The woman raised the comb to put a lock of hair behind Shuyu's ear, saying, "You know, you look good in this hairdo. From now on you should keep your hair like this." She turned aside and held up an oval mirror. "Now, how is that? Good?"

Shuyu smiled and nodded.

Thanking the woman again, she rose from the chair and limped out of the shop. Her hips hurt a little from the half-hour in the barber chair.

When Shuyu was out of hearing, the people in the shop

began talking about her. They all agreed she actually was not bad-looking, but she didn't know how to dress and make up. The cut of her dark-blue jacket was suitable for a woman of over sixty, with a slanting line of cloth-knots on the front instead of real buttons. If she hadn't worn the puttees, which made her trousers look like a pair of pantaloons, her bound feet would not have attracted so much attention. Probably womenfolk in the countryside had different taste in clothing. Another cause of her unusual looks might have been that she had worked too hard and burned herself out. They had noticed cracks on the backs of her hands and a few tineal patches on her swarthy face.

Gradually their topic shifted to the marriage. How could she survive by herself if Lin Kong divorced her? What a heartless man he was. Shouldn't the Political Department protect the poor woman by ending the relationship between Lin Kong and Manna Wu? This was a new society, in which nobody should found his happiness on another person's suffering. Besides, a married man ought to be duty-bound and must not be allowed to do whatever he wanted, or else families would break up and society would be in chaos.

By the next day Shuyu's answer—"I won't do that"—had become a catchphrase among the hospital's staff. When turning someone down, young nurses would utter that sentence jokingly, stressing every word and giving a long lilt to the final "that." Laughter would follow.

Under cover of darkness, a few curious young officers even went to the long dormitory house in which Lin had been assigned a room recently. They stayed outside at the window and the door, eager to find out whether the couple slept in the same bed. They stuck their ears to the keyhole and to the window screen, but the room was as quiet as if it were uninhabited. Three nights in a row they heard nothing except for a cough made by Lin. One of the men sprained his ankle on the granite doorsteps, having trodden on a sleeping toad; another had his eye whipped by a twig in front of the house. So they gave up and admitted the couple had done nothing unusual.

Word spread—"They don't do that."

2

Lin and Shuyu were sitting at the dining table, on which was a white enamel plate containing a melon, cut in half and with its seeds removed. They were having a talk because their court appearance was scheduled for the next morning. The room looked brighter after all the propaganda posters left by the former residents had been removed from the whitewashed walls. The buzzing of the fluorescent lights again drew Shuyu's attention. She raised her head to see whether a mosquito was in the air. Outside, in the cypress bushes below the window, an oriole was warbling now and then. The fragrance of early chrysanthemums wafted up from the roadside, where the long flowerbed was mulched with pulverized horse dung.

"Shuyu, have you ever thought about what Hua should do in the future?" Lin asked.

"No. I guess she can work at Bensheng's store. He's good to her and pays her well. He bought her a hooded overcoat last winter."

"No, no, she shouldn't remain in the countryside. I want to get her a job here. She's our only child and should live close to us in the city, don't you think?"

She made no answer.

He went on, "Tomorrow when the judge asks what you want from me, say you want me to find a good job for Hua, all right?"

"Why you want me to do that? I never wanted anything from you."

"Look, I've been in the service for over twenty years. According to the rule, the army should take care of our child.

Trust me, they'll find her a job. This is her only chance. Please tell the judge you want that, all right?"

"Okay, I'll do that."

He took a bite of the melon in his hand. "Try this. It's very sweet," he said, pointing at the other half.

She didn't touch it, saving it for him.

Early the next morning, Lin went to fetch breakfast for Shuyu and himself. Hundreds of people were eating in the mess hall. From inside the kitchen came the brisk clank of a shovel stir-frying something in a cauldron. The air smelled of sautéed scallions and celery. Manna turned up with a lunch tin in her hand. Coming up to Lin, she tried to smile, but the effort distorted her face, two wrinkles bracketing her nose and mouth. Her eyes were shining, glancing left and right; apparently she was uneasy about meeting him in this place. He noticed a flicker of resentment pass over her face, probably because he had not seen her for several days.

She said to him, "Don't talk too much in court, all right? And don't argue with the judge." She bit her lower lip.

"I know. There's no need to worry. I talked to Shuyu yesterday evening. She agreed to stick to her word this time. It's final."

"I hope so," she muttered. "Good luck."

She walked away, not daring to talk with him longer than necessary in the presence of so many people, some of whom had already begun darting glances in their direction. Since Shuyu's arrival, Manna had kept a low profile. She avoided meeting others, not going anywhere unless she had to, and wouldn't even eat lunch in the mess hall. As a result she looked anemic.

Lin brought back to the dormitory four steamed buns, half a pot of rice porridge, and a tiny cake of fermented bean curd. For the first time since she had come, he and his wife ate together.

While eating he had a strange realization. These days he had seldom met Manna, as though she were gone on vacation somewhere. He had stopped walking with her in the evening for fear that people would gossip about them and exert pressure on the leaders to stop the divorce. Somehow this temporary separation from Manna didn't bother him at all, just as sleeping in the same room with Shuyu did not discomfort him either. To tell the truth, he didn't miss Manna, though he felt sorry for her. Is this what love is like? he asked himself. No wonder people say marriage is the death of love. The closer we are to getting married, the less attached I feel to her. Does this mean I don't love her anymore? Don't be a fool. She and I have waited for each other so many years. Now it's time to be united. Yes, true lovers don't have to stay together looking at each other all the time; they look and move in the same direction. Who said that? It must have been a foreign monk. How about Manna, what does she think of my staying with Shuyu in this room? Is she irritated by it? She must be. Does she miss me?

His mind turned to the divorce, which became almost an inevitable thing to him now. He didn't need to make any effort to bring it about, as though the whole matter was like a ripe fruit that would fall after being touched by frost. He felt as if there was some force beyond his control, of which he merely served as a vehicle, that would realize the divorce and start him on a new life. Perhaps this force was what people called *fate*.

As soon as Shuyu had done the dishes, a Beijing jeep pulled up in front of the house. She put on the yellow taffeta shirt Lin had bought her a week before. The couple got into the jeep, which drove them to the courthouse next to the city Police Station. Together with them, in the front seat, was Ming Chen, representing the hospital. He was the director of the Political Department now; he had grown stout with thick shoulders and a fleshy face.

It was half past eight. The poplar-lined street was speckled
with people bicycling to work or returning home from their
midnight shifts. The concrete buildings, their red tiles covered with dew, were steaming and glistening in the sun. As the
jeep was passing an elementary school, groups of boys were
playing soccer on the sports ground, shouting and chasing
five or six balls. Girls were skipping ropes or kicking shuttle-
cocks. Obviously the pupils were at their first recess. At the
corner of Peace Avenue and Glory Street a walking tractor
was lying on its side, knocked over by an East Wind truck.
Zucchini were strewn on the ground; a crowd gathered there
watching and chatting; the truck was left on the sidewalk, its
fender bent against a thick tree trunk. Several old women
were pushing carts, each of which was loaded with a sky-blue
box; they were shouting, "Milk and chocolate popsicles, ten
fen apiece." A siren was screaming a few blocks away, growing louder and louder. The jeep carrying Lin and Shuyu nosed
through the crowd and then turned left into West Gate Road to
the Police Station.

At the entrance to the courthouse, which was a chapel built
by Danish missionaries in the 1910s, Lin saw a young couple
coming out. The husband looked sullen, while the wife
sobbed into a white neckerchief and was supported by an
older man, apparently her father. A guard told Director Chen
that the judge had just turned down the woman's plea for a divorce. She had accused her husband of physical abuse and
stealing her money. The judge had not agreed with the latter
part of the accusation. As a married couple, they lived under
the same roof, slept in the same bed, and ate from the same
pot; of course they should share a bank account. By no means
should the husband be charged with theft.

Several rows of benches occupied the center of the courtroom. A long table covered with green velveteen stood on a
low stage in the front. Above the table, a sign with these giant

words was suspended from an iron wire: *Secure the Law like a Mountain*. Beyond the slogan, on the front wall, the national emblem—five stars embraced by fat wheat ears—held the position once belonging to a crucifix. Lin was impressed by the chevron-shaped windows, the crystal chandeliers, and the high ceiling, which didn't need a single pillar to support itself despite the massive, well-hewn beams and rafters. He wondered what the chapel would have looked like if all the lights had been on and if there hadn't been any of these metal-legged chairs and tables. It must have looked splendid.

After everybody was seated in the front row, the judge, a middle-aged man with a wispy mustache and narrow eyes, walked onto the low stage and sat down at the table. He poured himself a cup of tea from a white porcelain teapot. To his right sat a fortyish woman, who was the court clerk, and to his left was seated a young man, the scribe, with a felt-tip pen in his hand. The judge coughed into his fist, then asked the husband to present his case.

Lin stood up and spoke. "Respectable Comrade Judge, I am here today to ask your court to allow me to end my marriage. My wife Shuyu Liu and I have been separated for eighteen years, although we have stayed in marriage nominally. There has been no love between us since our daughter was born. Please don't mistake me for a fickle, heartless man. During the eighteen years, I have treated my wife decently and had no sexual contact with another woman." He reddened at the word "sexual" and went on, "Please consider and approve my request for a divorce."

The judge had read the written petition, so he turned and asked Director Chen to testify to the truth of Lin's statement. Ming Chen didn't bother to stand up, because he held a higher rank than the judge. He said in a strong voice, "What Comrade Lin Kong said is correct. I have been his superior for many years. He has been elected a model officer several times, and there has been no serious problem in his lifestyle. He's a good man."

Lin cast a sidelong glance at Ming Chen. So I have "no serious problem," he thought. That means I have some small lifestyle problems. No wonder they haven't given me a promotion for the last ten years.

The judge asked the director sternly, "Do you, the hospital leaders, approve this divorce?" He lifted his teacup and took a sip.

"Of course we don't advocate divorce, but the couple have been separated for a long time. According to our rule, after eighteen years of separation, an officer can terminate his marriage without his spouse's consent. Lin Kong has been separated from his wife since 1966, already long enough. So we see no reason to decline his request."

The judge nodded as though he was familiar with this rule. He turned to Shuyu and asked what she would say.

"He can divorce me," she said unemotionally. "But I want something from—"

"Stand up when you speak," the judge ordered. She got to her feet.

"Now, what's your request?" he asked.

"We—we have a daughter, a big girl, almost eighteen. She's his child. He should get her a good job in the city."

Director Chen threw up his chin and laughed sonorously, the flesh on his neck folded. The judge looked puzzled. Ming Chen explained, "Our hospital is trying to have Shuyu Liu's residential status changed. This means their daughter will join her here, and we'll help the girl find a decent job. Because she is Lin Kong's child, she will be treated the same as the other officers' children. No problem, we'll see to this matter."

The judge then announced that according to the law Lin had to pay Shuyu thirty yuan a month in alimony. Lin agreed readily, but Shuyu waved her hand.

"What do you want to say?" the judge asked. "You want more?"

"No. I don't need so much. Twenty's enough. Really I don't need so much money."

The woman clerk and the scribe chuckled, and the three guards guffawed from the back of the courtroom, but they stopped at the stare of the judge.

Then the couple were asked whether they had property under dispute. They both shook their heads. Shuyu owned nothing, and the house in the village belonged to Lin.

The judge signed two divorce certificates, pressed a large seal into a case of red ink paste, stamped it on them, and handed the couple one apiece. He stood up and spoke in a resounding voice. "Although you two are divorced, you are still comrades belonging to the same large revolutionary family. Therefore you should treat each other with respect, care, and friendship."

"We will, Judge," Lin said.

"Good. The case is now settled."

The judge stood up; so did the woman clerk and the scribe. Another petition for divorce was waiting to be heard that morning, and the court had to hurry up a little.

Moving toward the entrance, Lin couldn't help feeling amazed by the whole process, which had turned out to be so easy. In less than half an hour, all the years of frustration and desperation had ended and a new page of his life was ready to start.

After the divorce, Shuyu didn't return to the country. She moved into another room in the same dormitory house. From now on she cooked her own meals and lived by herself. A young officer was assigned by the Political Department to deal with the district police in charge of residential registry and with the Splendor Match Plant, which was asked to employ Hua.

It occurred to Lin that his daughter might refuse to come to the city, because she must have been angry with him. When he returned home in the past few years, he had tried to talk with her and find out how she felt about his divorcing her mother, but she had always avoided being with him, saying she had to feed the pigs or go wash clothes in the creek. She seemed to have grown more and more remote from him. So now he decided to write a letter begging her to come to Muji.

At night when he sat at the table holding his Gold Dragon fountain pen, he was overwhelmed by the realization that this was the first time he had written to his daughter. What an awful father he was! Why had he been so absentminded all these years that he had never thought Hua might like to hear from him? No wonder she had been resentful.

He wrote:

My Dear Daughter Hua:

    Your mother and I went to the city courthouse last Monday, and we went through everything smoothly. We asked the army to help you find a job in Muji, and the leaders agree to have you transferred to the Splendor Match Plant here. As a matter of fact, this was your mother's only request in the court. So please respect her wish and come and join us after you receive this letter.

    Hua, please understand that this arrangement is absolutely necessary for you. You will have a better life in the city. Your mother is old, and I am reluctant to let her return to the village. Please come without delay. No matter how you feel about me, trust me just this once. I am your father; I want you to have a happy life. If you stay in the countryside forever, I will be filled with grief and regret.

Your father—Lin Kong

Uncertain whether she could be persuaded only by his words, he wrote another letter to Bensheng, asking him to urge Hua not to miss this opportunity.

Putting down the pen, he yawned, interlaced his fingers, and stretched his arms above his head until two of his knuckles cracked. He enjoyed the peaceful night and felt his mind was more alert when he was alone. A rustle of tree leaves attracted his attention to the window, whose panes were blurred with dewdrops at their corners. Outside a few maple leaves were falling. He stood up, wiped his face with a wet towel, then went to bed.

Some officers asked Lin when they could eat his wedding candies; he said it would be in a few months. Manna and he agreed that they should wait a while so as to prevent others from talking about their building a happy nest on the ex-wife's miseries.

Within two weeks Shuyu's residential status was changed, and all the procedures for Hua's employment were carried through. But Lin hadn't heard from his daughter yet and was worried.

Then, as he feared, her letter came, saying she was not interested in living in "an overpopulated city." She claimed that because the working class consisted of both peasants and workers, she decided to stay in the country as "a socialist peasant of the new type." Lin could tell that was a phrase she had picked up from a newspaper, and he was angry, but he didn't know what to do. Not having heard a word from Bensheng, he suspected that his brother-in-law must have played a negative role in this matter—trying to hold Hua back and keep her working for him. Even Shuyu couldn't help calling their daughter "a stupid egg."

When Lin talked with Manna about this impasse, she suggested he go and fetch his daughter personally. It seemed to be a good idea, because he also needed to sell the country property to get the cash for the wedding. So in the early fall he took annual leave and went back to Goose Village.

3

A dozen people were gathered in his yard when Lin arrived home. The afternoon heat had subsided, but flies were still droning madly. On the ground, near the wattle gate of the vegetable garden, was spread a bloody donkey's hide. It was almost covered up by dead greenheads. Judging by the sweetish odor still emanating from the skin, a lot of dichlorvos had been sprayed on it to prevent maggots. The air also smelled meaty and spicy, with a touch of cumin, prickly ash, and magnolia-vine. Hua, a violet towel covering her hair, was stirring something in a cauldron set on a makeshift fireplace built of rocks. Against a blue wheelbarrow leaned a signboard that carried these words in black ink: "The Best Delicacy—Donkey Meat on Earth like Dragon Meat in Heaven! Two-Fifty a Pound!"

At the sight of her father, Hua put down the shovel and went up to him. With a grin she said, "I'm so glad you're back, Dad." She took the duffel bag from his hand.

"What are you doing? Why are so many people here?"

"Uncle Bensheng's donkey died. I'm cooking five-flavored donkey meat for him. They're waiting to buy some."

"Where is he?"

"He's in our house talking with somebody. Let's go in now." She turned and put the wooden lid on the cauldron, but left a crack between the lid and the rim.

Lin wasn't happy about the scene, wondering why Bensheng had not used his own yard as a meat shop. What a greedy devil, he thought. He always tries to profit at others' expense. If I had come back a few days later, he'd have turned this home into his own.

Bensheng's only donkey had died two days ago. It had run out of its shed after midnight, gotten into a meadow, and then broke into a vegetable garden, where it ate a lot of alfalfa and beans without drinking any water. As a result it became too bloated to stay on its feet. A boy saw it lying behind the village's millhouse the next morning, and he ran to inform its owner. When Bensheng arrived to help the animal, it was breathing its last, its stomach burst. Bensheng was very upset, because he had depended on the donkey to transport groceries from Six Stars. All he could do now was sell its meat to get some money back. Though a few villagers wanted to buy raw donkey meat, he would only sell it cooked, figuring that in this way he could make more money. He told them, "I don't deal in raw material, only the finished product."

As Lin entered the house, he heard Bensheng speaking to someone in the main room. "I'll give you the donkey's hide, okay?"

Lin and Hua stopped to listen. Another voice countered loudly, "No, that won't do. Your beast destroyed my garden. I don't want its skin. What can I do with it? I can't even sell it at the salvage station."

"You can make a mattress out of it, can't you?"

"No. Who wants to sleep on a stinking ass? If it were a roe deer, I would take it."

"Some people don't even deserve the company of a dead donkey."

"I just don't want to have anything to do with it."

Lin stepped into the room, but the men didn't notice him. He recognized the other man as a neighbor, Uncle Sun. Bensheng said to the old man, "How about eight pounds of donkey meat, braised?"

"No, ten pounds."

"Nine."

"Damn it, I say ten!"

"Nine and a half."

"Ten!"

"All right, I'll let you have that much, Uncle Sun, only because I respect your old face."

Hua interrupted them by saying, "Uncle, my dad is home."

Both men turned to Lin. The old man looked a little embarrassed, flashing a toothless smile, and then said to Bensheng, "I must be going. I'll send my grandson over for the meat." He clasped his hands behind him and strode out with measured steps. A tuft of white hair peeked through a hole at the top of his felt skullcap.

Bensheng himself looked like an old man now. His forehead was seamed with wrinkles, and his thin eyes were dimmer than the previous year and slightly sunken, as though he hadn't slept for days. He seemed disturbed by Lin's sudden appearance, but quickly regained his composure. "Is Shuyu back too?" he asked Lin.

"No, I came alone to fetch Hua." He glanced at his daughter, whose face showed little response to his words.

Bensheng frowned, then said plaintively, "I received your letter, elder brother. I understand you got what you wanted. But we're still one family."

"I feel the same way," Lin managed to say, somewhat softened by his pity for him.

"My sis isn't here, so you come eat with us, all right?"

"Well . . ."

"Please Dad," Hua broke in. "I've been staying at Uncle's these days. We're one family."

"All right, I will."

Bensheng was apparently pleased with Lin's agreement. After telling Hua to get some water in a washbasin for her father, he went out to sell the five-flavored donkey meat.

Lin was also glad that he had accepted Bensheng's offer, because he wasn't sure how to put the property up for sale and might need Bensheng's advice and help. He wanted to sell it within a few days and return to Muji as soon as possible. In addition, he was unsure whether his daughter would be willing to leave with him. A good relationship with Bensheng would at least facilitate his job of persuading her. It seemed that Hua was quite attached to her uncle and aunt, who were childless and treated her like their own daughter. In his heart Lin resented the way Hua smiled at her uncle, as though there was something intimate between them, something to which he was denied access.

Another idea lurking at the back of his mind had come to the fore: he wondered if Hua had a boyfriend. The girl was becoming a handsome young woman and must have attracted some pursuers. If she already had a lover, his task of persuading her to go to Muji might get complicated. Perhaps she wouldn't give up her boyfriend for a job in the city. The more he thought about this, the more anxious he grew. He ought to find an opportunity to ask her so that he could know what difficulty he was facing.

At dinner that evening, Bensheng said that Second Donkey was thinking of buying Lin's house for his eldest son, Handong, together with the furniture. The young man planned to marry the next year, although he had no fiancée yet. These days matchmakers had been frequenting Second Donkey's home, because Handong, who worked full-time in Wujia Town, had finally agreed with his parents to look for a wife in the countryside. Lin was delighted that there was a buyer interested in the house, but his face darkened when Bensheng told him that Second Donkey had inspected the property and would pay no more than three thousand yuan. To Lin, the house and the furniture were worth at least four thousand.

"No, I won't sell it at that price," Lin said to Bensheng after dinner.

"Fine. Tomorrow when Second Donkey comes to my store, I'll tell him that. By the way, how much would you ask?"

"Four thousand."

"Keep in mind he can pay cash. He made a killing on cabbages last fall and on potato noodles this spring. His fish pond is a money cow. Few men in our village can come up with three thousand yuan at the moment."

"That's too low," Lin said firmly.

Though Lin turned Second Donkey down, he couldn't feel at ease because he might not have enough time to wait for a reasonable offer.

The next afternoon he talked with his daughter and found out that she did have a boyfriend. He was unhappy about it, believing she was too young to understand love, but he didn't blame her. While she was helping him pack up Shuyu's clothes, he continued to ask her about the young man. "Does Fengjin live in a nearby village?" he said.

"No, he's in the navy now, in Jiangsu Province."

"How did you get to know him?"

"We used to be classmates." She blushed almost to the ears, kept her eyes low, and went on folding a pair of her mother's pants.

"How serious is it between you and him? I mean, do you know him well enough to love him?"

"Yes," she replied confidently.

He was amazed by her answer, wondering how an eighteen-year-old could truly understand her feelings. Could love be so simple and so easy? Didn't it take time to achieve mutual understanding and trust? Maybe she just had a crush. She couldn't really love him, could she?

"Does he know you're going to have a new job?" he asked her.

"Yes, I wrote to him. He wants me to go to the city with you too."

"So that he can join you in Muji someday?"

"I think so." She nodded.

"Does Uncle Bensheng know you have a boyfriend?"

"Yes, but he's not happy about it."

"Why?"

"He said I should find a college graduate instead, because soldiers are not fashionable anymore."

Lin smiled. Then mixed feelings rose in his mind about her boyfriend. On one hand, he was pleased that Fengjin encouraged Hua to seize the opportunity to go to the city; on the other, the young man was undoubtedly a practical fellow, who knew how to use her to improve his future—because if Hua stayed in the village, he might have to come back to the countryside when he left the army. Lin was afraid her boyfriend might just be using her, but he didn't say a word about his suspicion. For the time being he would be satisfied if he could take her away without a hitch.

Outside the window a goose honked, which reminded him that he should get rid of all the poultry, the goat, and the sow within two or three days.

"Dad, do you think my mother can wear this? It's the only silk thing she has." Hua displayed a red tunic against her chest.

"No, it's too large for her. Have you ever seen her wear it?"

"No, I haven't."

He remembered that a relative of his had sent the tunic to Shuyu as a wedding present two decades before, but it had never fit her. Neither had she ever tried to alter it, always saying, "This is too fancy for me." That was why the tunic still looked new. Before he set out for the country, Shuyu had told him to give anything she couldn't wear to her brother's wife. He said to Hua, "Pack it in."

Bensheng came home with good news for Lin that evening. Second Donkey accepted the price, though he would pay only two thousand in cash initially and he would hand over the other half by the end of next year, after his son's wedding. Lin was suspicious of this way of being paid, knowing well that once the house was occupied, the new owner could delay giving him the rest of the payment forever, and that he might never receive the other two thousand yuan at all. Furthermore, Bensheng was Second Donkey's friend and might eventually get hold of the money without passing it on to him. That would be a good way to avenge his sister. Perhaps the two men had purposely worked out such an arrangement to take advantage of him. No, this wouldn't do. He had to forestall the trouble.

Without further consideration, Lin made up his mind to collect all the cash he could, and not to leave any balance behind.

That night he and Bensheng went to Second Donkey's home and clinched a deal. After a brief haggle, the buyer agreed to pay 3,200 yuan in cash on the spot. Lin hadn't seen Second Donkey for seven or eight years and was surprised that he had not aged much and that only his large eyes were no longer as bright as before. His long teeth were still strong, tea-stained along the gums; his donkeylike face remained smooth and even less swarthy, with just a few wrinkles. How he can take care of himself, Lin thought.

Second Donkey, his feet tucked up underneath him, went on saying, "We're all neighbors. I don't mind spending a bit more." He was drinking beer from a glass, which was so greasy that the liquid resembled peanut oil. Lin wouldn't touch the beer poured for him.

Second Donkey called in his son Handong to help draw up a contract. To Lin's amazement, the slender lad, who had an effeminate face and sensitive eyes, placed on the dining table a sheet of letter paper and a lumpy inkstone, which contained freshly ground ink. He climbed on the brick bed, sat cross-legged, and began to write with a small brush made of weasel's hair, which few people could use nowadays. From time to time he turned smiling eyes toward Lin. His posture, manners, and handwriting all appeared to be scholarly. In every way he didn't look like a son that the thickset, illiterate Second Donkey could father. Later, Lin heard from Bensheng, who thought a great deal of Handong, that the lad was a college graduate and a teacher in Wujia Middle School. Actually his father had given dinners and gifts to the commune leaders, who then had him elected for college as a worker-peasant-soldier student.

Besides the house and the furniture, the contract also included the shack in the backyard, the pigsty, the grinding stone, the vegetable garden, the eleven elm and jujube trees, the water well, the cauldron, and the latrine. Having read it through, Lin pressed his personal seal on the paper, beneath his name. Second Donkey did the same. Next, the buyer went into the inner room, in which his wife was shelling chestnuts, and came back with three bundles of cash, each consisting of a hundred ten-yuan bills. Then from a small envelope lying on a red chest, he pulled out forty brand-new fivers and put them together with the three thousand yuan on the dining table.

"Count this, please," he said to Lin, who was impressed, never having met a wealthier man.

Lin started counting the money, now and then pulling out a bill with a missing corner. Meanwhile Second Donkey poured another glass of beer for Bensheng, who frowned at Lin's white fingers.

All together Lin found seven damaged ten-yuan bills. "No store will accept these," he said to the buyer.

Second Donkey chuckled and said, "Smart man." He went into the inner room again and returned with seven intact tenners.

The transaction was completed, and Lin left Second Donkey a key to the house. Then he and Bensheng put on their caps, said good-bye to the father and son, and went out into the starless night.

On their way home, Lin gave the seven ten-yuan bills to Bensheng, who took the money but didn't look happy. A rooster crowed in the south. "Crazy. It's not midnight yet," Bensheng said. "They should kill or geld that damn cock who just confuses people, only makes noise and never lays an egg."

The next day Lin went to the village office and called his brother, telling him to come with a horse cart tomorrow after-noon to fetch things for his family. He had decided to give all the animals to Ren Kong. He told Hua of his decision, and she promised not to reveal a word to Uncle Bensheng, knowing her father had already given him seventy yuan and meant to leave him all their farm tools and the family plot.

Exhausted from sweeping and earthing up his parents' graves, Lin slept nine hours and got up late the next morning. His shoulders and elbows were still painful. After breakfast, he poured two bottles of sweet-potato liquor into the feed Hua had prepared—chopped radish greens and crumbs of soaked soybean cake. With a pair of chopsticks he mixed the alcohol and the feed, then fed it to the sow and the seven piglets, the poultry, and the goat. All the animals ate hungrily. He planned to leave for Muji the next day and was pleased that so far things had run smoothly according to his plan.

Ren and his two older sons arrived with a tractor in the early afternoon. Without delay they began to work. They put all the chickens, geese, and ducks into a large string bag, tied together the feet of the pigs and the goat with hempen ropes, then threw them into the spacious trailer. The creatures were all sound asleep and made no noise except to grunt vaguely once in a while. The boys were actually young men now, tall like their father with thick muscular arms. Lin was glad to see them, although he had never known them well. Ren had brought along a pair of brown leather sandals for Hua, the most fashionable and expensive kind in the county. The pre-sent delighted her so much that she immediately went about helping her cousins load into the trailer jars, vats, the meal bin, a pair of straw rain capes, pots, pans, two boxes of books, and a stack of unused notebooks for her youngest cousin who was still going to middle school.

"Hua, can you boil some water for tea?" her father asked.

"Sure." She went into the house to start the stove.

Meanwhile Lin and Ren sat under a jujube tree, chatting and smoking. Ren was puffing on his pipe, with an Amber cigarette tucked behind his ear, which Lin had given him and which he was saving for his eldest son. Again Lin expressed his admiration for his husky nephews. The eldest one was being trained to be a truck driver. Obviously Ren wouldn't lack wine and meat in the future, since the boy would have a lucrative job.

The trailer was fully loaded. Ren and his sons couldn't stay for tea because they would have to return the tractor to the commune Veterinary Station before five o'clock. After saying good-bye to Lin and Hua, they all jumped onto the vehicle, which rolled away with earsplitting toots.

As the tractor was put-putting down the road, Bensheng came in. His face fell at the sight of the yard, which was almost stripped empty. He asked his niece, "Hua, did you save the wheelbarrow for me?"

"I think it's still in the shed." She went there to see, but returned a minute later, saying, "Damn, they took everything, even the rakes and shovels."

Bensheng went up to Lin. "Elder brother, I thought you'd at least give me the sow."

"I'm leaving you our family plot."

"Forget it! The village is going to take it back."

"I—I told Ren to come with a horse cart so we could leave a lot of stuff for you, but he came with a tractor. We have some clothing for Hua's aunt in the house. Also, don't you want these?" He pointed to the stacks of brushwood and bean stalks, and a pile of manure.

"Damn you, such an ungrateful worm!" Bensheng stamped his feet, storming away. His left leg seemed shorter than his right; this caused him to wobble a little.

Lin and Hua decided to eat at their own home in the evening, not wanting to confront Bensheng. Lin took out some cookies and opened two cans, one of peaches and the other of fried minnow. Together father and daughter sat down to dinner, each drinking a cup of hot water.

As they were eating, Lin asked Hua whether he should give Bensheng some extra money, say, a hundred yuan, to make up with him. Hua thought for a moment, then said, "Don't do that. You should save the money for my mother. One hundred yuan is nothing for Uncle Bensheng. Sometimes he can make more than that in a week."

"All right, I won't give him any." Lin took a bite of a walnut cookie. "If he's so rich, I don't understand why he's so angry at me."

"Greedy. He has nothing but money on his mind. He even adds water to soy sauce and vinegar in his store."

"Really? Does your aunt know that?"

"No, she doesn't."

They smiled at each other. Lin was pleased with Hua's smile, which showed she had become his ally. He realized that since he had come home, he had been in good spirits and never felt lonely, perhaps because his daughter had grown close to him again. But she would soon belong to another man. If only he could have kept her around forever, or if only she were ten years younger. No, he said to himself, you've been alone all your life and will remain a loner. Don't be so mushy.

The house was quiet, as all the animals were gone. Most of

the flies had disappeared as well. Somewhere in the village a horse was neighing.

Dusk was descending after father and daughter had cleared the table and washed the dishes. They had to go to bed early so that they could rise before daybreak to catch the bus. There would be a long, exhausting day tomorrow, since they were to carry three large suitcases containing winter clothes and quilts. After bathing his feet, Lin lit two incense coils to repel mosquitoes, one for his room and the other for Hua's.

Having said good night to his daughter, he returned to his room. Hard as he tried, he couldn't fall asleep. The reed mat under his back was cool, but too hard to be comfortable. Besides, it was only eight o'clock, and the twilight outside wasn't dim yet. Someone was playing a fiddle in the village, the broken music quite jarring. Lin kept his eyes shut and tried not to think of anything. Gradually he grew a little drowsy.

A knock on the door woke him and he turned his head. Hua stepped in with a white toweling coverlet over her shoulders. "Dad, can I sleep in your room? I'm scared. That room is too quiet. With so many things gone, it feels spooky in there."

He remembered she had slept in her aunt's room since Shuyu left. "All right, you use the other end of the bed. Did you put out the incense?"

"Yes." She climbed onto the brick bed, whose breadth was the same as that of the room, and lay down on the other end. Without a word she closed her eyes.

Lin looked at her face carefully. Her nose was straight like his, but thinner; her forehead was full and her skin dark but healthy. When she was exhaling, her lips vibrated a little. He was amazed by her pretty looks, which she probably was unaware of. He was certain she would soon become an attractive young woman in the match plant. Why wouldn't she forget that boy in the navy? She could easily find a man who'd love her more and take better care of her.

As he was thinking, Hua opened her eyes. "Dad, what's Muji like?"

"It's a big city, with two parks, three large department stores, and six or seven movie theaters."

"My friends told me that there were lots of moons in Muji at night. That isn't true, is it?"

"Of course not. They must have meant neon lights."

"What are neon lights? They look like the moon?"

"Not exactly. They're colorful, blinking all the time."

"That must be scary. Is my mother afraid of walking alone in the city?"

"I don't think so." He regretted having answered in an uncertain tone, but on the other hand, he had never known how Shuyu felt when she was walking alone. "Hua, will you keep your mother company when she goes shopping in the city?"

"I will," she replied with her eyes shut. After a brief lull she said, "Dad?"

"Yes?"

"Were you scared when you left home alone? You were just a teenager then."

"Not really."

"Didn't you miss your friends in Wujia after you left?"

"I had few friends."

"Ah, I have so many here." Her voice turned pensive.

While father and daughter were conversing with their eyes closed, the night thickened. The table and chests in the room became obscure. Suddenly somebody yelled from the yard, "Come out, you pale-faced wolf!" It was Bensheng's hoarse voice.

Lin climbed out of bed, put on his pants, and went out. As he opened the door, sour, alcoholic fumes assailed his nose. Bensheng, in large white shorts and stripped to the waist, pointed at Lin's face and said, "Elder bro-brother, I want to settle accounts wi-with you tonight."

"What's this all about?"

"I want you to come h-home with me."

"All right."

Hua came out too, in a pair of pink pajamas. Her uncle waved his hand and croaked, "You're all su-such heartless beasts, so-so ungrateful."

"You've drunk too much, Bensheng," Lin said. "Let me take you—"

"No, my head isn't muddled. Everything is cl-clear in here." He pointed his thumb at his temple, but his legs buckled, shaking.

"Uncle, please go home."

"You're ungrateful too. You don't e-even want to eat m-my food. Your aunt made lamb dumplings for you, b-but you wouldn't show your face."

"Oh, I didn't know that!" Hua wailed.

"Tell me, how come Handong doesn't de-deserve you? Where can you find a better lad, a real scholar?"

"I've told you I don't want to think about him, Uncle."

"He loves you."

"I told you I don't want a bookworm."

Lin felt bad for Bensheng. "My brother," he said, "we were wrong, all right? Please—"

"Don't brother me! You snatched away my sister. Now you're taking Hua away from me. You bully me be-because I don't have a child. You, you're my born enemy. I want to get even with you." He collapsed to the ground, sobbing like a little boy.

"Uncle, don't be so upset. You can visit us and I'll come back to see you and Aunt. I promise."

"Don't sweet-talk me. I know you think I'm dirty and greedy, but my heart is pure, like gold." He thumped his chest with his fist.

As Lin bent down to help him up, Bensheng's stout wife

appeared from the darkness, wearing a white T-shirt and mauve slacks. "My old devil," she cried at her husband, "you come home with me."

"Leave me alone," he grunted.

"Get up right now!"

"Okay, my little granny." He tried to climb to his feet, but his legs were rubbery, unable to support him.

His wife turned to Lin and said, "I told him not to make any trouble here and let you and Hua leave in peace, but he sneaked out after a pot of horse pee."

"He can't walk anymore. Let me carry him back." Lin squatted down; Hua and her aunt lifted Bensheng by the arms and put him on Lin's back.

Lin carried him piggyback toward Bensheng's house, which was three hundred yards away, while Hua and her aunt followed, casting their long shadows ahead. As Lin plodded along in the damp moonlight, Bensheng breathed out hot air on the nape of his neck, making his skin tingle. Whenever Bensheng let out a feeble moan or a broken curse, Lin was afraid he would open his mouth to bite him. Hua was saying something to her aunt, her voice hardly audible.

Soon Lin began panting as the load on his back grew heavier and heavier.

4

Hua was hired by the Splendor Match Plant a week after her arrival at Muji. For the time being she stayed with her mother in the hospital at night. She liked her new job, which was lighter than any work in the village—just gluing a slip of paper on the top of each matchbox and wrapping every ten boxes into a packet. Besides, she made more money now—twenty-eight yuan a month. In her heart she was grateful to her father, but she never said a word about it.

A month later the plant assigned her a room in one of its dormitory houses; so one Sunday morning her mother moved out of the hospital to live with her in town. Lin bought bowls, pots, and some pieces of furniture for them, and he made sure they had enough coal and firewood. From now on, mother and daughter would be on their own. But their life was not worse than other workers'; Hua's earnings and the alimony Shuyu received could help them make ends meet each month.

After Shuyu and Hua had settled down, Lin began to attend to his own affairs. One day in October, he and Manna went to the Marriage Registration Office downtown. They gave each of the two women clerks a small bag of Mouse toffees. Without delay the older woman, who looked wizened and limped slightly, filled out a certificate for them. It was a piece of scarlet paper, folded and embossed with the golden words: *Marriage License*.

Then the preparations for the wedding began. They were allocated a one-bedroom apartment, which needed a lot of cleaning. For a week, in the evenings they brushed the cobwebs off the ceilings, scrubbed the floors and doors, painted the rusty bed that Lin had borrowed from the Section of General Affairs, and scoured the cooking range. They cleaned the windowpanes, which were speckled with fly droppings, and sealed the cracks around the window with flour-paste and strips of newspaper. The northern wall of the bedroom had some crevices; when it was windy outside, cold air would surge in, making the wallpaper vibrate with eerie noises. Two masons were sent over by the Logistics Department; they filled the crevices with mortar and then whitewashed all the walls.

In addition to the cleaning and repairing, Lin had to buy a large amount of candies, branded cigarettes, fruit, and wine. At the time these fancy things were in short supply, and he could get them only through the back door. Also, he was trying to buy a black-and-white TV set, which required a coupon he didn't have. So in the evening he bicycled about the city visiting people who might be able to help him, and he often returned late at night. Meanwhile Manna had a cold; she was coughing a lot.

The wedding took place in the conference room on the first Sunday of November. More than half of the hospital's staff and their families gathered there that evening. Most of the leaders and their wives attended the wedding, but Mrs. Su would not come because she abhorred the very idea of divorce. Somehow she couldn't stop calling Manna "Doctor Kong's concubine" whenever the couple came to mind.

Sodas, bottles of wine, platters of apples and frozen pears, and plates of roasted hazelnuts, sunflower seeds, pine nuts, cigarettes, and candies were laid out on twenty-four tables, which had been arranged into six rows. Children turned noisy at the sight of so many goodies; most of them were Young Pioneers, wearing around their necks a triangular scarf that represented a corner of a red flag. Some boys were running about and shouting at their pals while spitting out shells of sunflower seeds or cracking roasted pine nuts with their molars.

A few little girls were warming their hands on the radiators below the double-glazed windows, which were partly packed with sawdust in between. The panes were covered with frost, shimmering in the fluorescent lights; on them one could see the patterns of clamshells, seaweed, reefs, waves, capes, islands. It had snowed heavily that morning, and the whirring of the north wind could be heard through the windows.

On the front wall were posted two large words written in black ink on red paper: "Happy Marriage!" Six strings of colorful bunting intersected one another in the air. There were also two lines of balloons wavering almost imperceptibly; one of them was popped, hanging up there like a blue baby sock.

When the room was nearly full, Director Ming Chen went to the front and clapped his hands. "May I have your attention please," he called. People quieted down.

"Comrades and friends," he announced in a booming voice, "today we've gathered here to celebrate the happy union of Comrade Lin Kong and Comrade Manna Wu. I'm very honored to officiate at this wedding. You all know who they are, as you see them every day. So let us make the ceremony simple and short. First, let us meet the bride and the groom."

To loud applause Lin and Manna got up and turned around to face the people. Bareheaded, they both had on brand-new uniforms, with a red paper flower on their chests. Manna wore shiny patent-leather shoes while Lin was in big-toed boots, the standard army issue made of suede and canvas. She seemed nervous, not knowing where to put her hands, and kept smiling to a few nurses from her ward. Then at the request of Ming Chen, together the couple bowed to the audience, some of whom stood up and whooped while others applauded. More people were coming in from the doors at the back. A few women whispered about the bride's complexion, which had turned rather sallow the last few weeks. Someone said, "Look at Doctor Kong's face. He's such a gloomy man that you never see him in high spirits."

Director Chen announced again, "Now, the bride and the groom pay tribute to the Party and Chairman Mao."

The couple turned to face the side wall, on which hung a portrait of the late Chairman and a pair of large banners carrying the emblem of a crossed sickle and hammer.

Ming Chen began chanting: "The first bow . . ."

The couple bowed to the banners and the portrait, keeping the tips of their middle fingers on the seams of their trousers.

"The second bow . . ."

They bowed again, lower than the previous time, almost eighty degrees.

"The third bow . . ."

Done with the homage, the couple turned to face the audience again. For a few seconds the echoes of the director's chanting kept ringing in the room and the corridor. People remained quiet and seemed muted by the sheer volume of Ming Chen's voice. Then the director announced, "Now I declare Lin Kong and Manna Wu are man and wife. Let us congratulate them."

People applauded again; some boys whistled.

When the audience quieted down, the couple were asked to sing a song. Manna was good at singing, but Lin knew few songs, so they sang "Our Troops March Toward the Sun," which was so outdated that some of the young officers had never heard it. Their singing was unpleasant to the ear. The bridegroom's voice was too low and soft, while the bride's was rasping thanks to the cold she had. A few nurses couldn't help smirking; one said, "This gives me a toothache."

The moment they finished singing, a young officer raised his fist, shouting, "Eat a bobbing apple!"

"Yes, let them eat a bobbing apple together," several voices cried out. What they demanded was an apple strung by a thread in the air, so that the couple couldn't avoid kissing each other while eating it.

Director Chen held up his hands and calmed them down. He said, "We're revolutionary officers and soldiers, and the army isn't your home village, so the bobbing-apple stuff is not appropriate here. Now, enjoy yourselves."

As people were standing up and moving around, Ming Chen clapped his hands for the attention of the children. He cried, "Small friends—boys and girls—you can eat as many goodies as you want, but don't take any home. Understood?"

"Yes sir," a little girl shouted back.

Laughter followed. At once the room was filled with noise again. A baby burst out crying in a back corner. A young officer set off a firecracker; the explosion made a few girls scream; immediately he was prohibited from doing that again. The two doors at the back were opened to let out the smell of gunpowder.

One by one the leaders walked up to the bride and groom to clink glasses and give their congratulations. When Commissar Ran Su approached them, he seemed very moved. Unlike others, he didn't hold a glass of wine. He looked like an old man now—though he was merely fifty-one—with sparse hair and a gray mustache. Furrows spread on his forehead and at the corners of his eyes, whose lower lids hung down a little. He grasped Lin's and Manna's arms and drew them aside, saying in a somber voice, "You two must cherish this opportunity in your lives. Love and take care of each other. Don't forget that yours is a bitter love." He paused and said "bitter love" again, as though to himself.

His words touched the bride. After Ran Su left, she was unable to restrain herself anymore and broke out sobbing. Lin took her glass away. With his arm around her waist he steered her to a corner and tried to calm her down, but she was inconsolable, her mouth trembling and her face bathed in tears. She bit her lip, sniffling, her eyes shining at the happy crowd moving about under a 300-watt bulb.

"Don't be so upset, dear," Lin said.

She was still biting her lip, tears trickling down her chin and falling on the front of her jacket.

"Come, sweetheart," he said again, "this is our wedding. Try to put on a happy face."

She raised her face, which looked so contorted that for a moment he didn't know what to say. He touched her forehead; it was wet and hot.

He asked, "Is this too much for you?"

She nodded.

"Would you like to go home?"

She nodded again. He turned and saw Nurse Hsu sitting nearby with a few little girls and cracking hazelnuts for them with a pair of pliers. He asked her to take his bride home, since he couldn't extricate himself. Then he found Manna's fur hat and overcoat and brought them out to the corridor. There he helped her on with them, saying he would join her at home soon.

When he returned to the crowd, the room was full of noisy music. The tables were all pushed against the walls, and young nurses and officers were dancing together. After being banned for almost two decades, ballroom dancing had just come back into fashion. The young men and women were wheeling and swaying passionately as though they knew no fatigue. The older officers and doctors stood by, watching the dancers and chatting. Suddenly a nurse slipped and fell on the floor, having stepped on a pear core. Her fall brought on waves of laughter.

Haiyan and her husband Honggan came up to Lin and congratulated him. They were a middle-aged couple now. Honggan wore civilian clothes and glasses, which made him

resemble a ranking official; Haiyan was moonfaced and a little stout, wearing a saffron neckerchief. She beckoned to their
son. "Come here, Taotao, and meet Uncle Kong."

"No, I don't want to," whined the eight-year-old boy. He
skipped away with a wooden carbine in his arms and disappeared among his pals. His parents and Lin all laughed.

"You and Manna should never have a boy," Haiyan said to
the bridegroom. "It's much easier to raise a girl. By the way,
where is the bride?"

"She didn't feel well and went back home. She has a cold."

Honggan patted Lin on the shoulder and said, "My friend,
I'm very happy to be here. Listen, from now on if you need
any help, just let me know." His left hand was twirling an
empty glass.

Lin looked at his flat face, trying to make sense of his words.
He was amazed to see that Honggan had turned into a happy,
healthy man and had shed all traces of his peasant stock. His
face was quite smooth; only two small pinkish boils on his
forehead reminded Lin that the face used to be carbuncular.

"Don't be polite, Lin," Haiyan said. "He has power and
pull now. His company owns twelve trucks."

"Oh, thanks," he managed to reply. In his heart he still
couldn't embrace them as friends.

"If you need to bring home coal or firewood," Honggan
said, "just give me a call."

"Thanks."

Silence set in. The summer before last Honggan had been
demobilized and had become the vice-chairman of a lumber-
yard in Muji. Like her husband, Haiyan had also made
progress in life; after one and a half years of training in
Changchun City, she had become an obstetrician. They had
moved to downtown Muji so that their son could go to a better
school. Though Haiyan and Manna had made up long ago,

Manna still wouldn't trust her with any secret. Now Lin hoped the couple would leave him alone.

But Honggan was in a talkative mood. He said in a low voice, "Lin, have you heard anything about Geng Yang?"

Lin was perplexed by the question and shook his head, wondering why he mentioned that name at this wedding. Thank heaven, his bride wasn't around.

"Well, I don't mean to annoy you," Honggan went on, "but I heard he got rich, filthy rich. You know, a bad dog is always lucky."

Lin didn't say a word, his cheeks coloring.

Seeing the bridegroom's flushed face, Haiyan pinched her husband's neck and asked angrily, "Why the hell did you mention that thug here, moron?" She then gripped his ear and tweaked it.

"Ouch! Let go."

"Apologize to Lin," she ordered.

"All right, all right, Lin, I'm sorry."

Lin said with a bland smile, "Let him go, Haiyan. He meant no harm."

"He's stupid, such a killjoy." She released his ear. "As if he hadn't done enough damage and hadn't hurt Manna at all." She turned to her husband and asked, "Why did you try to spoil this wedding?"

Honggan realized his blunder. "Sorry, Lin, I didn't mean to do anything nasty. There was an article on Geng Yang in *Role Models* a month ago. I just want to say it's unfair that son of a bitch is doing so well."

"I understand," Lin said. He didn't read that magazine and had no idea how rich Geng Yang was.

"We should be going," Haiyan said to her husband.

"Yes." Honggan turned to the bridegroom. "Don't forget I'll be happy to help you. Any heavy work."

"I'll remember that." Lin wondered if the couple had drunk too much.

"Bye-bye." Honggan waved, then grasped his wife's arm. Together they merged into the crowd.

Most of the dancers were in sweaters or shirts now. The room seemed to Lin like a large cabin on a ship, foggy and swaying. This feeling made him giddy.

He couldn't dance, so he stayed with the older officers and their wives, receiving congratulations and answering questions. By now, most of the children had left with candies and fruit in their pockets and with all the balloons, so the room became less noisy and the tables were stacked with empty platters, plates, jackets, hats, mittens. Lin was tired and couldn't stop wondering how his bride was doing alone at home. How bored he was by their wedding.

5

Manna turned out to be a passionate lover, and her passion often unnerved Lin. He wasn't as experienced in bed as she had expected. He tired out easily, most of the time before she could calm down. At night when taps was sounded, they would go to bed immediately. They would make love for half an hour, not daring to remain awake longer because they would have to join the morning exercises at daybreak. If it snowed, they would get up early as well to clear roads with their comrades.

Manna seemed frustrated sometimes, but never lost her temper. One Saturday night she joked with Lin, saying good-humoredly, "I wonder how you could have made a baby with Shuyu. In just three minutes?" Her chin was resting on his chest while her eyes were dreamy and half-closed.

"I was young then," he muttered.

"So you had a different pecker?" She chuckled.

"She wasn't like you."

"In what way?"

"She didn't make me feel like an old man."

"Come on, you are still my young groom." She started kissing his mouth again and swung her leg across his belly.

"Sweetheart, I need more time," he said.

"Okay, take it easy." She lay still alongside him, but her hand went on caressing his thigh. It took a while to get him ready. They made love for an hour that night, since they wouldn't have to rise early the next morning.

Before the wedding Lin had feared that the rape of a decade ago might continue to trouble Manna, especially in bed; so he had often reminded himself to be gentle with her. But she showed no sign of discomfort. Every day she insisted they make love before going to sleep. Sometimes they even went to bed after lunch. What a woman, he would say to himself.

To satisfy her was not easy, yet he tried his best. Exhausted every night, he wondered if he should use an aphrodisiac—getting some ginseng or angelica roots or seahorses and steeping them in a bottle of wheat liquor. But he decided not to concoct such a drink, believing those things would help burn him out sooner. He hoped Manna could slow down a little, but she was passionate as ever. Are other newlyweds like us? he asked himself.

In bed, at the climax, Manna often moaned, "Oh, let me die. Let's die like this, together." At times she would weep and even bite his nipples or shoulders. In the beginning her words and tears frightened him, and he thought he must have hurt her. But she said he hadn't, claiming she was happy, so happy that she wished they could lie together in bed forever.

Once, however, she confessed to him, "I don't know why I feel so sad. If only we had married twenty years earlier." He gave thought to her words, but was unsure what they meant exactly. Did she imply that if he were younger, he would have been more virile?

Every time after sex he found her slightly different—tired and older, although pink patches would appear on her cheeks and make her a bit more charming. But the flaccid flesh on her stomach and arms, her soft breasts, and the small crinkles on her throat, all indicated that youth had left her. He would wonder how her body could generate so much desire, which seemed ageless and impossible for him to meet. He felt old and begged her not to indulge herself too much, but she didn't seem to care.

In two months he began to have a numb pain in the small of his back, and a soreness was developing in his right sole. He knew that too much sex might have hurt his kidneys, but he wouldn't shun it, feeling obligated to satisfy her in any way she wanted, because she had waited so many years for him. A large dose of vitamin B1 was injected into his foot, around the sore spot, to soothe the nerves. It alleviated the pain to some extent.

His colleagues noticed he had grown thinner. Since the previous summer he had lost fifteen pounds, and his chin jutted out further. When there was no woman around, his comrades would outdo one another poking fun at him. Shiding Mu, the head of the Propaganda Section, said one afternoon in the recreation room, "My goodness, Lin, you've been married for just three months. Look at yourself, you're running out of sap."

Lin sighed, not knowing how to reply. He went on writing the phrase "Warmly Welcome" with a brush on a large sheet of paper. They were making posters for a general's visit to the hospital. Lin was among the few skilled with the writing brush, so he had been assigned to the work.

Shiding Mu nudged him and went on, "Already tired out, eh? This is just the first step of a thousand-mile march." He gave a long laugh, which was so loud that it set the pane on a cabinet door rattling for a few seconds.

"Stop it!" Lin snapped.

But they wouldn't leave him alone. A junior officer chimed in, "Lin, by next summer, you'll be a skeleton if you go on like this. You must slow down."

Another man said to Lin with a wink, "You know, lust is the worm that sucks up your marrow."

Then a clerk in round-rimmed glasses dipped a small broom into a bucket, stirring the hot paste made of wheat flour, and recited loudly these lines from an ancient lyric:

> For her I have grown bony and pale,
> Yet I do not regret my robe
> Is turning baggier day by day.

They laughed out loud, then continued to talk about women. No wonder the saying went: "At thirty she is like a wolf; at forty a tiger." An old maid must be a wolf as well as a tiger, so only a young lion should engage her in battle. From the outset Lin should have known he was no match and should have set up a few rules with her. The office echoed with chortles. Their jokes made time pass so fast and the work so delightful.

Though he didn't show his anger, Lin was exasperated at heart. He told himself he had to do something to stop people from talking like this.

At home he looked at himself in the full-length mirror on the wardrobe, which was the only piece of furniture he had bought for the wedding. Indeed his eyes had sunk deeper and seemed larger. His face was pallid, and more white hair appeared at his temples and crown. The gray strands gave him a sense of finality. At medical school twenty-five years before, he had grown some white hair, which later turned black again. Now there was no hope of reversing the gray.

One day he and Manna jumped into bed after lunch and made love. Afterward, he was so exhausted he fell asleep. Manna didn't wake him when she left for work. He went on sleeping until a nurse came at about three to get the key to the storage room. She said a technician from Harbin had arrived to repair the inhalator Lin had locked away. How embarrassed he was. Without washing his face, he set out with the woman for the medical building. On the way he kept telling her that he didn't feel himself.

That evening he said to his wife, "Sweetheart, we can't continue like this. We're no longer young. People have been talking about us."

"I know it's bad," Manna said, "but I can't help myself. Something's eating me inside, as if I won't live for long and have to seize every hour."

"We should save some energy for work."

"In fact, I don't feel well these days. I had my blood pressure checked this afternoon. It was high."

"How high?"

"One hundred fifty-two over ninety-seven."

"That's awful. We shouldn't have sex so often."

"Maybe we shouldn't." She sighed.

They agreed to protect their health from then on. That night they slept peacefully for the first time.

6

"It's like a cinerary casket," Lin muttered to himself. He referred to a small sandalwood box underneath Manna's clothes in the wardrobe. A bronze padlock always secured its lid. He couldn't help wondering what was inside. Probably money, or her bankbook, or the certificates of merit she had received. Somehow the varnished box had begun to occupy his mind lately.

One evening he asked her in a joking tone, "What are you hiding from me in the box?"

"What are you talking about?"

"The sandalwood box in the wardrobe."

"Oh, nothing's in it. Why are you so curious?" She smiled.

"Can I see what's inside?"

"Uh-uh, unless you promise me something."

"What?"

"Promise you won't laugh at me."

"Of course I won't."

"Promise that from now on you'll tell me all your secrets."

"Sure, I won't hide anything from you."

"Okay, then I'll let you see."

She got up from the bed, went over to the wardrobe, and took out the box. Removing the padlock, she opened the lid, whose underside was pasted over with soda labels. A roll of cream-colored sponge puffed out, atop the other contents. She took the roll out and unfolded it on the bed, displaying about two dozen Chairman Mao buttons, all fastened to the sponge. Most of them were made of aluminum and a few of porcelain. Their convex surfaces glimmered. On one button, the Chairman in an army uniform was waving his cap, apparently to the people on parade in Tiananmen Square. On another, he was smoking a cigar, his other hand holding a straw hat, while talking with some peasants in his hometown in Hunan Province.

"Wow, I never thought you loved Chairman Mao so much," Lin said with a smile. "Where did you get so many of these?"

"I collected them."

"Out of your love for Chairman Mao?"

"I don't know. They look gorgeous, don't they?"

He was puzzled by her admiration. He realized that some-day these trinkets might become valuable indeed, as re-minders of the mad times and the wasted, lost lives in the revolution. They would become relics of history. But for her, they didn't seem to possess any historical value at all. Then it dawned on him that she must have kept these buttons as a kind of treasure. She must have collected them as the only beauti-ful things she could own, like jewelry.

As he was thinking, a miserable feeling came over him. He didn't know how to articulate his thoughts without hurting her feelings, so he kept silent.

He glanced at the box, in which there were about two dozen letters held together by a blue rubber band. "What are those?" he asked.

"Just some old letters from Mai Dong." She seemed to keep her head low, avoiding his eyes.

"Can I see them?"

"Why are you so inquisitive today?"

"If it bothers you, I don't have to see them."

"There's no secret in them. If you want, you can read them. But don't do that in front of me."

"All right, I won't."

"I won't lock the box then."

"Sure, I'll read them and see what a romantic girl you were."

In his heart he was eager to go through the letters, though
he didn't show his eagerness. Never had he seen a love letter
except in novels; never had he written one himself. Now he
could see a real love letter.

The next afternoon, he came home an hour early and took
out the sandalwood box to read the letters. Many of them
smelled fusty; they were already yellowish, and some words
were too fuzzy to be legible, owing to damp. Mai Dong's
writing wasn't extraordinary by any means; some of the letters were mere records of his daily activities—what he had
eaten for lunch, what movie he had seen the night before,
what friends he had met. But occasionally a phrase or a sentence would glow with the genuine feelings of a young man
desperately in love. At one place he wrote, "Manna, whenever
I think of you, my heart starts quickening. I couldn't sleep last
night, thinking about you. This morning I have a terrible
headache and cannot do anything." At another place he declared, "I feel my heart is about to explode. Manna, I cannot
live for long if this situation drags on." One letter ended with
such an exclamation, "May Heaven facilitate our union!"

Seeing those words, Lin almost laughed. Obviously Mai
Dong had been a simple, gushy fellow, hardly able to express
himself coherently.

Yet having read all the letters, he felt a doubt rising in his
mind. What troubled him was that the desperation Mai Dong
had described was entirely alien to him. Never had he experienced that kind of intense emotion for a woman; never had he
written a sentence charged with that kind of love. Whenever
he wrote to Manna, he would address her as "Comrade
Manna," or jokingly as "My Old Lady." Maybe I've read too
much, he reasoned, or maybe I'm too rational, better educated. I'm a scientist by training—knowledge chills your
blood.

At dinner that evening, he said to Manna, "I went through the letters. I can see that Mai Dong was really fond of you."

"No, I don't think so."

"Why not?"

"He jilted me. I hate him."

"But he loved you once, didn't he?"

"It was just a crush. Most men are liars. Well, except you." She grinned and went on wiping up the remaining pork broth on the plate with a piece of steamed bun.

Her words surprised him. If what she said about Mai Dong was true, then why had she kept his letters in the treasure box? Did she really hate him? He was puzzled.

Manna found herself pregnant in February. After that, she insisted Lin get another bed so they could sleep separately. "I don't want to hurt the baby," she explained, meaning they should stop having sex until the baby was born. He agreed. He borrowed a camp bed from the Section of General Affairs and set it up in a corner of the room.

Her pregnancy came as a surprise to Lin, who had thought that Manna, already forty-four, must be too old to be fertile. Now he was worried, because she had a weak heart. Since they had been married, once in a while she had suffered from arrhythmia, and her blood pressure had been high, though her cardiogram didn't indicate any serious problem. His worry was compounded by the fear that at her age she might not be able to give birth to a baby smoothly. He tried to persuade her to have an abortion, but she wanted the baby adamantly, saying that that was the purpose of their marriage, that she would not be a childless woman, and that this might be her last opportunity. She even told him, "I hope our baby is a boy. I want a little Lin."

"I don't believe in that feudal stuff. What's the difference between a boy and a girl?"

"A girl will have a harder life."

"Come on, I'm not interested in having another child."

"I want my own baby."

Unable to dissuade her, he dropped the subject and let her follow her wish.

Her reaction to pregnancy was severe. She vomited a great deal, sometimes even in the small hours. She didn't seem to care about her looks anymore. Her face became bloated, and the skin around her eyes grew dark and flabby as though she had just stopped crying. In addition, she ate a lot; she drank pork-chop soup with shredded kelp in it, saying the baby needed nutrition and tapping her belly, which hadn't bulged yet. What's more, her appetite was capricious. One day she craved sweet potatoes and the next day almond cookies. Then she remembered jellyfish and begged Lin to get some for her. Muji is far from the sea, and even dried jellyfish was a rarity after the Spring Festival. He bicycled about in the evening to look for jellyfish, but couldn't find any. He asked a few nurses, whose families lived in the city, to help, but none of them could do anything. Finally, through a relation of the mess officer, Lin bought two pounds of salted jellyfish at a seafood store.

Manna washed the sand and salt off the jellyfish, sliced them, and seasoned them with vinegar, mashed garlic, and sesame oil. For three days, at every meal she chewed the jellyfish with crunchy relish. She wanted Lin to try a piece, but he couldn't stand the smell.

Then from the fourth day on, she stopped putting the jellyfish on the dining table, as though the dish were unknown to her, despite half a bowl of the leftovers still sitting in the cupboard.

Aunt Cheng, Doctor Ning's mother, stopped by one

evening. She told Manna, "You're a lucky woman and can eat whatever you want. In the old days when I gave birth to my first son, I ate only ten eggs. That was all for two months. When I was big with my second child, I was dying to have a roast chicken. Every morning I went to the market to look at the golden chickens at a cooked-meat stand. I had no money even for a wing, just went there to smell some."

The old woman's words reminded Manna of what was good for her, and she began craving roast chicken. So every other day Lin bought her a chicken from a luncheonette nearby, though he was worried about the cost—on his monthly salary he could afford no more than fifteen roast chickens. Fortunately her appetite for chicken lasted less than two weeks. Then she remembered pomegranates, which were impossible to find here in wintertime. How she longed for those pink pearls, sour, pungent, and juicy! One night she even dreamed of a robust tree laden with pomegranates. She told Lin about the dream, saying the auspicious fruit portended that they would have a big boy. Somehow the impossibility of coming by a pomegranate corrected her freak appetite, and she began eating normally again.

Since they'd been married, Lin had read little. His bookcase standing by the door still held his books, but it was also loaded with cups, medicine bottles, eyeglass cases, flashlights, a tumbler doll, and knickknacks. Dust had gathered on the tops of the volumes, but neither he nor his wife bothered to wipe it away. By comparison, Manna was reading a lot, mainly about pregnancy, childbirth, and parenting. She checked out all the books the hospital's small library had on the subjects; she was amazed to discover how ignorant she was about parenting. At dinner she would brief her husband on what she had read that day. Most of the time he would listen to her absently; her words entered his head at one ear and left by the other. His lack of interest sometimes annoyed her.

In addition to reading, she was busy preparing clothing and diapers for the baby. She asked some nurses for their threadbare shirts and pajamas, because diapers should be made of soft, used cloth that wouldn't chafe the baby's skin. In the evening she often went to their neighbors' homes to learn how to make baby quilts and pillows and how to knit socks and booties. She bought three pounds of knitting wool, which cost her over seventy yuan and made Lin wonder why she had become so openhanded, even wasteful—the baby would hardly need so much woolen clothing. But he didn't complain, because she had spent her own money.

Hua sometimes came on Sundays. If Manna was at home, she would stay only for a short while. She told her father that Shuyu was very pleased to hear about Manna's pregnancy, because this meant their family would be larger. Lin was puzzled by Shuyu's response, which seemed to indicate that she thought she was still his wife. He wondered whether it was the alimony he paid that made her feel this way. What a simpleminded woman. At times Hua brought along scallion pancakes, which Shuyu had made for him, but she wouldn't take the food out of her bag if Manna was around. She talked more and smiled more now, telling her father that she liked her job and that the fellow workers treated her well. She looked cheerful, the corners of her mouth going upward a little when she smiled, and a gleam appeared in her eyes. Without Manna's knowledge, Lin bought Hua a Phoenix bicycle and a Shanghai wristwatch. Though Manna knew Hua couldn't afford them by herself, she said nothing. She never greeted the girl wholeheartedly.

Sometimes Lin thought about the twenty years before this marriage. The peaceful time seemed as remote as if it had belonged to another man's life. He couldn't help imagining what this home would have been like if Manna and he had gotten married fifteen years earlier. At that time she had been such a pleasant woman that he had always believed he would be a happy man once he married her. But now she was so different and rather boring. He realized how suffering had changed her.

Once in a while he was bewildered by a strange emotion that would shoot a tingling pain to his temples. It made him wonder whether he cared for this married life, which was so tedious, so chaotic, and so exhausting.

7

Lin told Manna that he would go to his office after dinner. He had been asked to give lessons in basic chemistry to a group of orderlies, who were going to take exams for nursing school. He taught in the evening twice a week.

"Why do you have to go to the office tonight?" Manna asked.

"I can get more work done there," he replied nonchalantly.

"What work?"

"I told you I have to brush up on my chemistry in order to teach the class."

"Can't you do that at home?"

"I need to concentrate." His voice was marked with resolution.

She said no more, though unhappy about his words. His eagerness to be away from home unsettled her. Recently she often saw a hard light appear in his eyes when he talked with her, as though he were out of patience. To her mind, his irritation might have resulted either from her refusal to abort the baby or from their abstaining from sex. She had asked several older women to see whether she could continue to share her bed with him, but they all assured her that for the baby's sake, the parents ought to remain abstinent during the pregnancy. She believed them, since some books she had read had given the same advice.

After Lin left for his office, she became restless. More doubts came to her mind and set her imagination on the wing. She couldn't help wondering if he still loved her.

It seemed unlikely that their abstinence from sex had estranged him from her. She clearly remembered that when she asked him to set up a bed for himself, he had approved of the idea readily, as if quite pleased. Does this mean he's tired of me? she asked herself. Probably so. Is he looking for another woman? That's impossible. We've stood together through all the bad times. He couldn't change his heart all of a sudden. Still, why is he so eager to stay away from me? Does he want to have a good time with someone else? Is he attracted to other women? Did he really go to his office? Is he there alone?

The more she thought, the more wretched she felt. An intense loneliness overcame her, and the dim home seemed like a deserted sickroom. She felt as if the whole world were conspiring to make a fool of her. No, she said to herself, even if I were a millstone on Lin's back, I wouldn't let him drop me so easily. He's all I have. Without him there would no longer be this home. Besides, he should concentrate on loving and taking care of his pregnant wife, shouldn't he? I must try every means to keep hold of him.

The next evening, after Lin finished dinner and left with an umbrella, she flung her raincoat on and followed him out. She kept about a hundred yards behind him as he was slouching through the rain, which was falling in white threads that were slanting, swaying, and swirling with the wind. A few sparrows were chirping tremulously under the eaves. It was still chilly, though the roadside trees were already softly green with budding leaves. Lin's heavy gait reminded Manna that he was no longer a young man. How could you think of him going to see another woman? she wondered. How absurd you are. You're too jealous and too possessive. Why not let him have some freedom?

He entered the medical building, but she didn't follow in. Instead, she stood beneath a basketball hoop in the front yard. She wouldn't go in until he reached his office on the second floor.

She waited and waited. Ten minutes passed and still the

lights in his office remained off. The window was dark like the mouth of a well. Where was he? In the men's room? Impossible, he had relieved himself just before leaving home. He must be doing something secret elsewhere.

As she wiped rainwater from her face with her hand, laughter rang out from the west end of the building. She walked over to see what was going on. There, in the lecture room on the first floor, Lin was talking to seven or eight young orderlies, who were all women of around twenty. They looked engrossed in his talk. The windows were open, but she couldn't hear what he was saying. Every now and then Manna caught a phrase like "a different structure" or "molecular formula." She could tell he was happy, his face expressive and his gestures full of life. He looked taller than usual as his back was straight now. He turned around and began writing something on the blackboard. All the students' eyes were still fixed on him. Suddenly the tip of the chalk sprang away from his fingers and he said, "Whoops!" That brought a silly laugh from one of the women.

Anger and jealousy surged up in Manna's chest. She thought two of the orderlies were quite good-looking and must have been attractive to most men, especially the one nicknamed Snow Goose. That young woman had been transferred to this hospital five months ago on account of an affair with a senior officer at Shenyang Military Headquarters. She had been an actress in an opera troupe there and was sent down to this remote city after the officer's wife had written a dozen letters to his superiors, threatening to publicize the scandal if they didn't punish "the itching bitch." Observing Snow Goose now from a distance of twenty yards, Manna noticed her neck was indeed white and long like a goose's, partly covered by jet-black hair. Her nose quivered and she couldn't stop smiling at the teacher. There must have been something wrong with this woman, who seemed unable to live without seducing a man, like a weasel spirit. Manna had heard that at work one night Snow Goose had wandered about in her white gown without any underclothes on. Some male patients must have smelled something in her and would follow her whenever she was within sight.

The more Manna looked at that woman's bewitching face, the more miserable she became. What angered her most was that pair of apricot eyes, which hadn't left Lin since Manna began observing her. How she hated her, and hated them all! Lin was no good either. He obviously enjoyed flirting with these young women. Shameless, he could be their father. Small wonder he was so eager to leave home the moment he put down his chopsticks. Their home was no more than a guesthouse to him—he just went back to eat and sleep. Damn him! Damn them all!

The rain turned heavy, larger raindrops falling on the greenish tiles and the concrete ground with a thickening, crushing sound. Two women in the lecture room stood up and came to the windows to close them, so Manna swung around, heading home. Her legs felt weak like water.

Manna ran into Commissar Su the next morning on her way to work. Since they had been on friendly terms, she asked him why the hospital couldn't use somebody else to teach the chemistry course. As a pregnant wife she needed her husband to stay home in the evening. For a moment Ran Su was bewildered by her question, saying he had never heard of such a class, not to mention assigning Lin the work. Indeed there were a good number of recent college graduates available; why should they bother Lin with it?

"Don't worry, I'll look into this matter," he said to her as they parted company. His bowlegs seemed more bent than last year.

Commissar Su's answer surprised Manna, and she wondered who had assigned Lin to teach the class. The night before, after returning from the medical building and arguing with herself for two hours, she had decided not to confront Lin, as she remembered the price he had paid for their home. It would be unimaginable that Lin was not serious about their marriage. Otherwise he wouldn't have waited for her so many years and struggled so hard to obtain the divorce. In no way could he be a frivolous man. But now that she had met Ran Su and found out the class was not officially established, Manna changed her mind. She wanted to question Lin so as to get to the bottom of this.

"Lin, I want ask you something," she said after lunch.

"What?"

"Who told you to teach the chemistry class?"

"They asked me to help."

"Who did?"

"Those orderlies who want to take the exams. They went to my office the other day and asked me to give them a crash course."

"So no one assigned you the job?"

"No. They begged me and I agreed to help."

"Then why didn't you talk with me before you agreed?"

"Did I have to?" he asked derisively. Behind the lenses his eyes again glinted with the hard light she dreaded.

"This is our home, not a guesthouse where you can check out as you please."

"I know." He looked annoyed.

She broke into tears and spoke toward the ceiling. "Heavens, as if he really has no idea what he's been doing. How can I make him understand!"

"What's wrong? They asked me for help, why shouldn't I help them?"

"Let me tell you what's wrong. You have a pregnant wife

moping alone and worried sick at home, while you're having a good time with other women."

"That's not fair. I didn't spend time with any woman."

"Who are those orderlies then? Who's Snow Goose? A gentleman?"

"Come on, you're being unreasonable."

"This is not a matter of reason but of feelings. Let me tell you this: no decent husband would do such a thing to his wife."

"Well, I've never thought of that." He sounded quite innocent.

She went into the bedroom, burying her face in a pillow stuffed with duck down. He sat smoking for a while. Then he wiped clean the dining table and did the dishes. Without a word he left for work.

For a whole afternoon Manna was fidgety, unsure whether Lin would come home for dinner and whether he would continue to go out in the evening. She even blamed herself. Maybe she shouldn't have blown up like that. He must think of her as a jealous shrew now. Had he really changed his heart about her? Probably he had become so tired of her that he had begun running after another woman. No, he couldn't be so heartless. Then what did he really want?

The more she thought, the more agitated she became. Yet deep down, she felt she was not wrong.

She made wontons for dinner, hoping he would come home on time. She boiled a pot of water and waited for him. Lin returned at six sharp as usual. How relieved she was at the sight of him; without delay she dropped the pork wontons into the boiling water.

As the pot was seething, she shredded two sheets of dried laver, cut a tiny bunch of cilantro, and put them into a large tureen. Meanwhile Lin placed spoons, bowls, and cups of soy sauce and vinegar on the dining table, saying she should have waited for him so that he could prepare the stuffing and help her make wonton wrappers.

"I didn't know when you'd be back," she told him, although that was only partially true. She had worried that he might not come home for dinner at all.

When the wontons were cooked, she poured them, together with the water, into the tureen, then dropped in a spoonful of chili oil and stirred the soup counterclockwise for a moment with a stainless steel ladle.

Dinner was ready. Lin carried the tureen to the dining room, which was also their living room.

While eating, Lin said he had seen Ran Su in the afternoon. Actually they had talked for a long time about women. "It was a nice chat," he told her.

"Who did you talk about?"

"Just women in general."

"So he thinks I'm out of my mind?"

"Oh no, he said I was in the wrong and I didn't understand you."

"What did he say exactly?"

"He said a woman couldn't live long without attention and love."

She tittered, amused that the commissar could talk that way. No wonder he was so patient with his crazy wife. She said, "That's not true. How about nuns?"

"Well," Lin paused, then went on, "they have the attention of monks, don't they?"

They both laughed.

"Manna," he said, "if I had known you'd feel so strongly about my teaching the class, I'd never have agreed to do it."

Seeing the honest look on his face, Manna smiled and told him never to make such a decision on his own. They should always discuss it first. "A married couple must work like a team," she said.

From that day on, he would stay home in the evening to prepare the lessons. Because the class was already in motion, it was impossible to change and he had to go to teach it twice a week. Though Manna was glad about the reconciliation, the two lonely evenings each week still irritated her. Sometimes she felt depressed when he wasn't home, and she couldn't help imagining how to give him a piece of her mind.

8

As her belly bulged out in the summer, Manna grew more grumpy. She resented Lin's absence from home two evenings a week. She knew the class would be over soon, but she couldn't help herself, treating him as though he were having an affair. Her peevish face often reminded Lin of what she had said the day after their wedding, "I wish you were paralyzed in bed, so you'd stay with me all the time."

Is this love? he would wonder. Probably she loves me too much.

One late afternoon in August, Manna returned from the grocery store with four cakes of warm tofu in a yellow plastic pail. Putting it down on the kitchen range, she said to Lin, "Something is wrong with me." Hurriedly she went into the bedroom, and he followed her in.

She looked down at the crotch of her baggy pants and found a wet patch. "Oh, I must've broken my water."

"Really?" He was alarmed. The pregnancy had not reached the ninth month yet.

"Quick, let's go to the medical building," she said.

"Don't panic. It may be too early and could be false labor."

"Let's go. I'm sure it's time."

"Can you walk?"

"Yes."

Together they set out on their way, he supporting her by the arm. The sun was setting, but the heat was still springing up from the asphalt road, which felt soft under their feet. A few lines of green and white clothes were swaying languidly among the thick aspens behind a dormitory house. A large grasshopper whooshed away from the roadside, flashing the pinkish lining of its wings, then bumped into a cotton quilt hanging on a clothesline and fell to the ground. The leaves of some trees on the roadside were shriveled and darkened with aphids because it hadn't rained for a whole month. Here and there caterpillars' droppings were scattered on the ground. Lin was paying close attention to the road so as to avoid places where Manna might make a false step; at the same time he grew more apprehensive, thinking of the baby that would be premature.

When they arrived at the building, Manna was rushed into a small room on the third floor, in which an examination table, upholstered with sponge rubber and shiny leather, served as a birth bed. Nurse Yu spread a sterile cloth on the table and helped Manna climb onto it. A few minutes later Manna's contractions started and she groaned.

Nurse Yu ran out to send for Haiyan, the only obstetrician in the hospital, who had left for home. At the entrance of the building she bumped into her friend Snow Goose, who agreed to come up and help.

In the room upstairs Manna groaned again, clutching Lin's arm.

"You'll be all right, dear," he said.

"Oh, my kidneys!" She was panting and rubbing her back with her free hand.

"It can't be your kidneys, Manna," he said as though examining a regular patient. "The pain must radiate from your pelvis."

"Help me! Don't just talk!"

He was baffled for a moment; then he pressed his palm on the small of her back and began massaging her. Meanwhile she was moaning and sweating. He had no idea what else he should do to alleviate her pain. He tried to recall the contents of a textbook on childbirth he had studied two decades before, but he couldn't remember anything.

Haiyan didn't arrive until an hour later. She looked calm and apologized for being delayed by traffic. After examining Manna briefly, she told Nurse Yu to test the patient's blood pressure and then shave her. Next she ordered Snow Goose, "Flick on the fans and boil some water." Then, turning to Lin, she said, "Her cervix is only three centimeters open. It will take a while." Putting her palm on the patient's forehead, she said, "Everything will be all right, Manna."

Lin drew Haiyan aside and whispered, "Do you think she can survive this? You know her heart isn't very strong."

"So far she's doing fine. Don't worry. The baby is coming and it's too late to think about anything else. But I'll keep that in mind."

She moved back to the table and said, "Manna, I'm going to give you an oxytocin drip, all right?"

"Yes, do it. Let me get through this quickly."

"Can I do something?" Lin asked Haiyan.

"Did you have dinner?"

"No."

"Go eat and come back as soon as you can. This may take a whole night. We'll need you to be around."

"How about you? Did you eat?"

"Yes."

He was impressed by Haiyan's composure. He left the room while his wife was groaning and rubbing her back with both hands.

In the mess hall Lin bought a spinach soup and two buns stuffed with pork and cabbage, which he began to eat without appetite. He couldn't tell whether he was happy about the baby, whose arrival took him by surprise. He belched, and his mouth was filled with acid gastric juice, which almost made him vomit. He rested his head for a moment on his fist placed on the edge of the tabletop. Fortunately nobody was nearby; around him were stools turned upside down on the tables.

Outside, pigs began oinking from their sties behind the kitchen as the swineherd knocked the side of a trough with an iron scoop. A group of nurses and orderlies came in, gathered around two tables at the other end of the hall, and began stringing green beans.

Lin let out a sigh. His heartburn prevented him from finishing dinner. In the air lingered a stench, coming from the hog-wash vat by the long sink. He got up and went across to dump the soup into the vat. After washing his bowls and spoon, he gargled twice, then put the dinner set into his bag made of a striped towel and hung it on the wall, among the bags of his comrades. At the other end of the hall the young women were chatting and humming a movie song. A puppy was whimpering, leashed to a leg of a table.

When Lin came back to the medical building, his wife's groaning had turned into screaming. Haiyan told him that the baby seemed to be coming sooner than she had thought. In fact Manna was in transition. Lin wet a towel and wiped the sweat and tears off her face. Her eyes were flashing and her cheeks crimson.

"I can't stand this anymore! No more!" she cried. The corners of her mouth stretched sideways.

"Manna," he said, "it will be over soon. Haiyan will make sure that—"

"Oh, why did you do this to me?" she shouted.

He was taken aback, but managed to say, "Manna, don't you want the baby?"

"Damn you! You don't know how this hurts. Oh, you've all abused me!"

"Please, don't yell. Others in the building can hear you."

"Don't tell me what to do, damn you!"

"Come on, I didn't mean—"

"I hate you!" she screamed. "I hate you all."

"Please, you'll disturb—"

"Miser! Too late. Oh, help me!"

"Okay, you yell as you like."

"Miser! Miser!"

He was bewildered, wondering why she suddenly called him that. She seemed angry at Haiyan too; that must have been why she said they had all abused her. Then the thought came to him that by "miser" she must have been referring to the two thousand yuan they had talked about paying to Bensheng to get his support a decade before. She must have thought that if they had married ten years earlier it would have been easier for her to give birth to the baby. This realization stunned him, because he hadn't known she had harbored her deep resentment all these years. He turned to the door, telling Snow Goose that he was going to the bathroom.

Once alone in a toilet stall, he tried to sort out his thoughts. Manna must have hoped he would spend two thousand yuan to buy off Bensheng at that time, though she had never made her wish explicit to him. He remembered clearly that she refused to share such a cost. Then why did she call him "miser"? He felt something clutching his lungs, and a pain gnawed him in the chest. Had he had that much money, he would certainly have brought about the divorce sooner. He had told her that he only had six hundred yuan in the bank, and she wouldn't even reveal to him how much she had saved. She must have thought he was a rich man and could easily afford two thousand yuan. After so many years, how come she still didn't believe him? Why on earth had she always kept her secrets from him, never allowing him to see her bankbook?

In his mind a voice replied, Because money's more precious and more effective than love. If you had spent the money, everything would have worked out all right and you could have enjoyed a happy marriage.

No, it wasn't that simple, Lin retorted.

It was simple and clear like a bug on a bald head, the voice went on. Say you had owned ten thousand yuan and spent one-fifth of it on your brother-in-law, counting that as a loss. Then you could have married Manna a decade ago. If so, she would have had no difficulty in giving birth to a baby and wouldn't have harbored a grievance against you. You see, isn't money more powerful than love?

That's not true, Lin countered. We needed no money to help us fall in love, just as we need no money to consummate our marriage.

Really? Then why did you spend eleven hundred yuan for the wedding? Why have you two kept separate bank accounts?

Lin was at a loss for an answer, but he suppressed that cold voice. For a long while he remained in the bathroom, which was the only quiet place where he could be unobserved. Now he was sitting on the windowsill with his back against the wall, absentmindedly watching the backyard. It was already dark; beyond the screen mosquitoes were humming and fire-flies were drawing little arcs. From a dormitory house a harmonica was shrieking out "The Internationale" disjointedly. A truck driver was burning oily rags at the corner of the garage, a bucket of water standing by him. Far away on the hill a cluster of gas lamps were flickering in a temporary api-ary. Some beekeepers were still busy collecting honey over there despite the nightfall.

Somehow Lin's right eye began smarting, as though a for-eign object had entered it. He removed his glasses and rubbed his eye with his fingertip. But the more he rubbed it, the more it hurt. He stood up, went to the sink, and put his head side-ways beneath the spout so that the stream could rinse his eye. The cold water, falling over his cheeks and forehead, re-freshed him.

No sooner had he turned off the faucet than a piercing scream came from Manna, which reminded him that he must have stayed in the bathroom at least half an hour and that it was time to go back. He wiped his face with his handkerchief, put on his glasses, and hurried out.

As he entered the delivery room again, his wife was wailing, "Oh! I hate you . . . Too late . . . So many years . . . I'm dying, too old for this baby."

"Manna, I'm sorry," he said. "Don't bring up old scores, okay? Concentrate on——"

"All right, no cervix left." Haiyan waved to Nurse Yu and Snow Goose to come closer and help. "Manna, let's push. Take a deep breath. Ready?"

She nodded.

Haiyan counted, "One . . . two . . . *go.*"

She pushed, her face purple and swollen. Lin noticed that Haiyan's face was puffy, as red as a boiled crab.

The second Manna exhaled, she yelled at him again, "Damn you, it's too late. Rice Bag . . . Chicken Heart!"

"Please don't be so nasty," he begged.

"Ah, I'm dying. Damn your mother!"

Snow Goose turned aside and tittered, but she stopped at Manna's stare. Ashamed, Lin let go of his wife's shoulder and made for the door again. Haiyan grasped his arm and whispered, "Lin, you should stay."

"I—I can't."

"It's common for a woman in labor to go berserk. She called me names too. But we shouldn't mind. You know, this makes her feel better. You mustn't take her words to heart. She's frightened and needs you to be with her."

He shook his head and went out without another word.

Manna yelled after him, "Go to hell, coward! I don't want to see your face before I die."

Haiyan returned to the birth bed and said, "Come on, let's push again."

"No, I can't," Manna cried. "Cut me open, Haiyan. I beg of you. Please give me . . . a cesarean."

The corridor was lit dimly, though some people were on night duty in the building. Lin paced up and down in the hall, chain-smoking; his mind was numb, blank, and slightly dazed. Meanwhile his wife's screams and curses were echoing through the floor. Some people went past the delivery room time and again to try to make out what she was shouting. Lin sat down on a long bench, his face buried in his hands. He felt pity for himself. Why do I have to go through this? he thought. I never wanted a baby.

He remembered that half a year ago a peasant woman had lain on this very bench, bleeding and waiting to be treated. Her husband had thrust two large batteries into her vagina, because he had incurred a thousand-yuan fine for having a second baby and she had once more failed to give him a son. The barefoot doctor in the village couldn't get the batteries out, so she was carted to the army hospital. Lin vividly remembered that she was skinny and young, her face half-covered by a sky-blue bandanna and a blood vessel on her temple pulsating like an earthworm. Her round eyes gazed at him emotionlessly as he paused to observe her. He was amazed by her eyes, which were devoid of any trace of resentment, and he saw lice and nits like sesame seeds in her permed hair.

Now he couldn't help thinking, Why do people have to live like animals, eating and reproducing, possessed by the instinct for survival? What point is there in having a dozen sons if your own life is miserable and senseless? Probably people are afraid, afraid of disappearing from this world—traceless and completely forgotten, so they have children to leave reminders of themselves. How selfish parents can be. Then why does it have to be a son? Can't a girl serve equally well as a reminder of her parents? What a crazy, stupid custom, which demands that every couple have a baby boy to carry on the family line.

He remembered the saying "Raise a son for your old

years." He reasoned, Even though a boy is believed superior
to a girl, his life may not be easy either. He will have to become a provider for his parents when he grows up. Selfish.
How often parents have sons so that they can exploit them in
the future. They prefer boys to girls mainly because sons will
provide more, are worth more as capital.

His thoughts were interrupted by a burst of squalling from
the delivery room. The door opened and Nurse Yu beckoned
him to come in. He stubbed out the cigarette on his rubber
sole, dropped it into a spittoon by the bench, and rose to his
feet, shuffling to the door.

"Congratulations," Haiyan said the moment he stepped in.
"You have two sons."

"You mean twins?"

"Yes."

The nurses showed him the crying babies, who looked almost identical, each weighing just over five pounds. They
were bony, with big heads, thick joints, flat noses, red
shrunken skin, and closed eyes. Their faces were puckered
like old men's. One of them opened his mouth as though
wanting to eat something to assert his existence. The other
one had an ear whose auricle was folded inward. They were
so different from what Lin had expected that he was overwhelmed with disgust.

"Look," Haiyan said to Lin. "They take after you."

"Like two exact copies of you," Snow Goose chimed in,
gently patting the back of the baby she was holding in her arms.

He turned and looked at his wife. She smiled at him faintly
with tear-stained eyes and mumbled, "Sorry, I was so scared.
I thought I couldn't make it. My heart almost burst."

"You did well." He put the back of his hand on her cheek.
Meanwhile, Haiyan began giving Manna stitches to sew up
the torn cervix and the incision of the episiotomy. The sight of

the bloody cut made Lin's skin crawl, and he turned his head, nauseated.

An hour later two male nurses came. They placed Manna on a stretcher, covered her with blankets, and carried her home. Lin followed them, holding the babies in his arms and shivering with cold. The moon was glistening on the willow and maple crowns; beetles and grasshoppers were chirring madly. The leaves and branches, heavy with dew, bent down slightly, while the grass on both sides of the road looked spiky and thick in the coppery light of the street lamps. A toad was croaking like a broken horn from a distant ditch partly filled with foamy water. Lin felt weak and aged; he was unsure whether he cared for the twins and whether he would be able to love them devotedly. Watching their covered faces, somehow he began to imagine trading places with them, having his life start afresh. If only he himself had been carried by someone like this now; then he would have led his life differently. Perhaps he would never have had a family.

9

Manna was given fifty-six days of maternity leave. During the first week she could hardly move about, so Lin did all the housework and cooked for her. She didn't have enough milk for the twins, though Lin made her eat a large bowl of pigs' feet soup a day to increase lactation. The babies had to be fed every three or four hours; because it took at least a month to secure the daily delivery of fresh milk, for the time being Lin had to get powdered milk for them, which was in short supply. Luckily Haiyan helped him buy eight pounds of milk powder in town, though at a higher price.

In the second week after Manna's delivery, Lin hired a maid from a suburban village, a short, freckle-faced girl with a pair of long braids. Her name was Juli. On weekdays she cooked and helped Manna look after the babies, but she returned home at night and couldn't come on Sundays.

Manna meanwhile was getting weaker and weaker. Sometimes she had heartburn and breathed with difficulty as though suffering from asthma. A murmur was detected in her heart. The cardiogram indicated she had a heart condition, which shocked Lin. He withheld the information from her for a week, then decided to let her know. When he told her the truth, she shed a few tears, not for herself but for their babies.

"It doesn't matter for me," she said. "The earlier I die, the sooner I can free myself from this world."

"What nonsense," he said. "I want you to live!"

She lifted her face, and the desperate look in her eyes disconcerted him. "Lin, I want you to promise me something."

"What?"

"Promise me that you'll love and take care of our babies when I'm gone."

"Don't think of that. You'll—"

"Promise me, please!"

"All right, I promise."

"You'll never abandon them."

"I won't, of course."

"Thank you. You've made me feel better." Unconsciously her right palm was rubbing her sore nipple.

Her words upset him, but he had no idea how to distract her from thinking of death. All he could do was insist she must not exert herself in any way or worry about anything. Let him do the housework and receive any visitor she was reluctant to meet.

After an extended argument between the parents, the twins were finally named River and Lake. Their father didn't like the names very much because they sounded too common, but their mother believed the commonness was a major advantage, arguing that with plain names the boys would be easier to raise. Besides, both the characters "river" and "lake" contain the element of water, which represents natural vitality and is pliable, enduring, and invincible.

Many officers' wives came to see the twins, who looked identical to them. The visitors kept asking Lin and Manna, "Which one is River?" or "Is this Lake?" Indeed it was difficult to tell who was who. Even the maid sometimes had to remember that River had a slightly folded ear.

The visitors brought along eggs, brown sugar, dried dates, and millet, saying these things could enrich Manna's blood. Several women told her that she should eat a lot of eggs, at least six hundred in two months, to strengthen her bones. By tradition it was believed that if the mother was well cared for and well nourished in the weeks after childbirth, most of her

illnesses would naturally disappear. So some women advised
Manna to take care not to catch cold when she went out and
not to be too stingy to spend money on nutritious food. Their
words saddened Manna, reminding her of her heart condition,
of which few people knew.

The visitors all congratulated the couple on having two
sons. "You landed two birds with a single bullet," one would
say. And another, "What a lucky man!" In everybody's eyes
Lin was extraordinarily fortunate, because since the 1970s a
rule had allowed no couple to have more than one child. But
Lin now had two sons and also a grown daughter. His old
roommate Jin Tian was upset when he heard Lin had two
boys, because his wife had borne him only a girl. He suggested that Lin do something to celebrate this great fortune,
either throw a party or distribute some candies and cigarettes.
But Lin was too exhausted to think about that.

Though she managed to eat six or seven eggs a day,
Manna's health kept deteriorating. It was beyond her ability
to breast-feed and look after the twins. Juli, the maid, could
help only a little, because the babies slept a lot in the daytime
and would remain awake at night, playing and crying. To stop
them from disturbing the neighbors in the same dormitory
house, Lin had to hold them by turns. In the beginning, his
holding could calm the babies, but soon they wanted more
motion and wouldn't allow their father to sit down, so Lin had
to pace back and forth to stop them from crying. In addition,
he had to hum tunes incessantly. Though exhausted and
heavy-eyed, he dared not discontinue. At times he was so miserable that he felt like crying together with his sons, but he
controlled himself.

Soon neither of the twins wanted to be left in bed for a
minute; the moment Lin put down the calmed one to pick up
the screaming one, the babies would join forces crying loudly.
So Manna began to take part in pacing the floor. As a result,

neither of the parents could get enough sleep. This was too much, but they had no choice. A few weeks later Juli suggested that they get a swaying crib, the rocking of which might keep the babies quiet. Lin bought a large crib immediately and tied its ends to ropes secured to the window frame and the door lintel. The crib worked miraculously; the parents didn't have to pace the room at night anymore. Instead, Lin would sit on the bed and go on rocking the crib, while the babies made noises continually as though talking to their father.

In the meantime, the boys were growing rapidly, each having gained two inches and six pounds in two months. River was now slightly bigger than his younger brother Lake.

One morning Juli pushed the baby carriage out of the hospital to watch a column of police trucks parading criminals through the streets. Two drug dealers had been sentenced to death and a rapist to life. Each of the criminals carried above his head a wooden placard whose base was tied to his back. A young woman was also among them; she, who had once been a teacher in a kindergarten, had locked a naughty boy in a basement to teach him a lesson, but she had forgotten to release him. The child had starved to death, and she was going to serve fourteen years in prison.

When the twins returned home, their faces became bluish. Manna was unhappy and told Juli never to take them out in the freezing weather again. That afternoon the babies began to have loose bowels.

Their father took them to Doctor Min, a young pediatrician who had just graduated from the Second Military Medical University. The diagnosis was dysentery. Like deflated balloons, the twins seemed to have withered all of a sudden, their heads drooping and their eyes lusterless, both whimpering a little and breathing heavily. Juli was scared, declaring tearfully that she hadn't fed them anything unclean. Neither Manna nor Lin blamed her more, though they were baffled by the cause of the disease. Probably the babies' drinking water hadn't been boiled long enough to kill all the bacteria.

To prevent dehydration, the twins had to be given an intravenous drip of glucose and salt water without delay. The nurses went about working on Lake and River at the same time, but the babies' blood vessels were hardly visible and were so thin that the nurses tried several times unsuccessfully to lodge a needle into them. The twins were screaming hoarsely. To Lin, his sons' arms looked almost transparent, so he was impatient with the nurses who couldn't find their blood vessels. Yet he dared not try to do it himself; neither could he watch for long the needles probing beneath his sons' tender skin. They made his heart twinge and his chest contract. For the first time in his life he was experiencing this kind of paternal suffering, which caused him to tremble a little. He realized that he did love the babies, his nose twitching and tears welling up in his eyes. If only he could substitute for them!

Doctor Min prescribed coptis powder, which is said to be the bitterest thing on earth and which the babies had to take three times a day. No matter how much sugar the parents mixed with the yellow powder, the twins would cry hard when forced to swallow the medicine. The parents and the maid worked as a team, one holding River, another pinching his nose shut and prying open his mouth with a spoon, and the third thrusting the spoonful of coptis powder mixed with sugar into his mouth, then washing it down with warm water. Done with River, they went on to Lake, who had been bawling furiously.

A week later the dysentery still persisted; every day each of the babies would relieve his bowels six or seven times. Juli had to take them to the medical building for the drips every afternoon. Their parents were desperate.

Hua came on Sunday morning. At the sight of her stricken half brothers she couldn't stop her tears. She reminded her fa-

ther that purslane might help, since in their home village people always used this herb to treat loose bowels. Lin remembered that several years ago when he visited a clinic in the
countryside, he had seen barefoot doctors cook purslane stew
in a cauldron. The villagers who suffered from diarrhea or
dysentery would go to the front yard of the clinic and eat a
bowl of the stew. At most it took three bowls to cure the illness. But now it was wintertime; where on earth could he find
purslane?

Nevertheless, he bicycled downtown right away, believing
some medicinal herb stores might have dried purslane. He
went to every one of them in Muji, but was told that this was
an item that no herb store would carry.

"Why not?" he asked.

"It's a tradition, I don't know why not. Perhaps because it's
just a vegetable," a beardless old clerk told him.

The babies were getting weaker and weaker. Apparently
the coptis powder didn't work. As a last resort, Doctor Min
decided to give them enemas, to wash their bowels with coptis solution directly. This treatment turned out to be very effective. Within three days, new tests showed that the bacteria
had disappeared from the babies' intestines. Yet the symptom
did not diminish; the twins continued to have loose bowels. In
addition, they wouldn't pass water: their urine was excreted
through their anuses.

Doctor Min was totally bewildered by this case. After two
days' thinking she decided that though the dysentery had been
cured, the twins still suffered from a nervous disorder that
was impossible for her to treat. She said to the nurses, "I'm
afraid we have to let nature take its own course."

Lin and Manna were at their wits' end, since nobody knew
what to do about the babies' nervous disorder. A cook suggested they give the twins some mashed garlic. They told him
that the babies were too young for that. Besides, garlic mainly

works as an antibiotic, and the bacteria in the babies' intestines had been eliminated.

Then Hua came one evening and told her father, "Mother said you should feed them some mashed taro mixed with white sugar and egg yolk."

"How come she's so sure it will work?" Lin asked. Manna moved closer, listening intently.

"Mother said it helped me once," Hua answered. "When I was five and had dysentery, Mother made me drink a lot of herb decoction, but it didn't cure the disease. Our neighbors thought I was dying and couldn't be saved. Uncle Bensheng ran to Wujia Town and got the recipe from an old doctor."

"How do you cook the egg yolk?" Manna broke in.

"Just hard-boil the eggs."

Though still doubtful, without delay Lin bought five pounds of taros from a vegetable shop and prepared the folk remedy. The twins enjoyed eating the mashed taro, opening their mouths like baby swallows receiving food from the mother bird. To everyone's amazement, that very night the babies stopped defecating. Within two days they began to urinate normally. Many doctors and nurses harbored misgivings about folk remedies, but this time everybody was impressed.

At long last the twins were cured, and Lin was possessed by a new, mysterious emotion, which occasionally brought tears to his eyes. He felt the babies had almost become a part of himself. The week before, he had read in *Heilongjiang Daily* that a retired clerk had donated a kidney to his son. These days Lin kept asking himself whether he could do the same for his children.

10

Along with their dysentery, the babies' nightly wakefulness was also cured. Now they would go to sleep early in the evening and remain peaceful until daybreak. Even when they were given the bottle at midnight and when their father changed their diapers, they would make no noise. Their normal sleep made it possible for their parents to spend some time together in the evening. After the babies fell asleep, Lin and Manna often lounged on the sofa, chatting or watching news or a movie on TV. At last they could enjoy a little peace.

One evening in late November there was a featured report on TV entitled "To Get Rich Is Glorious," which showed how some people in the South had responded to the Party's call and grown affluent. A young man had bought dried mushrooms and ginseng roots from Manchuria and sold them in Fujian Province at higher prices, and within five years he owned seven stores in different cities. An engineer had quit his regular job and made a fortune by running two chicken farms, which employed 130 hands. A middle-aged woman had opened a clothing shop just three years ago, but now she had become a local magnate and had hired sixty workers to make fashionable garments in her shop. At the last Spring Festival she donated ten thousand yuan to an elementary school, so she was admitted into the Communist Party and elected a model citizen. Every one of these entrepreneurs became a legendary figure. A few years ago their ways of making money had been illegal, but now the nouveaux riches were held up as examples for the masses to follow.

Manna was grating turnips over a terra-cotta basin, while Lin, never interested in making money, was reading a back issue of *Popular Medicine,* fascinated by an article about a folk way of getting rid of kidney stones. As he was wondering why sesame oil and walnuts were prescribed in the recipe, the woman reporter announced on TV, "Now we have another rich man, from Feidong County, Anhui Province. Comrade Geng Yang."

At the mention of that name, Manna let out a moan and dropped the steel grater into the basin. Lin turned his head and asked, "What's wrong?"

She didn't respond, her eyes riveted on the TV screen. He turned and saw Geng Yang's face growing larger and closer. It was almost the same as eleven years before, sallow and long, only less stern and marked with a few wrinkles. Geng Yang had some gray hair now, but he was bulkier and darker, a picture of health.

The young reporter asked him, "Are you the richest man in Feidong County?"

He beamed, licking his upper lip. "Well, I never thought I could get rich. I owe it entirely to our Party's great policy." Behind him a crane was hoisting a load of bricks onto a building under construction. Three clusters of white sparks were radiating from welding torches in the air. Somewhere a steam hammer was clanking rhythmically.

"How much did you make last year?" The woman raised the microphone close to his mouth.

"Twenty thousand yuan."

"Wow, that's about twenty times the amount you pay a worker. How come you made so much?"

His eyes flickered as though fireflies were flitting in his pupils. Manna recognized the same lustful look in those eyes. "Well," he said, "this construction company used to lose money all the time. Three years ago they set up a new policy: Whoever managed this company would get ten percent of its profit; but if the company lost money again, the manager would have to pay three percent of the loss out of his own pocket. Nobody would take the risk of steering such a sinking boat. I was the daredevil that stepped in to try." He tipped his head back and gave a hearty laugh.

"How did you make this company profitable within a year?"

"By strengthening discipline and order, by rewarding and punishing the workers fairly and strictly. Everyone here must do his job efficiently, or else we'll dock a certain amount from his wages. Now the company is organized like an army unit— a battalion, I should say. Each team must carry out its task on time, and I hold its leaders responsible for any delay and sloppy work."

"How about this year? How much profit do you expect to get personally?"

"Probably twenty-three thousand."

"So you're having another banner year?"

"Yes."

"Thank you, Manager Geng."

As the camera panned away from Geng Yang to a roaring bulldozer on the construction site, Manna burst out sobbing, wiping her cheeks with the sleeve of her shirt. Meanwhile Lin was flabbergasted at Geng Yang's appearance on TV. How could that devil be doing so well? So full of vitality? Enjoying so much fortune and publicity? No wonder Honggan had called him a lucky dog at their wedding last winter.

Lin got to his feet and went over to Manna as she was screaming, "It's unfair, unfair!"

"Shh, don't wake up the babies." He sat down beside her, removed the half-grated turnip from her hand and put it into the basin. He held her hand, lifted it up, and pressed it against his cheek. Her fingers were still wet and flecked with bits of turnip, giving off a pungent smell.

"How come an evil man like him can get rich and famous so easily?" she asked. "The Lord of Heaven has no eyes!"

Lin sighed, shaking his head. "Life's always like this, ridiculous—a monster thrives for a thousand years, while the good suffer and die before their time."

"How I'm scared of him!" she moaned in tears.

He turned and embraced her, whispering, "Don't be scared. He's not here. I won't let him hurt you."

Gently he twisted the tip of her ear to calm her down, as though she were a little girl who had just come in from a pitch-black night. He went on murmuring, "Don't be scared." She put her arms around him and buried her face in his chest.

His words and the warmth of his body invoked in her the old overpowering pain that had arisen from the absence of consolation during the first days after the rape eleven years before, so now she simply couldn't stop crying, holding him tight and whimpering incoherently. Something in her chest snapped as tears flowed out of her eyes. It was so good to have a trustworthy friend in whose arms she could cry without feeling embarrassed, without being afraid of the kind of ridicule unleashed by the hostile world, without worrying about becoming the target of endless gossip and mockery, and without having to say, "Forgive me." For the first time she was weeping with abandon, like a child. Her tears soaked the front of his woolen vest. Her thick hair kept touching his chin. He grew tearful too and stroked the nape of her neck.

From that night on, they slept in the same bed again. Many days in a row Manna had nightmares, which were bizarre and indecipherable. In one of them, she was on her way to a nunnery atop a mountain, carrying the twins on her back. It was a sunny day, the breeze sweet-scented, full of scattered blossoms. As she approached a reservoir, which she had to cross to reach the mountain, an old man in a conical bamboo hat was coming along the rocky dam from the opposite direction.

From the distance she couldn't see his face clearly, but his gait was so tottery that he didn't look dangerous. The babies on her back were sleeping, exhausted by the heat, saliva dribbling from the corners of their opened mouths.

As the man was coming closer, suddenly a gust of wind blew his hat off, revealing his face. It was Geng Yang! Manna was too shocked to shout or escape. He rushed over, grabbed her by the scruff of the neck, snatched the twins off her back, and ran away along the dam. She shouted while chasing him, "Give them back to me! Geng Yang, you can do anything to me if you give my babies back! I promise I'll come to you if you let them go." The babies were screaming and kicking their legs.

Without turning his head, Geng Yang swerved and ran down the dam toward a sandy bar, his boots throwing up a thin mist of dust. She was gasping for breath, but went on pursuing him. Then she saw him put the twins each into a giant wooden shoe, which he pushed into the water. A wind came and blew the shoes away toward the center of the vast reservoir. He burst out laughing. "Now you lost your sons. See if you dare to report me again!"

She collapsed on the ground, shouting, "I've never reported you. Please, please, I beg of you, have a heart, bring them back for me!"

"No, they're on their way to see the Dragon Emperor in the Water Palace, ha-ha-ha."

"Lin! Come and help me!" she called out.

"That chicken can't do a thing," Geng Yang said.

"Lin—come and save our children!" she yelled again. Still Lin was nowhere to be seen.

At this moment Mai Dong, her first love, came out of the osier bushes on the bank and began capering about on the beach. He waved his hands and then clapped them above his head, chanting to her merrily, "You can't have them back! You can't have them back!" He was still in his mid-twenties, wearing the army uniform and a crew cut.

She became murderous and picked up a few large cobblestones and threw them at Geng Yang and Mai Dong with all her might.

"Ouch!" Lin yelled as Manna's fist landed on his forehead. He pulled the lamp cord, and the blinding light woke her up. She kept rubbing her eyes.

"Why hit me like that? Oh, my eyes—" Lin stopped, seeing his wife in tears, her face horror-stricken.

"Sorry, sorry, I was having a terrible dream," she said and turned aside. "I dreamed that we lost our children and couldn't get them back." She began sobbing while her arm covered the sleeping babies.

Lin sighed. "Don't think too much, darling."

"I won't," she said. "You go back to sleep now."

He turned off the light and soon resumed snoring softly. Meanwhile Manna's eyes were wide open, watching the clouds being torn to strips by the bare branches waving outside the window. She was wondering why Lin hadn't appeared in her dream, whereas Mai Dong had turned up and ridiculed her so maliciously. What does this mean? she asked herself. Why didn't Lin come to our rescue? Where was he? Is he really too timid to fight to protect us? Why was Mai Dong as mean as that bastard Geng Yang?

Question after question rose to her mind, but she couldn't answer any of them. Her thoughts were in disorder.

Outside, the moon was pale, wavering beyond the dark treetops. The wind was howling and reminded her of the wolves she had often heard at night when she was a child in the orphanage.

11

Manna's heart grew weaker, her pulse more irregular and sometimes thready. Severe pains occurred in her chest and left arm, and at nightfall she would feel dizzy and short of breath. Her heart murmur often turned into a gallop rhythm. The results of a new examination shocked Doctor Yao, an expert in cardiopathy. One afternoon, holding Manna's X-ray against a desk lamp in his office, Doctor Yao told Lin, "Medication may not help her anymore. I'm afraid she doesn't have many years left. Heaven knows why her condition has deteriorated so rapidly."

Hearing the prognosis, Lin almost broke into tears. He said in a choked voice, "Why—why did I let this happen? I'm a doctor, why didn't I detect the real condition of her heart?" He covered his face with both hands.

"Lin, don't blame yourself. We all knew she had a heart problem, but we didn't expect infarction would develop so soon. Some of her coronary vessels must have been blocked long ago."

"Oh, I should have known this. I told her not to eat too many eggs, but she wouldn't listen." Lin struck his knee with his fist.

Doctor Yao sighed. "I wish we had diagnosed it."

"So there's no cure?"

"I've heard some experts in Europe can dilate the coronary arteries, but the technology is not available in our country."

"What should I do?"

"Lin, I'm sorry." Doctor Yao held Lin's upper arm and shook it gently, meaning he had no idea either. "But you must not be too emotional. Cheer up a little—she depends on you."

He paused for a moment while Lin rubbed his stomach with the palm of his hand as though assuaging a pain. Doctor Yao went on, "Don't let her do any physical work, don't make her lose her temper, just make life easy for her."

Lin lowered his head and muttered, "I'll try my best."

"If I were you, I wouldn't tell her about her heart condition, just keep her happy."

"I won't let her know, of course."

Despite Lin's effort to guard the secret, word of Manna's illness soon began circulating in the hospital. The rumor went wild and even claimed that she would definitely die within a year. In a few weeks Manna heard about the true condition of her heart, but she took it with surprising serenity, saying to Lin that she knew her life would be over soon. Her words distressed him.

As she got weaker, her temper became worse. She often yelled at Juli and Lin; sometimes she cried for no apparent reason, like a self-willed child.

Lin tried to do as much housework as he could. He washed diapers on weekends when Juli didn't come to work. In midwinter the tap water was ice cold. His hands ached and itched while he scrubbed at the faucet in front of the house. He had never expected that washing laundry would be a part of his married life. Throughout those years before the marriage, he had washed only his socks and underwear since Manna did his laundry for him. Now, a pile of diapers would be waiting for him every weekend. He dared not complain or think too much, for things could be worse. In spite of all the difficulties, they could afford to hire a maid and he didn't have to wash laundry on weekdays.

On Saturday evenings he would carry out to the faucet a load of baby clothes and diapers and a kettle of hot water, which he would pour over two or three fistfuls of soap powder, and then he would soak the laundry in the suds for a moment. Under the mercury street lamp, the water would glisten in the large basin. Through the loudspeaker atop the roof of the medical building, a soft female voice often sang "A Large River Long and Wide" and "The Five-Starred Red Flag Flies High." Lin would set the washboard against the rim of the sink and start scrubbing the laundry piece by piece with a squishing sound. Soon the detergent water lost its suds and turned cold, and he had to blow on his fingers again and again in order to continue. The toughest part was to rinse the soaped, scrubbed laundry, because there was no hot water available after the initial soak and the tap water was so cold it seemed to bite his fingers with teeth. Yet he kept washing quietly and always avoided greeting those who came to fetch water.

People noticed that Lin's face had grown bony, his cheeks more prominent now. His trousers became baggy on him. Commissar Su's wife would tell her neighbors, "Lin Kong has lost his hips. It's heaven's retribution, serves him right. See who dares to abandon his wife again." Whenever she saw Lin, she would glower at him, spit to the ground, and stamp her feet. He ignored her as though he hadn't heard or seen her. But unlike the crazy woman, his colleagues had stopped joking about him; instead they would shake their heads behind his back.

He was grateful that Hua often came on weekends. She sometimes helped him with the laundry and looked after the babies. She liked feeding them with only one nursing bottle, which made them compete to suck it and crow with pleasure. They would laugh and put out their fat little hands whenever she teased them, calling them "my little precious" while pressing her chin against their chests. She had made them each a bunny hat with frills. By now Manna had become friendly to Hua and had even bought her a pink cardigan. She once told Lin that if only she could have had a daughter like Hua.

After a long sick leave, Manna returned to the Medical Ward. She could work only half a day, but she was paid a full salary. She spent afternoons at home.

One Sunday morning in January, Lin was cooking rice for lunch. While the pot was boiling, he set out for the mess hall to buy a dish. The previous evening, he had seen a notice on the small blackboard at the entrance to the kitchen, saying there would be beef and fried potato for lunch, seventy fen a helping. On his way there he ran into Commissar Su. They talked for a while about initiating a crash program for training paramedics from the local counties the next spring. The prefecture's Department of Public Health had just asked the army hospital for help and was willing to finance the program. This meant the hospital's staff would receive a larger bonus at the end of next year.

Because of the talk, Lin forgot the rice boiling at home. When he got back with a bowl of potato and beef, the kitchen was white with smoke. He rushed to the cooking range, put the bowl down, and removed the pot. The second he opened the lid a wave of steam clouded his glasses and made him unable to see anything. After wiping the lenses with the end of his jacket and putting the glasses back on, he saw that the rice was already burned through. He picked up an iron scoop and was about to put a little water into the pot when Manna came into the kitchen, coughing and buttoning her jacket. "Put a scallion into the pot, quick!" she shouted.

Lin planted a scallion stalk into the rice to get rid of the burned smell, but it was too late, a good part of the rice was already brown. He pushed the transom open to let the smoke out.

Suddenly Manna yelled at him, "Why did you leave while the rice pot was boiling? You can't even cook such a simple thing, idiot."

"I—I went to buy a dish. You were home, why couldn't you keep an eye on it?"

"You didn't tell me, did you? Besides, I'm too sick to cook. Don't you know that?" With her fingertips holding the cuff of her sleeve, she swept the pot and the bowl off the cooking range; they crashed to the cement floor; beef and potato cubes and smoking rice were scattered about. The aluminum lid of the pot rolled away and hit the threshold, where it came to rest, leaning upright against two bricks piled together as a doorstop.

"Even pigs won't touch this," she added.

From inside the bedroom Lake broke out crying, then screamed at the top of his lungs. A few seconds later River started bawling too. Manna hurried back in to calm them. Without tending to the stove or cleaning up, Lin turned and stormed out. His green mittens, connected by a string, flapped wildly beside his flanks as he strode away. "I hate her! I hate her!" he said to himself.

He went to the hill behind the hospital grounds. It was a cold day. The orchard on the slope was deserted, the apple-pear trees thick and bulky, their frosty branches sprawling and looking feathery. For a while he couldn't think of anything, his skull numb and his temples tight. He climbed toward the hilltop, which was covered by snow except for two clusters of brownish rocks. Beyond the hill, on the riverbank, there was a village that had a deer farm and a boat house, which Lin for some reason wanted to watch from the crown of the hill. The scent of winter was clean and intense. It was windless, and the sun was glinting on the boulders here and there and on the tree trunks crusted with ice. In the distance a flock of rooks were circling and cawing hungrily.

As Lin calmed down, a voice rose in his head and said, Do you really hate her?

He made no reply.

The voice continued, You asked for this mess. Why did you marry her?

I love her, he answered.

You married her for love? You really loved her?

He thought a while, then managed to answer, I think so. We waited eighteen years for each other, didn't we? Doesn't such a long time prove we love each other?

No, time may prove nothing. Actually you never loved her. You just had a crush on her, which you didn't get a chance to outgrow or to develop into love.

What? A crush! He was taken aback and paused in his tracks. His sinuses became congested.

Yes, you mistook your crush for love. You didn't know what love was like. In fact you waited eighteen years just for the sake of waiting. You could have waited that long for another woman too, couldn't you?

I waited for Manna only. There wasn't another woman involved.

All right, there were only the two of you. Let's assume you and she loved each other. Were you sure that you both would enjoy living together as husband and wife?

We really loved each other, didn't we? Lin's temples were throbbing, and he took off his hat so that the cold air could cool his head.

Really? the voice resumed. What do you know about love? Did you know her well enough before you married her? Were you sure she was the woman you'd spend the rest of your life with? Be honest now, among all the women you've known, who are you most fond of? Isn't there someone else who is more suitable for you than Manna?

I can't tell. Besides her there's only Shuyu in my life. How could I compare Manna with someone else? I don't know much about women, although I wish I did.

Suddenly he felt his head expanding with a shooting pain. He was giddy with the intuition that this marriage might not be what he had wanted. He sat down on a rock to catch his breath and think more.

The voice went on, Yes, you waited so many years, but for what?

He found his mind blank and couldn't answer. The question frightened him, because it implied that all those years he had waited for something wrong.

Let me tell you what really happened, the voice said. All those years you waited torpidly, like a sleepwalker, pulled and pushed about by others' opinions, by external pressure, by your illusions, by the official rules you internalized. You were misled by your own frustration and passivity, believing that what you were not allowed to have was what your heart was destined to embrace.

Lin was stunned. For a moment he was at a loss for words. Then he began cursing himself. Fool, eighteen years you waited without knowing for what! Eighteen years, the prime of your life, gone, wasted, and they led you to this damn marriage. You're a model fool!

What's to be done now? the voice asked.

He heaved a deep sigh, not knowing what to do or whether he should try to do something. Tears were sliding down his cheeks and reached the corners of his mouth; time and again he raised his hand to wipe them off. His ears were freezing, so he put the fur hat back on and turned down its earflaps.

Then the image of Manna in her late twenties emerged in his mind. She had a vivacious face smiling radiantly; on her palm perched a tiny green frog, its mouth quivering. A few sky-blue dragonflies were flying around her, their wings issuing a whirring sound. As Lin stretched out his hand to touch the frog's back, it jumped and plopped into the limpid stream flowing along the edge of an eggplant field. She turned and looked at him, her eyes dim with affection and kindness, as though full of secrets that she was eager to share with him. The end of her loose hair was thrown up a little by the warm breeze, revealing the silky nape of her neck. How different she was now from then! He realized that the long waiting must have changed her profoundly—from a pleasant young woman into a hopeless spitfire. No matter how he felt about her now, he was certain she had always loved him. Perhaps it was the unrequited love that had dragged her down. Or perhaps it was the suffering and despondency she had experienced in the long waiting that had dissolved her gentle nature, worn away her hopes, ruined her health, poisoned her heart, and doomed her.

The voice interrupted his thoughts. Yes, she has loved you. But isn't it this marriage that has been debilitating her?

He tried to answer, She wanted a family and children, didn't she? She must have been starved for human warmth and affection, any bit of which she might have taken as love. Yes, she's been blind to the true situation, always believing I loved her. She doesn't know what a true lover is like.

His heart began aching. It dawned on him that he had never loved a woman wholeheartedly and that he had always been the loved one. This must have been the reason why he knew so little about love and women. In other words, emotionally he hadn't grown up. His instinct and ability to love passionately had withered away before they had had an opportunity to blossom. If only he had fallen in love soulfully just once in his life, even though it might have broken his heart, paralyzed his mind, made him live in a daze, bathed his face in tears, and drowned him in despair!

What are you going to do? the voice kept on.

He could not think of an answer. Being a husband and a father, he felt he ought to carry out the responsibilities imposed on him by his marriage. What else could he do to alleviate his sense of guilt and convince himself that he was a decent man? What else could he do other than to endure?

He sighed. If only he had had enough passion and energy left in him so that he could learn how to love devotedly and start his life afresh. If only Manna were healthy and not dying. He was too old to take any action now. His heart was weary. He only hoped that before his wife died their sons would be old enough for kindergarten.

Down below, along the brick wall behind the hospital, a man and a woman were strolling eastward despite the cold weather. Both of them wore uniforms; the man was a head taller than the woman, who looked rather small and delicate. Every once in a while she would run a few steps to catch up with him. They looked familiar to Lin. Lin strained his eyes to make out who they were, but his sight failed him. It occurred to him that the rule that prohibited two people of opposite sex from walking together outside the wall had been almost abandoned in the past year. Few leaders would now bother to criticize young men and women who walked in pairs outside the compound. He had heard that some nurses had even gone into the woods with their patients. Yet somehow to him and Manna, there still seemed to be a wall around them. They had never walked together outside the hospital since they were married, and Manna still could not ride a bicycle.

A moment later Lin stood up and whisked the snow off his lap with the mittens. Instead of going up to the summit, he turned back at the middle of the slope, coming down slowly, weak at the knees. A few goats were bleating from the birch woods on the left; a line of cow dung dotted the white road, still sending up curls of steam. Up on the slope a cart was climbing toward the hilltop, its iron-rimmed wheels rattling away on pebbles and ice. Down there, at the foot of the hill, a tiny whirlwind was hurling dried leaves along the bank of the frozen brook, swirling away toward the vast field studded with corn stubble.

He reached home twenty minutes later. On opening the door, he was suddenly nauseated by the smell of rice vinegar, which had been blown into the air to deactivate the flu virus and which, before now, had always been pleasant to his nose. Manna came and told him in a soft voice that lunch was in the bamboo steamer on the cooking range. She had made noodles and fried some soy paste. But he didn't go to the kitchen. Instead, he went into the bedroom, flopped down on the camp bed, and pulled a blanket over his face. The bedsprings under him creaked as he turned now and then.

Manna began sobbing. For a while he didn't want to comfort her, for fear that he might join her in weeping if he tried. But a moment later he pulled himself together, got out of bed, and went up to her. Sitting down beside her, he put his arm around her shoulders and said, "Come, stop now, dear. You've cried enough. It's bad for your health." For the first time he felt she was as fragile as though her bones might fall apart at any moment. His heart was again filled with sadness and compassion. He kissed her cheek.

She raised her eyes and said with shame, "I was nasty. Can you forgive me?"

"Forget about it, darling. I should have been more careful."

"Say you forgive me."

"It wasn't your fault."

"Just say it!"

"I forgive you."

"Please eat lunch."

"I'm not hungry."

"Please eat."

"All right, if you say so." He tried to smile, but the effort distorted his face, which he turned aside to avoid being noticed. He got up and went to the kitchen.

12

"Why don't you escape?" That question came to Lin's mind now and then.

He couldn't help forming imaginary plans—withdrawing all the 900 yuan from his savings account, sneaking away at night to the train station, using an alias from now on, restarting his life in a remote town where no one knew him. Ideally he'd like to work as a librarian. But in the depths of his heart he knew he would have been weighed down with remorse if he had abandoned his family to seek his own happiness. Wherever he had gone, the hound of his conscience would have hunted him down.

When the Spring Festival was at hand, Manna said to him, "Why don't you take something to Shuyu before the holiday? Just to see how she's doing."

"Why do you want me to do that?" He was surprised.

"She must be lonely, no family around except Hua. Besides, don't you miss them?"

"All right, I'll go see them."

At first he thought perhaps Manna had suggested the visit because her illness had softened her feelings, or because she knew that the twins might depend on Hua and Shuyu's help in the future. Then he wondered, Isn't Manna a lonely woman herself? Did she imply that she didn't feel as lonely as Shuyu because she had a family intact? Can my role as a husband make such a difference? Do most married women feel the same way?

To some extent, he was eager to see how Shuyu was getting on, though he had heard from Hua that she was well. Her sciatica was greatly alleviated by hot baths she often took in

the match plant. But his daughter had also told him that sometimes her mother missed their home village. Shuyu would
say, "I'm like an old tree that can't be moved to another
place." She made Hua promise that next April the two of them
would go back to Goose Village to sweep the graves of Lin's
parents. Despite complaining, she enjoyed her life in the city.

Two days before the Spring Festival, Lin put into a duffel
bag four frozen mackerel and a bundle of garlic stems, both of
which had been allocated to their family by the hospital for
the holiday, and he was ready to set off for the Splendor
Match Plant. As he was leaving, Manna got up from the bed
and gazed at him. He had on his fur hat, with its earflaps tied
around his chin, and his hands in leather gloves were holding
the handlebars of their Peacock bicycle, which was an eco-
nomical brand, the only one that didn't require a coupon at the
time. Manna's eyes were glowing and wide open as though
unable to close. She bent down and kissed the elder baby
River, who was sleeping with his brother Lake in the suspended crib.

"Be careful," she said to Lin.

"I will."

"Come back early. I'll wait for you."

"Sure, I'll be home for dinner."

It was half past four in the afternoon and traffic was surging in the city. The sky was overcast with gray clouds and
smog. One after another lights flickered on in the two- and
three-story buildings on Spring Street, along which Lin bicycled. He was going to the city's west end. The tops of the
houses, covered with red pantiles and ice, turned murky in the
dusk, and the road was slippery with the snow pressed hard by
carts and automobiles. He told himself not to pedal fast. A
week ago a girl had been killed by a truck while bicycling on
this very street.

When he arrived at the plant, it was already dark; all the

houses had their lights on. Without difficulty he found Unit 12, which had been assigned to Hua recently and was in the middle of a dormitory house. Hearing his daughter singing from inside, he didn't knock on the door. He couldn't make out what she was singing, perhaps a dance song.

It had begun to snow lightly. From a tall smokestack in the south, a loudspeaker was announcing the evening news after the music of "The East Is Red, the Sun Is Rising." Outside the plant a few firecrackers exploded on the balconies of some residential buildings.

Uncertain whether he should go in, he remained at the window, whose panes had almost frosted over. He bent forward and looked in with one eye through an uncovered spot. Inside, Shuyu, in a white apron and a green cotton-padded jacket, looked healthy and happy. Mother and daughter were making pies together. A round bamboo grid on a kneading bowl held three rows of pies. Hua was rolling out the dough with a wooden pin, while her mother was using a spoon to stuff the pies with sugared red-bean paste. Shuyu looked younger now, somewhat urbanized; she reminded Lin of a professional cook. For some reason he was overwhelmed by the peaceful scene, and his throat tightened. He straightened up, looked around, and saw a few white cloth sacks, which must have been filled with frozen dumplings and pies, hanging outside some windows of another dormitory house. He remembered that back in their home village each family would make thousands of pies and dumplings at the end of the year and have them frozen in the storehouse, so that they wouldn't have to spend a lot of time preparing meals during the holiday season. Winter was the time to relax and enjoy themselves, and many men would gamble and get drunk every day.

Should he go in? He remembered that a few months ago a retired official had died of a stroke while getting together with his former family. The old man had left his home village with

the Communist army in the fall of 1943 and later divorced his
wife when he became a middle-ranking official in Harbin.
Forty years later, when he retired and went back to visit his
home village, he found his former wife still waiting for him
and their four children already raising their own families.
Overwhelmed by the family gathering, which consisted of
sixteen members of three generations, the old man had a
stroke at the dinner table and died two days later.

Now, standing outside the apartment, Lin was afraid he
might not be able to control his emotions if he went in. So he
left the duffel bag on the briquets piled beside the door. But
before he could move away, the bag fell to the ground, together with a thick bunch of frozen scallions that had hung
above the coal.

"Who is it?" Hua cried from inside.

The door opened. "Dad! Come in." She turned around and
shouted, "Mom, my dad is here."

Shuyu came out, rubbing her floury hands. "Don't stand in
the snow. Come on in," she said with a broad smile, as though
he had returned from a long trip.

Lin locked the bicycle and went in. The room was so warm
he took off his hat and glasses, which misted up instantly. He
kept wiping the lenses with his thumb and forefinger.

Both Shuyu and Hua urged him to get on the brick bed,
which was shiny and well heated, so he unlaced his boots and
climbed on it. He crossed his legs, covered them with a small
quilt, then removed his jacket. In no time Shuyu placed a large
mug of black tea on the low table before him. She said, "Drink
this to warm yourself up. It's so cold outside."

Sitting on the brick bed made him feel cozy. How he would
like to lie down and warm his back for a while. He was tired,
and the feeling of being at home moved him as he sipped the
tea and listened to his wife and daughter talking in the kitchen
and cooking dinner.

His heart was full, and he was breathing heavily. He looked around and saw four Spring Festival pictures on the walls, similar to those in their village home and each having at least one fat baby and a pair of giant peaches in it. The thought came to him that Shuyu and Hua could live quite well without him. This realization saddened him and made him feel like a good-for-nothing. "I'm a superfluous man," he muttered. That was a phrase he had read in a Russian novel long ago. The author's name escaped him.

He tried to recall the holidays in recent years and found himself at a loss—not a single one of them was distinguishable from the rest. He couldn't say that he had ever had a happy Spring Festival since he left Goose Village. His mind shifted from holidays to love, which perplexed him more because he had never spent a day with a woman he loved wholeheartedly—no, there had not been such a woman in his life and that emotion had been alien to him. Yet one thing he was certain about now: between love and peace of mind he would choose the latter. He would prefer a peaceful home. What was better than a place where you could sit down comfortably, read a book, and have a good meal and an unbroken sleep? Deep in his heart he knew this was merely wishful thinking, because soon he would have to return to Manna and their babies in the other home. He closed his eyes. What a mess he had made of his life and the lives of others!

Dinner was ready. Hua put on the table a cabbage salad mixed with cellophane noodles, a plate of stewed chicken, a small basket of fried pies made of glutinous-rice flour, and a casserole of sauerkraut and pork and tiny shrimps. Shuyu opened a bottle of wheat liquor and poured a full cup for Lin, telling him, "Bensheng asked Second Donkey to bring this bottle for you when he came to town."

"When did Second Donkey come?"

"Last week. He was here with his son Handong to buy a used truck. He's so rich now he wants to start a hauling business."

"How's Bensheng doing?"

"He's fine. Second Donkey says he envies you a lot."

"Your brother envies me?"

"Yes. Bensheng said, 'How come all good things happen to Lin? Why am I never that lucky? He has the best education, a high rank, and three kids.' "

"Why did he say that? Didn't he make a lot of money from his grocery store?"

"Don't know. Second Donkey said Bensheng burst into tears when he heard you got two sons. Never so jealous."

Lin raised his head, facing the sloped ceiling. He thought, How we're each sequestered in our own suffering! He turned to his daughter. "Get two more cups, Hua."

"We have only one cup, Dad." But she went out into the kitchen anyway.

"We have more good news," Shuyu said.

"What?"

"Hua's boyfriend, Fengjin, is going to leave the navy soon. He'll come here and join her. He wants to be engaged. Lin, in a few years we'll become grandparents, and our family is going to get bigger."

"Mom, don't talk about that please," Hua cut in, having returned with two small bowls.

Shuyu's words made Lin want to smile and weep at the same time. He closed his eyes for a few seconds, then he poured some liquor into the bowls and said, "We should all drink for this family reunion."

"Happy holiday!" Hua said to him.

They clinked the cup and bowls and drank. Shuyu said to him, "Try a pie and see how good we made it." With her chopsticks she put one of the two chicken legs in his bowl.

As he was eating, he remembered that this was the first time he had celebrated the Spring Festival with Shuyu and Hua, if he could call this a celebration. The holiday was still two days away. Every winter he had stayed at the hospital, and he had always returned home in summer. This memory upset him. Somehow he wished Shuyu and Hua had hated him and barred him from this home. That might have made him feel better, at least less attached to them. It was harder to bear their kindness.

He drank one cup after another, as though wanting to numb his mind and make himself forgetful.

"Dad, don't drink too much. You'll get drunk," his daughter said.

Shuyu glared at Hua, as if saying, Shut up, girl!

"I'll be all r-right," he said, raising his cup again.

Soon he was unable to control his emotions. He felt pathetic, eager to say something that could make them understand him, but his tongue seemed no longer his own.

He grabbed Shuyu's hand and said tearfully, "Sweetheart, I didn't mean to hurt you. Can, can you forgive me?"

"All right."

"I'm a bad, bad man, sweetheart."

"No, you're a good man."

"Oh, I don't want to be a good man. I just want to be a normal man."

"All right, you're not a good man then." Shuyu couldn't stop her tears by now, because this was the first time he had ever said an endearment to her.

"Don't, don't cry, dear," he went on. Somehow his vision blurred, and he saw Manna weeping before him, together with his sons. He rubbed his eyes and they vanished.

"I'm so happy, Lin, at last you came home," Shuyu said and glanced at their daughter, whose eyes were traveling between her parents' faces. Shuyu believed that now he was showing his true feeling about her, because a man would speak his heart when drunk.

"Oh, I was so stupid." He turned to his daughter. "You

know, Hua, Manna will die soon. She's a goner. Ah, she isn't a bad woman, but her heart can't last long."

"Daddy, stop please!"

"All right, all right, I'll shut up." But he embraced Shuyu with one arm, touching her face with his free hand, and asked, "Is that you, Shuyu?"

"Yes, it's me, your wife Shuyu."

"Sweetheart, will you wait for me? I'll come back to you soon. We are still, still one family, aren't we? Don't leave me. Manna's going to die in a year or two. Oh what—what should I do about the twins?"

"Please, don't talk like this. Don't worry your head about that."

"Will you help me?"

"All right, we'll help you, I promise. Don't be so upset." She turned to Hua and ordered, "Get a bowl of vinegar, quick. Your dad is real drunk."

He went on, "My dear, I'm so sad. My heart is so full, about to burst. I can't stand this damn life anymore!"

They made him drain a bowl of diluted vinegar. He fell on the warmer end of the brick bed, and an instant later began snoring tremulously. Having covered him with a thin cotton quilt, Shuyu told Hua, "Go call the hospital and let that woman know your dad is too drunk to go back tonight."

Wrapping a scarf around her head, Hua rushed out into the rustling snow. She ran toward the guard office, which had a telephone.

After breakfast with Shuyu and Hua, Lin returned to the hospital, his footsteps still infirm because of the hangover. Manna was relieved to see him back, saying, "You should've taken care not to drink too much. You're no longer a young man."

"I'm sorry." He put on the table the duffel bag, stuffed with hazelnuts and chestnuts.

"I only slept two hours last night. How I worried!" she said.

"I didn't mean to stay there. I left the fish and the garlic stems at their door, but Hua saw me before I could leave."

"How are they?"

"They're doing well, better than in the village."

"That's good to know."

Since the babies were sleeping, Lin and Manna began to prepare for the holiday. She stewed pork feet and a hen to make aspic, while he took their kettle out to do some scouring and descaling at the faucet. As the aluminum pot was boiling, Manna put roasted peanuts and sundry candies into two cookie boxes for the people who would come to pay them a holiday visit the next morning.

Hua came early in the afternoon. She looked so happy that even her eyes seemed to be smiling. While Lin and Manna were cleaning the home, Hua looked after the twins, humming a folk song to them and telling them the story of a big gray wolf and two little lambs, as though they could understand her. The room was filled with the babies' prattle and laughter. Hua cut a rooster and a prancing cat out of red paper, showed them to the babies, then pasted them on two windowpanes. Manna was pleased with the paper-cuts, which made their home more festive, especially to the eyes looking from the street.

With a broom tied to a bamboo pole, Lin was sweeping the cobwebs off the ceiling. As he was passing by, his daughter patted his knee. Seeing Manna shaking a flour sack outside the front door, Hua said, "Dad, my mom is very happy at home. She said she'd wait for you."

Suddenly he remembered what he had babbled at dinner the night before. Embarrassed, he asked, "I made a fool of myself last night, didn't I?"

"No, no. We were so glad you came home. You should see
Mom—she's a different person today. She said she'd come
and see them in the spring." She referred to the twins, her
forefinger pointing at the crib.

A miserable feeling arose in Lin. He pondered for a moment, then said, "Hua, your mother's getting old. Will you
take good care of her?"

"Yes, I will, Dad." She smiled.

"Tell her not to wait for me. I'm a useless man, not worth
waiting for."

"Don't be so hard on yourself, Dad. We'll always wait for
you."

He felt a clutching in his chest and turned away to sweep
the kitchen ceiling, trying hard to hold back his tears. He was
upset and touched at the same time. Outside, Manna was
cheerfully wishing "Happy Spring Festival" to someone passing by. She sounded so pleasant that Lin noticed her voice was
still resonant with life.

ACKNOWLEDGMENTS

The author wishes to express his thanks to Emory University for a grant that enabled him to complete an early draft of this book. He also wishes to thank his editor, LuAnn Walther, for her consideration and suggestions, and his agent, Lane Zachary, for her comments.